RESURRECTING
SUNSHINE

RESURRECTING SUNSHINE

LISA A. KOOSIS

Albert Whitman and Company
Chicago, Illinois

This book is, in large part, a love letter to the people
we've all loved and lost. So to my grandfather, who always
encouraged me to follow my dreams; to my grandmother,
who I still miss every day; to my beautiful Aunt Carol;
and to my dear, dear friend, Elisabeth Daneels, who was
taken way too soon...this book is for you.

Library of Congress Cataloging-in-Publication
data is on file with the publisher.

Text copyright © 2016 by Lisa A. Koosis
Published in 2016 by Albert Whitman & Company
ISBN 978-0-8075-6943-6 (hardcover)
ISBN 978-0-8075-6944-3 (paperback)

Printed in the United States of America
10 9 8 7 6 5 4 3 2 1 BP 24 23 22 21 20 19 18 17 16

Cover illustration and design by Jordan Kost

For more information about Albert Whitman & Company,
visit our web site at www.albertwhitman.com.

Chapter 1

This is the memory that visits my dreams.

We're walking through a concrete underpass that smells like piss and stale beer and rotting fish. Marybeth is framed by the rectangle of light at the tunnel's end, her dark hair in ponytails, her eyes hidden behind huge plastic sunglasses—probably stolen from her foster mom's dresser—that should make her look stupid but instead make her look incredibly hot. Her sneakers slap on the concrete, and her knapsack, slung carelessly over one shoulder, bounces at her side.

We step out onto the beach. Dark, flat-bottomed clouds hang low over us, and fat raindrops crater the sand. There's no one here but us and the gulls, which tip their heads back and screech, cries that sound like laughter.

The wind yanks strands of Marybeth's hair free from her ponytails and turns her cheeks pink. She kicks off her sneakers, abandoning them.

We walk along the water's edge. The ocean is all whitecaps. Salty spray wets my face.

Near the jetty, Marybeth plops down onto the sand. She pushes the sunglasses on top of her head and digs in her knapsack, pulling out a plastic boat, red with a yellow sail, the kind every cheapo toy store sells.

"I never had one of these," she says. She smiles at me, one of her weird smiles that I can never decipher as happy or sad or maybe a little of both.

She takes a black marker from her bag and, on the side of the boat, in block letters, writes: ADAM.

Then: ♥

And below that: MARYBETH.

She stands, wiping sand from her jeans, and carries the boat to the water.

The ocean rushes up around her ankles, soaking her jeans. A sign on the jetty warns: No Swimming. Hazardous Currents. I want to tell her to be careful, but I don't dare, so I stand beside her instead.

She squats down and drops the ADAM ♥ MARYBETH boat into the water. It immediately rides out on a trail of foam.

I think, *It's going to sink.* I want to make her turn away before she can see it happen. But I don't, and it doesn't sink. Instead, we watch the little boat ride the current out until it's no more than a red-and-yellow speck.

I close my eyes, and when I open them again I'm looking back at Marybeth. She's standing on shore, waving, which makes no sense, except suddenly I feel the motion of waves beneath me, the rise and fall of a boat on rough water.

What...?

I wrap my hands around the boat's rail, which shouldn't flex beneath my fingers. But it does, because it's not metal. It's plastic and red. Only now it's life-size.

I lean over the side. Sure enough, there are the words Marybeth wrote.

Except the MARYBETH is scratched out, and now it reads: ADAM ♥ ~~MARYBETH~~ SUNSHINE.

"Marybeth?" I call to her. But the wind swallows my words.

Above me, a sail flaps, the sound sharp and clear. I look up at it, searching for a way to lower it, because it's pulling me away from shore, from Marybeth. But when I look, it's not a sail at all. It's nothing but a yellow dress, catching the wind.

And when I look back to shore, Marybeth is gone.

Chapter 2

When I roll over, my traitorous body still expects to find her beside me, sleepy and warm. But the only curves my hands find belong to my buddy Jose Cuervo, the bottle mostly empty, and a reeking mound of blankets. My little freaking pearl of a world.

Out in the hall, the intercom for the security gate buzzes.

I shove Jose out of the bed. "Oh for fuck's sake!"

Who is it now? NBC? MTV? StarStreamz? I thought I was done with this. But no, here they are again, probably revving up for the one-year anniversary of her death. Like if just the right amount of time passes, a death is something to celebrate, with balloons and ice cream and stupid paper streamers. Yellow, of course.

My brain races ahead. To five years, ten years, the possibility that they'll never stop. That they'll still demand that I stand in front of their cameras and microphones and keep some piece of her alive.

Here's your news flash, assholes. She's gone. Dead. Not coming back for some ten o'clock special report.

The buzz of the intercom continues—bzzzz, pause, bzzzz, pause, bzzzzzzzzzzzzzzzzzzzzz—like Morse code for hornets.

I yank off the sheets and get up, finding last night's jeans on the floor and pulling them on. From the bedroom window, I can see the high wrought iron fence that surrounds our—I mean my—home. But no satellite-dish-topped news vans wait at the curb, no online reporters waving streaming holocams. Not even some hopeful fangirls, thumbs ready to tweet: "I saw him. I saw *Adam*!" Only a single dark blue SUV stands outside the gate.

I open the window and lean out. "Get off my property."

The intercom buzzes again and this time doesn't stop. Why didn't I disable that damn thing months ago?

"We're really going to do this, huh?" I slam the window shut and head down the hall. In the intercom's monitor, I can see a blond woman waiting. As best I can tell, there's no camera crew, no microphones, just her.

I stab the talk button. "In thirty seconds I call the cops."

She jumps, which gives me a second of satisfaction. "Mr. Rhodes?"

"You heard me. No interviews. Twenty-nine, twenty-eight..."

"I'm not..." She shakes her head and her ponytail wags. "Mr. Rhodes—Adam—I'm not here for an interview."

"Then what do you want?" I mean for it to come out angry, rough, the voice of someone in charge. Instead, it sounds small and sad.

Her image warps as she leans in toward the camera. "My name is Dr. Trixie Elloran. I'm the scientific director of a very special research project, and I'm here with a proposition I know you'll want to hear. If you'd please let me have five minutes—*five minutes*, Adam—I promise you'll find it worth your time."

As if my time is worth anything.

As if she can possibly say something that matters.

Way down in the pit of my belly, something churns. And maybe it's boredom or curiosity or just being tired of the silence in this damn house, but before I can stop myself I hit the release for the gate.

The woman gets into the SUV and drives through the gate. By the time I reach the front door, she's knocking.

She isn't dressed like a reporter. No voice-of-authority, five-o'clock-news clothes, but also not the I'm-thirty-but-trying-to-look-twenty-hipster/interviewer look that you see on most of the net streams. And with her white blouse and faded jeans, the messenger bag slung over her shoulder, she isn't dressed like a doctor either.

When she extends her hand to shake mine, I turn away.

"Five minutes." I step aside to let her in, making a point of looking at my wrist only to realize I'm not wearing a watch.

She heads immediately into the living room and sits in one of the armchairs without waiting for an invitation, as if she knows one won't be coming. She puts her bag on the floor.

"Why don't you sit?" she says, like this is her house instead of mine...instead of Sunshine's.

My heart pounds. "No thanks."

It's been ages since anyone besides me sat in this living room, and for a second I see the room as she must: thick dust on everything, pizza boxes—some still hiding petrified slices—on the floor, the stained couch, sweaty T-shirts caught in the cushions, bottles everywhere.

But she keeps her eyes locked on me. "I'll cut to it."

"Good idea, lady."

She nods. Her voice is soft but direct.

"Adam, what if I told you we could give Sunshine back to you?"

Chapter 3

"Lady, what kind of bullshit joke...?" I take a step toward her. "Are you wearing a mic?"

She just sits there, calmly watching me. "Adam—"

"Your time is up." I grab my phone from my pocket and tap 9, then 1. "Get out before I call the cops."

But she doesn't move. She just says, "I'm not with any television show, and this isn't a joke."

I tap the second 1 and let my finger hover over the green Call icon. *Do it*, I tell myself. *Did you lose your motor functions, loser?*

Maybe it just feels good to have someone to yell at.

"No? Then maybe you didn't get the same memo as the rest of the world, because Sunshine is dead. So tell me. How are you going to 'give her back'?"

And even as I say it, there's a small, pathetic voice somewhere in my brain that's saying, *Tell me. Please tell me.*

"I would like to explain." She leans forward. "If you would like to listen."

My finger shakes, a fraction of an inch over my phone, but I stand, silent, both listening and cursing myself for listening.

"I'm with Project Orpheus. We're a private research venture dedicated to advancing scientific knowledge of genetics and neuroscience. Our DNA and our brains. The two things that make us who we are.

"We're doing amazing things there, Adam." She whistles. "We're developing cutting-edge techniques: hormone-driven controlled aging, artificial wombs, memory reconstruction. We've created implantable memory archiving chips that will be affordable to everyone. These are things that nobody else in the world is even close to attempting."

I shake my head. "I don't understand."

"Let me say this." She smiles. "Our ultimate goal is to give the world the greatest gift it will ever get. The ability to bring back the people we've lost. And we want to start with Sunshine."

I drop down onto the couch and let my phone fall from my hand. I want a drink, and then I want to go back to sleep. And when I wake up again, this will have been just another drunken dream, one that'll fade and leave me to the routine I've carved for myself in this post-Sunshine world.

"Don't screw with me, lady." My voice shakes and it pisses me off.

"I promise you I'm not." She sounds so sincere that my throat tightens. "What I'm offering isn't magic. Science can't bring Sunshine back from the dead, you understand. Flesh decays. But we have the"—she smiles a hesitation—"*means* to reconstruct the Sunshine that we all knew and loved. Exactly as she was."

Exactly, I think. "You're talking about…"

She nods.

"Last time I checked"—which, okay, was maybe never—"we cloned *sheep*, not *people*."

"We're there now, Adam."

"Is that even legal?" I ask.

She shrugs. "Oh it's against, shall we say, the advice of the government. But we have a state-of-the-art facility in a private, off-shore location."

"So it's illegal," I say.

She waves that away, as if it's a minor detail.

I sag back against the couch. "This is nuts."

"It is," she says. "But it's real."

We stare at each other for a minute while I try to process even a small fraction of this, while I try to process the fact that I'm even having this conversation.

"And you want to bring back Sunshine?" I finally say.

"Sunshine," she says, "is our ideal candidate. She's our proof of concept, Adam. There are thousands of people all over the country hooked up to MAP machines even as we speak, their memories saved and ready. And some of them—well, some of them have loved ones with very deep pockets who would pay anything for the ability to bring them back from the dead, memories and all. But they aren't going to just hand over their money on our word. If we can resurrect Sunshine, Adam, put her back on the world stage exactly as she was, that will be the ultimate validation of what we're doing."

"So you just bring back a dead girl, stick her on a stage, and ask her to sing? And then what? You tell the world she's a"—I hiccup over the word—"a *clone*? You tell *her* she's a clone?"

"No," she says. "Of course not. Discretion is in the best interest of everyone, most of all the people who will want this technology. And beyond that, there will be ironclad nondisclosure agreements. Our prospective clients are people who stand to lose a lot, Adam. They know how to keep their mouths shut."

"So you do what then?" I ask.

"Well, truths can be bent, and particularly in the instance of Sunshine, people are eager to believe." She pauses and then says, "So here's a for instance. Maybe Sunshine was weary of the spotlight. Maybe she faked her death, and now...Now she's changed her mind, and she's ready to come back to the public that loved her."

She's right about this much: truths can be bent, and people believe what they want to believe. Including me.

"Now here's the thing. We've had the ability to re-create a physical body for years, even to artificially age it. And maybe that's enough for a pet—the body, the basic shell, the *potential* that exists in DNA. But a *person*? We aren't just genetics, Adam. The joys. The tragedies. Our collective experiences—our memories—*that's* what makes us who we are."

I take another breath. "Still listening."

"Good," she says. "I'm sure you're aware that before Sunshine was taken off life support, the hospital had her hooked into the MAP?"

Her question takes me instantly back to the hospital. I'm slouched in a chair in a dark-paneled office trying to listen to the doctor as he explains how the MAP, the Memory Archiving Port, a sort of neural computer, will download and preserve her memories, in case her brain swells, in case the cells are dying even now. *If she wakes up,* he tells me, *and the pathways in her brain can't connect to the places that tell her who she is, where she's been, the MAP can return them to her.* Except all I can hear is the word "if"—*if* she wakes up—and my brain is screaming, *She's dying, she's dying, she's dying.*

"Adam?"

I pull myself back to the now and rake a hand through my hair. It feels greasy and way too long. "Yeah. I knew about the MAP."

"The MAP has another benefit. Sunshine may have died, but her memories didn't. We've acquired them, and we can implant those stored memories into a"—she meets my eyes—"into Sunshine. She'll know you. Her memories will *be* Sunshine's memories. Her thoughts will be what Sunshine—your Sunshine—would have thought."

"If you can do all this, then why are you here?" I narrow my eyes at her. Because here it comes. "You want Sunshine's money?"

"Money?" She surprises me by laughing. "No. And I will tell you this first. The project will go forward with or without you. No matter what you say, it's already started."

"You mean...?" The words won't come.

"Her new body has been"—she hesitates—"born, created from nothing more than a few stolen skin cells, Adam. It—*she*—is currently undergoing an artificial aging process. We're already implanting memories into her, starting to form her into who she'll eventually become."

"Sunshine," I say.

She nods. "Sunshine."

Her words penetrate. But it's like those first few seconds after you cut yourself really badly, when you see the blood but you don't feel the pain.

"But here's our dilemma," she says. "Even with the MAP, after the oxygen deprivation from the drowning, some of Sunshine's memories are corrupted, incomplete. Have you ever watched television and had a blip in the cable signal? All of a sudden the screen fills with random pixels? That's pretty much what I'm talking about, and it could jeopardize our project. That's where you come in, Adam—completing her memory set. The person who knew her best of all." She looks at me as if I'm an adult, capable of making a decision, and not some reeking, hungover kid whose whole life has been an epic fail.

"Whatever your fucking-fantastic science can do, Dr. Whoever-You-Are, she's still dead. And I'll always know she's dead."

She doesn't answer, and she doesn't seem at all disturbed by my outburst. She leans over and rummages through her bag, pulling out a tablet and sliding it across the coffee table toward me. At the motion, the screen winks on.

She nods toward it. I hesitate and then pick it up.

The image on the screen is one I recognize. And well I should, since it made a tour of all the major media outlets a few months ago. It shows me on my knees by Marybeth's grave. But I wasn't crying. I was falling-down drunk.

"Keep going," the doctor says.

I want to tell her to go to hell, but instead I swipe to the next image, which is a black-and-white shot of me, fist ready, running at a cameraman. The caption reads: NO CHARGES PRESSED AGAINST GRIEVING GUITARIST.

I drop the tablet back onto the table.

"This can be a second chance for you too." She drops a business card on top of the tablet. It's completely blank except for a phone number. "And looking at the path you're on, you'd be foolish not to take it."

Chapter 4

After Dr. Elloran leaves, the house feels strange. Maybe because every unbelievable word she spoke haunted this place with hope. But she didn't take the hope away with her when she left. Oh no. She left it here, and now it's like a goddamn ghost following me around.

Sunshine. Alive again.

Not Sunshine, my brain whispers. *Marybeth.*

This is crazy.

Sick crazy. A-worm-wriggling-around-my-brain crazy.

I walk from room to room, the Hope-Ghost drifting behind me. I don't know what I'm doing. But that's nothing new.

I pick up the business card and put it down again about thirty times.

From the closet, I grab my old laptop and plug it in. After it groans to life, I SmartSearch "Project Orpheus." But all that comes up is a dead link for some old band from like 2016.

I try "Trixie Elloran," which, weirdly, gives me no hits at all.

I take a deep breath and key in "cloning." Now that nets me upward of sixty-six million results. Jesus. Randomly, I click on several and read about cloning techniques and governmental regulations and how scientists managed to successfully clone a primate after years of failure.

If you only knew, I think, clicking out of the site.

After a moment's hesitation, I type in "human cloning," which still gets me more than a million results, though most of them seem to deal only with cloning single organs and not actual people.

I slam the laptop shut and pick up the phone to text the only person I can think of: my manager.

Need ur help, I text.

All of about two seconds later, my phone rings. Typical, old-school Jack.

"Well, well," he says. "Look who crawled out from under his rock."

"Hilarious, Jack. Listen. I need a favor."

"Oh I'm fine, fine. Thank you for asking. And yourself, Adam? Are you ready to rejoin the world?" Then his voice turns serious, and I can picture him twisting his salt-and-pepper beard into a point. "Have you at least considered the idea of a memorial tour, getting back on the road, being with people? It might be good for you, kid. And maybe it's time to—"

On top of everything else, I can't listen to this. I close my eyes. "A favor, Jack. Please."

There's a pause and then a sigh. "Sure, kid. Name it."

"Put out some feelers. Find out what you can about..." I start to say *about Project Orpheus*, but something stops me. "About a Dr. Trixie Elloran."

"I'll call you back in ten." And then he's gone.

Nine minutes later—but who's counting—my phone rings.

"Beatrice—aka Trixie—Elloran," he says and spews a stream of PhDs and MDs and RSVPs or whatever-the-fuck abbreviations follow her name. "She's a hotshot neuroscientist, won all sorts of awards for her research into memory, particularly on eidetic or 'photographic' memory. Three years ago she was credited with a breakthrough in..." He pauses. "'The untapped human capacity for remarkable recall in all of us.' Shortly thereafter, she disappeared."

"Disappeared," I echo.

"Completely." He pauses. "Adam, why are you asking me this? I haven't talked to you in weeks, and now you call me asking about a missing scientist."

For a second, I consider telling him. After all, he cared about Marybeth too. But I don't. I think I'm afraid to hear how crazy it would sound if I said it out loud.

Or worse, saying it out loud would make it too real.

So I say, "It's for a research paper. I'm getting my GED."

I can almost hear him deciding whether to call bullshit.

"Adam, is everything all right?" he asks instead. "Are *you* all right?"

Which is maybe the stupidest question ever.

"I'm fine," I say. "But I might be going away for a while."

Chapter 5

When I disconnect from Jack, something's different. Everything's different. With shaking hands, I dial the number on Trixie Elloran's card.

"I'm in," I say, as soon as I hear her voice.

"You won't be sorry," she says. "Do you have a pen?"

Beside me, that Hope-Ghost ripples, becoming something so real I could poke it with a stick. I fumble in the junk drawer for a pen. Then I listen and write down a date, time, and flight number. I also write down her single rule.

Stay sober.

Shit.

I head for the kitchen, straight to the cabinet beneath the microwave where I stash my bottles, and I kneel on the filthy floor. Tequila. Vodka. Gin. My mouth is so dry. I wipe my lips with the back of my hand and pull out a bottle. Inside, the liquid sloshes, calling me.

I unscrew the top, press the bottle against my cheek. The glass feels cool on my skin.

In my head, Trixie Elloran's voice says, *No alcohol. At all. We cannot risk compromising the memory feed for Sunshine.*

My grip tightens around the bottle. I wish I could shatter it with my bare hands. Finally, I stand and upend the bottle over the sink.

When it's empty, I push it aside and grab one of its buddies, pouring out every drop. Then I grab the next. And the next. And the next.

When that's done, I move to the living room, where empties lurk beneath the couch. Spiders nesting inside the bottles skitter against the glass when I grab their homes.

"Moving day, guys." I can't help but think of Marybeth, who would never let me kill a spider, so I evict them into a dead plant on the windowsill before tossing the bottles.

There are bottles beneath my bed. Bottles behind the overflowing garbage. Bottles in the toilet tank.

Next is the grass. From my bedside drawer, I grab the bag of weed and dump that too. There's also a bag in the pantry, stashed in an empty box of Rice Krispies.

I can do this. If not for myself, I'll do it for her. I'm not going to give Sunshine stoned or drunken memories.

Not Sunshine though. Not really.

Marybeth, the Hope-Ghost whispers.

To the world, they were one and the same. The beautiful singer in the yellow dress. Sunshine was Marybeth and Marybeth was Sunshine. But what did they know?

"Shut the fuck up," I say, but then I try out the name myself. "Marybeth."

I haven't spoken her name for so long.

My stomach heaves. I race for the toilet and drop to my knees and puke up the only alcohol left in the house.

Once my stomach is empty, I run the shower so hot that the spray bites my chest and neck. I rinse away a layer of grime from the bar of soap and then scrub my skin raw, as if I could wash away months of grief and loneliness and regret. Or maybe I'm just scrubbing away the person—the nonperson—I've become without her.

Or was I a nonperson even before that? Even then, was I just an extension of Sunshine, the guy playing guitar in the background while all eyes focused on the girl in the yellow dress with dark hair and bare feet?

After the shower, I find clean-ish jeans and a too-loose T-shirt at the back of my closet. They used to fit. And though my head still throbs, I feel more human, my mouth minty from toothpaste.

Back in the kitchen, I make a breakfast that isn't 100 proof. All these activities, things that should be routine, are alien, like I've borrowed another guy's body and it doesn't quite fit. My hands can't butter the toast right. My teeth don't know how to chew.

It's like I'm testing myself, trying out the moving parts of a person who hasn't functioned for the last seven months.

I think about Project Orpheus. About what Trixie Elloran said. About the idea of New Marybeth, maybe a baby even now in some artificial womb, growing and thriving.

Waiting for me. As if I were someone to pin hopes on.

When I finish the toast, I wash the dishes and take out the garbage. Flies buzz inside the bag. The sun burns against my face. How did these things become so strange?

* * *

I put clothes into a suitcase and then take them out and put other things in. My bedroom becomes an obstacle course of discarded jeans and tees and sneakers.

Twice I pick up my phone to dial Trixie Elloran's number, planning to tell her I've changed my mind, that this is nuts and she should be locked up. Once, in the middle of the night, I wake up soaked in sweat, sure that I dreamed the whole thing, and tear the house apart looking for her business card to make sure it's all real. Once, I even almost call the Bureau of Unparented Minors— in my head, I hear Marybeth saying, *Don't bother calling the useless BUM*—to ask for permission to travel, even though I've been emancipated for so long now.

And seven hundred times I ask myself: *What am I doing?*

Finally, at 9:00 a.m. on Friday, a car pulls up to the curb. As I get into the passenger seat, I feel the vultures watching from windows and doorways, whispering to each other over their coffee and doughnuts.

I lean back against the seat. I could disappear now, and unlike Sunshine, nobody would ever miss me.

Chapter 6

At home, I can control everything. I can take pictures down from the wall. I can stash the vintage watch she gave me that last Christmas someplace where I won't stumble upon it, where it won't accidentally rip my heart out again. I can stream mediacasts that run nothing but cartoons or old sci-fi movies or holovids. I can smash phones with photos and songs to pieces.

But in the real world, even a small airport like this, I never know when I'll turn a turn a corner and find something that will smack me down. A random stranger in a yellow dress or a concert T-shirt. A few notes of a song on someone's ringtone.

I pass check-in and baggage check. Beside the employee lounge, two flight attendants huddle, whispering. One looks at me just long enough that I'm sure she's recognized me.

I keep walking, head down, past the airport bar. The clink of ice in glasses is too loud, a siren song.

From inside, a girl's voice squeals, "OMG. I think that's *Adam*."

She may have just saved me from myself, I think.

Still, this was a bad idea.

I tug my baseball cap low over my eyes and hurry toward the Private Departures sign. Only once I've gone through, to an empty waiting area, do I breathe. Outside the floor-to-ceiling window, a small jet waits on the tarmac.

Almost instantly, a guy in a suit appears. Without checking me in, without taking my bag, without even speaking, he leads me out to the plane, which is unpainted and unmarked, except for a tail number.

I jog up the wobbly mobile staircase to the plane's open door, where a dark-haired flight attendant in a sky-blue uniform smiles at me. "Adam, welcome. Take a seat anywhere. You can stow your bag in the overhead compartment. And I'll need to take your phone."

"My phone?"

She nods. "Sorry. Orders."

"Fine. Whatever." I dig it out of my pocket but then hesitate and pull up my contact list.

I look at Jack's number and try to commit it to memory. The flight attendant waits, hand held out. Finally, I hand it over.

"Thank you. Make yourself comfortable. We'll be cleared for takeoff shortly."

Instead of a traditional aisle with seats on either side, a padded bench lines one side of the plane. On the other side, several over-stuffed chairs and pullout desks are scattered around. Everything is beige and brown and completely generic. Except for a single photograph, blown up, the frame bolted to the wall that separates the main part of the plane from what must be the toilets or the flight attendants' area or something.

In the photo, Sunshine stands onstage, the spotlight like a halo around her. Her eyes seem to look right out of the picture and meet mine.

My breath catches. It's been so very long since I've even glimpsed her image. I sink into the nearest seat and think about Dr. Elloran's words. *She'll know you. Her memories will be Sunshine's memories. Her thoughts will be what Sunshine—your Sunshine—would have thought.*

Crazy words. Impossible words.

The flight attendant shuts the plane door, and maybe that's

what does it, but it's like I'm awake for the first time in days.

What am I doing?

"Please buckle your seat belt. We're preparing for takeoff." The woman's voice, right beside me, startles me.

I look up and try to hide how bad I'm shaking. And the sympathy on her face, sympathy that says *I know who you are and what you've been through and my heart goes out to you*, makes me want to hurl.

I can't do this. If I let myself want this and it doesn't work, I'll never recover.

As if I'd ever recovered the first time. As if I'd even started.

There's still time to get off the plane. I could stop at the nearest liquor store and be home by noon.

"Adam," she says, "your seat belt."

The engines start to whine. Vibrations hum in my feet and move up, right through the seat and into the backs of my legs.

What's it going to be? I ask myself.

I snap my seat belt closed around me. Sunshine's image looks down over me. And then the plane taxis forward.

Chapter 7

The plane touches down on a narrow landing strip. There's no airport, no signs, nothing to tell me where we are. There's only the runway and palm trees and, surrounding everything, ocean.

I expect the pilot to announce that we've landed in...well, wherever it is that we've landed, but we taxi to a stop without a word. Through the window, I watch a guy wheeling over a mobile staircase.

I unbuckle my seat belt and stretch. I feel like I've spent days traveling, but probably only sixteen or seventeen hours have passed.

At the door, I ask the flight attendant, "Where are we?"

She smiles. "I'm not allowed to disclose that."

Well, I know that we took off heading west and hit the Pacific a few hours into the flight.

"Somewhere in the Pacific, maybe?" I try. "The Philippines?"

She just shakes her head. "I'm sorry. I can't."

Because the media would be all over this if word got out, I think.

I duck my head and exit the plane. Warm, moist air hits my face. It's like breathing through a wet washcloth, but it feels good. I'm a long way from home, a long way from the reporters and the photographers, the gawkers and the people who want to hold on to me because, even if I'm not nearly good enough, I'm all they have left.

This place, it doesn't look like home. It doesn't smell like home. And in the strangeness I feel more comfortable than I've felt in a long time.

At the bottom of the stairs, Dr. Elloran smiles and waves. Dressed even more casually than before, she wears long khaki shorts, a pale blue T-shirt, and flip-flops. Her legs are tanned.

I jog down the stairs, which shudder like they're going to collapse.

"Welcome." She holds out her hand and I shake it. "I'm glad you didn't have a change of heart."

"Yeah. Well, what we talked about, all that stuff…" I shove my hands into my pockets. Sweat already sticks my shirt to the back of my shoulders. "It's kinda hard to believe any of this is possible. You know?"

"I know." She wags a hand in the air, as if to shoo away my skepticism and then points to a path that disappears between palm trees. "Shall we? Leave your bag. Someone will bring it."

As soon as we step beneath the trees, the air cools. Sunlight stripes through the broad leaves. Hidden birds cry out.

The path leads to a landscaped area with benches and picnic tables and a stone drinking fountain. Jagged chunks of black lava rocks line the edges. All the flowers here have bright yellow blooms.

Of course they're yellow.

Beyond that stands a low white building.

"We're coming in the back way. Pretty, isn't it? Feel free to explore. There's a beach nearby, and town is only a short walk, if you feel like a change of scenery or a shaved ice. Of course we'll be asking you to sign a nondisclosure agreement." She pauses for a breath. It's hard to remember that she's an important scientist—a *missing* scientist—and not just a tour guide. "This is a good place, Adam. I think you'll be happy here for the duration."

"Happy?" I clench my teeth. "This isn't a vacation."

"Bad choice of words," she says. Her voice is lower now, not that of a tour guide anymore, but of a scientist once again. "I promise you, everyone here takes this very seriously. Me most of all."

Something about the way she says it, that low voice appearing as if there were a different person underneath her bright shell, makes me shiver.

"But…" I lock my hands together and cup them against the back of my skull. My heart beats too fast. "How are you so sure you can do this?"

She meets my eyes. I've had hundreds of thousands of people watching me onstage, but I've never felt as exposed as I do now. Sweat runs down my neck.

"Because we've done it before," she says.

The Hope-Ghost hovers beside me, its mouth—like mine—hanging open, catching flies or *cucarachas* or whatever bugs live here.

"You've cloned someone before?"

"We have."

Dr. Elloran is already walking again toward the building.

"Wait." I hurry to catch up with her. "Who?"

"That, I'm afraid, is not public information. For the ultimate success of our project, it's vital that our clones don't know they're clones. You wouldn't want me sharing that information about Sunshine once we're done, would you? And neither would the clients we're ultimately hoping to attract."

"So how do you find the clients then?" I ask.

"You've heard of lawyers who get clients by ambulance chasing, right?" She shrugs. "This will not be much different. Wealthy people who lose loved ones almost always make the news."

We reach the building. The building where Sunshine is growing. No. Not Sunshine. Marybeth.

Growing and breathing and *alive*.

The thought is too big. It balloons inside me until I can't breathe.

How old is she now? Is she just a toddler, living once again through her last days with her drug-stupid birth mom before the woman finally overdosed and died? Is she a schoolgirl reliving something brain-numbingly dull like a spelling test? Is she dreaming that someday she'll be a famous singer or…

I stop myself before the chain of my thoughts paralyzes me and follow the doctor through a door into an alcove. After the tropical heat, the air-conditioning is a shock.

Dr. Elloran beams. "Welcome to Project Orpheus."

Past a set of swinging doors, a long hallway has life-size photographs of Sunshine lining both walls.

Dr. E walks ahead. She can't see that the photographs are like kryptonite, that my legs have morphed into eels or jellyfish or gummy candies or some other boneless, worthless things.

The first photo is a concert shot. Sunshine stands at center stage wearing her trademark yellow dress. No jewelry. No sparkly crap. Her hair is straight and long, her feet bare, and her toenails painted a blush color, like the inside of a shell.

Behind her, off to the side, I sit on a stool with my guitar, watching over her.

Always watching over her.

For a second, I'm transported back to that stage, blue spotlights crisscrossing overhead, tinting my hands and the strings of my guitar, the curve of Sunshine's cheek. Something roars in my ears and I don't know if it's the memory of the audience or the air-conditioning or just the rush of my own blood.

Whose photos were there before? I wonder. *And when I'm gone— when Sunshine and I have left for our happily ever after (if I can believe Dr. E's promise)—will they repaint the walls and hang up new pictures that will rip someone else's heart out or maybe give them the hope that they'd lost for so long?*

Jesus, Adam, stop.

I realize I've stopped walking completely, and my hand is hovering an inch from the image of Sunshine. Worse, the doctor has stopped walking too and is watching me with this stupid, pitying shine in her eyes.

My face burns. I jam my hands into the pockets of my jeans and start walking again, looking at the floor instead of the photos.

Dr. E starts to narrate, as if she knows that I need her to fill the silence that's heavy with Marybeth's presence. She points to an open door—cafeteria—and another—rec room—skipping a few that are closed, and then to the library (which has half a dozen deep leather armchairs, as if this were a resort and not a cutting-edge research facility). And though every nerve in my body jitters, I listen to her talk about laundry (there's staff for that) and telephone calls (room phones connect only to other places inside the building) and exercise rooms (there are two).

Suddenly I'm more exhausted than I've ever been in my life. All I want is a drink—*oh no, you don't*—and then to fall into bed. Or onto the floor for that matter. It wouldn't be the first time.

But no, that's not even what I really want.

"Can I see her?" I ask Dr. E.

She turns to me and smiles. "Eventually, yes. But now, no. We have a long road ahead of us first."

Finally, she stops at a door marked 1013 and zips a key card into a slot in the wall. A green light flashes. She presses the key card into my hand.

"I know it's a lot to take in," she says, "and I know the process is going to be taxing. But you won't be sorry."

She holds my gaze. My throat feels too tight.

"Get some rest. Tomorrow morning we'll begin," she says. Then she walks away.

I watch until she turns the corner. And then I'm alone.

Only I'm not.

Because somewhere in this maze of a building is Marybeth.

Chapter 8

Marybeth stands at the edge of the low stage. Her cheeks are pale. Her eyes look too large, moon eyes, because the skin around them is so sunken.

She wears a yellow dress. The color wrenches my heart, as if my heart hasn't been wrenched enough already over the last few days.

"You can change your mind, MB."

She looks at the place where the band's instruments should be. But instead of keyboards, drums, a writhing snake pit of wires for the amps, there's only a microphone. Then she looks at me. "I can't. I have to do this for them."

I shake my head because it won't bring them back. I can't follow her logic.

"Do this with me. Please, Adam."

I take her hand. Her fingers feel cold. Around us, stage curtains the color of eggplants sway. They rustle, the sound like insect wings. I feel clammy, sick.

Don't make me do this, MB. The words swell my tongue and won't come out.

Beyond the stage, the crowd claps and claps. They whistle, cheer. Like the curtains, they sway. Like the curtains, they sound like insects.

MB pulls me up the stairs, one, two, and then we're onstage.

"Marybeth…" I start.

She touches my cheek. "I'm not Marybeth, Adam." And in that

moment, she doesn't sound like Marybeth. She sounds hollow, a seashell held to my ear. "I'm Sunshine. Don't you remember?"

* * *

I jerk awake, with the sheets falling away. But when I fumble in the dark for the bottle that's always on the nightstand, it's not there. I take a shaky breath. Instead of sweat and old alcohol, I smell fabric softener.

A sick fist of disorientation squeezes my stomach as the blue glow of an alarm clock outlines an unfamiliar room. For a few heartbeats, I don't know where I am. I only know I need a drink.

A voice in my head says, *You can't; you promised.*

And then I remember. All of it.

I press the heels of my hands against my eyes.

When I look at the clock again, it says 3:40, but I don't know what time zone I'm in, or if it's a.m. or p.m.

I stumble to the bathroom, which is all pale stone and soft light and thick towels. The shower looks like a grotto, with two shower-heads. I run them both full throttle.

Afterward, I'm calmer, and my stomach rumbles. I remember we passed a cafeteria on the way here.

I get dressed and venture out. Except after maybe ten turns down ten different hallways, I'm lost. I haven't hit the cafeteria. I haven't hit the lobby. I haven't hit the alcove that leads to the back door. And the only sounds are the breath of the air conditioner and the tapping of my own footsteps.

The dream lingers, and I wonder if maybe I never actually woke up. Maybe this is a new part of the nightmare. But then I hear the click of a door lock up ahead.

"Hey." I pick up my pace. "Hey!"

A girl exits from one of the unmarked doors. Seeing me, she lets out a little "oh" and pulls the door shut.

She slaps one hand over her heart. "You scared me."

She's a tiny thing, her short hair blond and wavy and pinned back to one side with a dragonfly barrette. She can't be any older than I am.

"Sorry." I hesitate. "I'm Adam."

"Of course you are," she says.

"Of course I am. And you are…?"

She grins. "Genevieve. You can call me Gen. Did you just get off the plane?"

"No. This afternoon."

"Seriously?" She beams at me, rocking up onto her tiptoes to look me in the eye. Her directness is like a spotlight. I'm not sure where to rest my gaze. "I can't believe nobody told me you were here!"

"Were they supposed to?" I ask.

She disregards the question. "Anyway," she says, "you do know it's the middle of the night now, right?"

"Yeah. I—uh—got that memo. But it might be morning before I find the cafeteria." I try a smile, but my mouth feels too stiff.

"This place is a maze, right? You'll get used to it."

"Or they'll find me half-starved and raving down a dead-end hallway some night."

She laughs. "Well, there's a cheery possibility. But not on my shift. I'll show you the way to the caf. I wouldn't mind a monster BLT. I'm just getting off work."

I imagine this little slip of a girl wolfing down a giant sandwich, and I almost smile for real.

She heads back the way I just came from and gestures for me to follow.

"Aren't you a little young to work here?" I ask.

"Oh, it's just an after-school job," she says. "Or sometimes a before-school job. Island time is a little, well, loose, as you might guess from the fact that I'm getting off work in the middle of the night."

"And here I thought you were the resident vampire," I say.

I feel like I'm out of my body, floating up by the fluorescent lights, looking down at myself bantering with this girl as if I were still just Adam the nobody, rather than Sunshine's Adam, rather than the kid who's hidden away from the world for most of the last year.

"So you're here with your parents?" I ask.

"With my dad."

"He works here?"

The girl—Genevieve—tips her head. "More or less."

She doesn't volunteer more, and I don't ask.

"So there are other kids around?"

"Some." She shrugs. "Mostly little ones."

We turn left at the corner.

"So what do you do for an after-school job at a place like this? Flip burgers? Babysit? Deliver pizzas to the memory donors?"

And since we're asking so many questions, who is this guy who keeps talking, anyway?

"Ha-ha. Something like that," she says. A few doors down, she stops. "Come on, comedian. Do you want food or not?"

We step into the cafeteria, which is otherwise empty. At the counter, Genevieve dings a gold bell. A middle-aged man appears from a back room. Lights reflect from the top of his balding head, though a silver ponytail hangs down across his collar.

"Hey, Genevieve. Just get off work?"

"Yup. And look who I found."

"Aha." The man reaches across the counter to shake my hand.

For the second time in just a few minutes, I almost feel as if I'm a real person. "Welcome, Adam. I'm Jay. What can I get for you?"

"Well, Genevieve got me thinking about a BLT. And maybe some chips."

"Make that two," Gen says.

After Jay disappears into the kitchen, Gen plunks down at a table. "I like coming here late. Most folks do room service after eleven, but I like sitting here by myself. I can hear myself think."

"Hearing myself think? Now that I could do without."

"That's a shame," she says. "I'd bet you have some pretty interesting thoughts."

I arch my eyebrows. "'Interesting' isn't the word I'd use."

We sit in silence, the smell of bacon wafting out from the back. My mouth waters.

"This is weird," she finally says.

"What's weird?"

"Sitting here with you."

Just then, Jay emerges, carrying a tray holding two plates—each with a gigantic sandwich and a duo of pickles—a big bowl of potato chips, and two large sodas. He sets it on our table.

"Enjoy," he says.

"Thanks." I inhale. "Smells amazing."

Jay pats Gen on the shoulder and then disappears again.

"So, you were saying?" I prompt.

"I was...? Oh yeah. That it's weird sitting here with you. And you know why. You were famous last time I checked."

"Famous. Right." I grab a handful of potato chips and stuff them in my mouth.

"You look different." Gen gives me a weird half-smile. "Thinner. And your hair. No spikes."

She half stands and reaches across the table to pat the top of my head, where my hair used to stick up in sharp points. Now it's too long and kind of shaggy.

The touch is like a bee sting. A year ago, hands constantly reached for me, thousands of them grabbing at me, wanting me because I was somebody famous or wanting me because I was Sunshine's somebody. But now? Nobody's touched me in so long.

I flinch without meaning to.

She pulls her hand away. Her cheeks flush. I look down at the table. We both go back to our sandwiches.

When we finish eating, she says, "I'll walk you back to your apartment so you don't get lost. Maybe you should do like the blind and count your steps so you'll be able to find your way next time."

She grins at her own joke, and the tension disappears.

"Thanks for the tip." I hesitate. I'm still not sure what to make of this girl. "And thanks for the company."

Even as I say it, I realize I mean it.

"No problem," she says.

Back at my apartment—which ironically is only a few turns from the cafeteria—she says, "You need anything, just dial the front desk and ask them to connect you to Gen. I'll take care of you. Deal?"

I smile and, weirdly, it feels comfortable. "Deal."

"Okay then."

She stands there, so close I can see the mix of blue and gray that makes up her eyes.

"Good night, Adam," she finally says, and with a wave she disappears around the corner.

Chapter 9

In the morning, I wake to a phone ringing. The room is filled with light. When I find the phone and answer it, a woman's cheery voice says, "Mr. Rhodes, wake-up call. Dr. Elloran will come for you in one hour."

In the tiny kitchen, beside the coffee pot, a pamphlet encourages me to "Rethink Drinking." There's an extension number in the bottom corner. I toss it in the garbage and put on a pot of coffee, then down two mugs of it with tons of sugar. It helps, at least a little, with the I-need-a-drink shakes.

Finally, Dr. Elloran appears. As always, her blond hair is in a ponytail. This time she's wearing a sky-blue lab coat.

"Adam, good morning." She smiles. We've come a long way from me threatening to call the cops on her. "How are you settling in?"

I shrug. Maybe it's best to make light. "Well, the shower is epic and the cafeteria makes a kick-ass BLT."

She laughs. "Wait until you try the burgers."

"I'll keep that in mind."

"I'm glad to see you in good spirits. Come on then. There's a video I'd like you to see. Then we'll talk."

The room we enter looks like a screening room. Half a dozen chairs form a semicircle around a small screen.

"What is this?" I ask.

"An introductory film. The beginnings of what we'll show prospective clients." She gestures for me to sit and then takes a seat herself. "Of course, we can't complete it yet. Not until we've succeeded in what we're doing with Sunshine, but I'd like you to view what we have so far. To give you an idea of what we're all about."

She clicks something on a remote control, and the screen fills with blue. The voice of a little girl says, "Project Orpheus," and the first notes of a song play.

My fingers instantly try to find the familiar chords, but the guitar I once played them on is rotting in pieces at the bottom of the ocean. I threw that fucker into the water the day Sunshine died.

Layered over our music, Sunshine sings, sweet and soft and sad, her voice telling the story of a man who'd stood by the sea and turned to stone. My lungs shrink.

The narration starts, a woman's voice. "In the year 2023 a young singer, known to everyone as Sunshine, rose to worldwide fame." In the video clip, Sunshine steps onstage. It couldn't have been too long after the bus crash. She still has that too-thin look, all ribs beneath her loose dress.

I want to yell for Dr. Elloran to turn it off, because I really can't breathe. But instead I clench my fists and watch as Sunshine—as *Marybeth*—stares at me from the screen.

I'm in the footage too. Perched on a tall stool, one foot propped on the rungs, the guitar slung across my lap, I play.

And that's all it had been since the crash. No matter how big the craze got, no matter how large the audience, it was just me and Marybeth on the stage. Her voice and my guitar.

I can't focus on the words being spoken. I can only concentrate on trying to breathe.

Then, thank God, the song ends and the concert footage disappears. A building now fills the screen, redbrick, its front window painted in Day-Glo images of steaming coffee mugs. The Hip Sip.

Our old haunt.

The stage at the Hip Sip was just a few stacked pallets with plywood nailed over the top. Playing there never paid much, barely enough to buy us each a cup of coffee. But we'd loved that place. Our band, Constellation, had played some of our first sets there. Marybeth had been so happy on that stage.

The image changes to the club in New York City where Marybeth became Sunshine.

I force myself to listen to the narration.

"The Sunshine phenomenon began in a small club in New York City, when singer Marybeth Travers decided to take the stage despite the tragic deaths of her bandmates, Larissa 'LaLa' Laramie and Jed Price."

The images flash by: Sunshine, myself, larger and larger concert halls, screaming fans, album covers and concert T-shirts and awards and…

I should remind Dr. Elloran that I could *tell* this story myself. That I lived it.

The slide show races toward the conclusion I already know. If only I could hit pause and freeze-frame it at a point when there still was hope.

The rush of pictures slows. Finally, there's a deserted beach, waves, an old wooden pier. Tied to the pilings are yellow ribbons and teddy bears in yellow dresses and sunflowers wilting on thick stems.

My throat closes.

"April 16, 2025," the narrator says. "The world lost one of the most beloved performers of all time when Sunshine drowned in a tragic accident."

On-screen, one image remains: a headstone.

Then the video moves forward, oblivious to the fact that I'm stuck in that one moment, and the screen fills with more familiar images. Masses of fans waving cell phones, singing her songs as tears stream down their faces. Vendors selling memorial T-shirts on every city street corner, ready to make a buck from tragedy. Everyone grieving for the beautiful young singer in the yellow dress.

Everyone except me. I'd never grieved for Sunshine, but for a ponytailed girl named Marybeth.

Worse still are the scenes of her funeral, her mahogany casket decorated with a 14-carat gold sunburst, bouquets of yellow roses and sunflowers everywhere.

I look away, but other images bubble up on the one screen I can't look away from. My own damn brain.

The buzz of my cell phone, a stranger on the other end telling me, "You should get here as quickly as you can." And then later, long hallways and closed doors and the doctor, a man whose expression beneath his horn-rimmed glasses said what his words didn't have to. That Marybeth was gone.

Mercifully the video switches to show the building we're in now. The camera pans over the low white structure, the landscape of palm trees and lava rocks.

"Built on advances in the fields of genetics and neurosciences, Project Orpheus is dedicated to assuring that those who have passed need not be lost forever."

Another slide show slips through a series of images: scientists wearing lab coats in the same sky blue that's everywhere around here, some comparing notes on oversized clipboards, others monitoring screens of data. Technicians tend to smiling people in dentist-office-type chairs.

Then Dr. Elloran appears on-screen. She sits, legs crossed, on the edge of a desk, leaning forward as if she were talking to me and not some camera. "The work we're doing here is groundbreaking. We're making great strides in the understanding of the science of memory, of what makes us who we are, and the applications are limitless."

The intensity in her eyes makes me shiver, even as her image fades away to be replaced by others: silver-haired old people in wheelchairs, couples huddled together over tiny coffins.

I swallow hard.

The screen returns to images of Sunshine. I wait for a picture of the new Sunshine. No…the new Marybeth. Because that's where this is going, right?

I ache for that picture. To see her. To know that her heart's beating, that she's breathing, maybe smiling as she dreams her way into this second chance at life.

But abruptly, the screen darkens to blue, and I realize Dr. E is watching me. "We'll have footage of the 'new' Sunshine for the ending once we complete the project, of course, and maybe a few more technical details."

I'm not sure what she expects me to say, so I say nothing. I just stare at the blue screen until she leads the way out of the room.

* * *

A few hallways later, we enter her office. On the wall directly across from the doorway hang a series of diplomas and awards—the kind with gold seals and official-looking signatures—as if to let anyone who enters know that this woman is seriously hot shit.

Dr. E gestures toward one of two swivel chairs beside a lacquered black desk. I sit, and Dr. E takes a seat behind the desk.

Between us stand stacks of books with titles I can't even pronounce and a computer. I glance around for pictures, something that might give me a clue about who Dr. E is besides a scientist, but there's nothing. No wedding photos, no smiling, gray-haired parents. Not even a golden retriever or a cat.

She moves a pile of books to one side, apparently unconcerned that my eyes are being incredibly nosy. "I'd like to chat a little bit about Project Orpheus itself, what's going to happen over the next few months and what'll be expected of you."

I nod.

"The project you are about to take part in is like nothing you could imagine, Adam." Her eyes shine. They're such a dark brown that I can't see the pupils. "We're developing technologies and processes that will change the world. That will change, in fact, life and death. You are now a part of that."

Her words feel too big for the room, too big for me. I shift in the chair. "If you don't mind, Dr. E, I'll leave the Nobel Prize to you. I just want to do whatever it takes to bring Marybeth"—I correct myself—"Sunshine back."

She nods, seeming to return from whatever award podium she was standing at in her imagination. "Of course. So let me explain how your part will work. This afternoon we'll start a series of baseline memory tests. Having you bite into an apple, look at colors, visualize places, objects, things like that, so we can understand how your mind is mapped."

"I'll be wired in or something?"

"You'll be wired in, yes. The equipment we use for this phase is similar to the MAP machine that captured Sunshine's memories."

I picture Marybeth lying in her hospital bed, her eyes closed, tubes and wires everywhere, glowing lines on monitors, the MAP machine humming as it held on to her memories and thoughts and knowledge the way I held on to her limp hand. I swallow hard.

"Our equipment is modified for the purposes of harvesting memories—yours—and then ultimately, restoring memories—hers.

So what we'll be doing is essentially calibrating the equipment to you."

"Okay." I try to concentrate on listening to what she's saying and not letting my brain run away.

"Once that's done, we'll begin mapping your memories. All the pieces related to Sunshine. Even the things you don't know you remember."

"How is that possible?"

"Your memory is like a massive file-sharing service, Adam. What we've learned only recently is that every time a memory goes into storage, it's tagged so it can be found again. Basically, every memory you have of Sunshine will have a tag attached to it that tells the brain that 'file' is related somehow to Sunshine. Even when you *think* you've lost it, it's findable once we know how it's tagged."

"Okay…"

"When we calibrate, we'll be able to see the areas of your brain that 'light up' when we search for those Sunshine files."

I imagine little gray file cabinets in my brain, tiny tags on each drawer that say things like "Mr. Solomon's algebra class," "Guys whose asses I've kicked," or "Hip Sip gigs."

Or: "Things better left unremembered."

"Sounds impressive," I say.

"It is. Now this part of the process is tedious, I'll confess, and it might take up to a week, week and a half. But once that's done to our satisfaction, we'll be able to get to the heart of our project."

"Which is harvesting my memories of Sunshine?"

My stomach squeezes at the thought of someone harvesting my brain for memories, as if they were nothing more than apples. I'm afraid they'll find something more like old bones.

"Yes," she says. "Those harvested memories of yours will be added to the ones the hospital recovered from her after the accident.

They'll make up for any memory loss or degradation. We'll have to modify them, of course. 'Switch the point of view' is perhaps the least technical way to put it. And then those memories will be transplanted into Sunshine."

"But won't that…" How do I finish that sentence? *Won't that be cheating? Won't that make her someone else completely? Won't that make her a girl created from memory rather than reality?*

She nods as if she knows the question I'm going to ask better than I do.

"Don't worry. We're not going to make some Franken-Sunshine. We're creating a backup of recollections of important moments in her life. But most of the memories will be her own. She'll be *your* Sunshine, Adam, the girl we all know and love."

The Hope-Ghost floats over to Dr. Elloran and plants a smack-eroo right on her cheek. But my heart pounds. I stare at the awards on the wall.

The girl we all know and love. We.

But they only know Sunshine. Not Marybeth.

But even as I'm thinking it, Dr. Elloran is moving on. "You asked me yesterday if you could see her. Right now, she's undergoing a strenuous artificial aging process. We control the rate she ages through special synthetic hormones, but it's taxing on the body, and we need to keep her closely monitored. But maybe more importantly, we don't want a visit with her to affect you, Adam. We need you clean for this.

"When we hit Phase Three of the project, when her cloned body has advanced to a sufficient age, then I promise you'll see her. Often. In fact, that's part of why your presence here is so important."

I don't trust myself to speak. My throat feels dry, and I want a drink desperately. Not even alcohol. Just a tall glass of water.

Something to help me swallow.

"We have reason to believe that too many virtually implanted memories have the potential to become phantom memories."

"Phantom memories?"

"It's exactly how it sounds. Memories that feel insubstantial, less than real. Like they belong to someone else."

I nod. The whole two years of the Sunshine craze seem like phantom memories.

"Our fear is that it could cause mental illness," she continues. "Schizophrenia or bipolar disorder. But we're certain we can counteract this phantom memory syndrome by physically re-creating vital memories, particularly more recent memories."

"Re-creating?"

"Reenacting, essentially. It'll be a high-tech illusion. We'll plug you into a virtual reality with Sunshine, where you'll replay life experiences with her. It'll be kind of like putting on a play."

The prospect of what she's suggesting is both exhilarating and flat-out terrifying.

Because I'm going to see her.

And because I'm going to have to live through everything all over again.

"I just want to make sure you understand this, Adam. To Sunshine, it'll all be new, but you will know that these are re-created memories."

"That's…" I shake my head. I'm going to see Marybeth in a matter of…what? Months? Weeks maybe. "It's okay. It's…more than okay."

She nods. "Good."

"And then what happens?"

In answer, she smiles a broad, beaming smile. "Then the future. Then Project Orpheus will have succeeded in our immediate goals. But for you…Well, that part's still unwritten, isn't it, Adam?"

PHASE 1

Chapter 10

We enter a door marked Memory Room A. The interior of the room looks like a mash-up of a spa and a spaceship, curved walls and weird, colorless, minimalist chairs. A white recliner sits dead center.

A back wall made of tinted glass reveals a second room, filled with panels of levers, slides, and a ridiculous amount of seizure-inducing lights. Off to one side, I see the silhouette of a man.

"Sorry about that." Dr. E taps a button on the side wall and the window becomes a mirror. "You're not supposed to see our inner workings. Someone goofed. Take a seat, please."

"Who was the man back there?" I ask as I drop into the recliner. I imagine other people who I can't see joining him now, all clustered behind the window watching me. That's the way it is onstage with the spotlights blazing down, blinding. You know the audience is there. You can almost feel them breathing, like they're a single creature rather than thirty thousand people, but you can't see them.

"One of our scientists, I'd imagine. Now lean back," she says.

She wallpapers me with circular pads, each with a clip at its center. They're cold and squishy. Soon, wires trail from my head to a small, boxy gadget. Reflected in the mirrored wall, I look like something out of a mad scientist movie or maybe the guitar player from Planet Ooga-Booga.

In the mirror, I see another woman enter the room. She has fiery red, waist-length hair. She wears a lab coat too and looks like she's been sucking on lemons.

"Adam," Dr. E says. "This is Rita. She'll be overseeing your calibration."

"Hey," I say, but when Rita looks at the machine instead of saying hello, I get a bad feeling.

"Let's start," she says once Dr. E is gone.

She fusses with the wires on my head, as if Dr. E didn't do a good enough job. And she's not gentle. I want to ask her who pissed in her Cheerios.

She rolls over a cart and a chair and sits beside me. The machine I'm wired into beeps like it's waking up.

"The first thing we're going to do is calibrate the sense of taste. You'll be given items to sample, and I'll ask you a series of questions about each item, including whether it's something you like or dislike, your level of familiarity with it, and the frequency of it in your life. Is that clear?" She sounds annoyed, as if I've already fucked something up.

"Perfectly," I say.

"Okay." She takes an apple from the cart and holds it up. "Do you like apples?"

"McIntosh ones."

She huffs. "Yes or no."

I grit my teeth. "Yes."

"Thank you." She doesn't sound thankful at all. She holds the apple out to me. Her fingernails are painted an ugly orange. "Now just look at it for a minute."

Look at it? I take the apple and stare at it, feeling incredibly stupid.

"Now take a single bite. Don't chew yet."

I bite into the fruit. And I imagine my brain waves going out through my skin, traveling across the wires and into the mapping machine. But what is it telling them? How I see an apple? What it feels like to bite into it and get that first flood of sweet tartness?

"Okay. Now chew it and swallow it."

The apple sticks in my throat, trying to choke me.

After I answer all her questions, Rita Lemonsucker takes the rest of the apple and drops it into a trash can, then holds out a pretzel rod. "Do you like pretzels?"

We go step by step through the pretzel.

After that it's very tart lemonade—ha! I bet that's what she drank before coming in the room—and then bubblegum and dry cereal and soda...

...and spaghetti (I wonder briefly if Jay, the brilliant BLT-maker, cooked it)

...and waffles

...and peanut butter

...and hard-boiled eggs

...and lemon meringue

...and a whole host of things that come out of the drawers in her bottomless cart.

And then she pours vodka into a shot glass and holds it toward me. Instinctively, I reach to take it, but then push it away. Liquid sloshes out of the glass onto her fingers.

My mouth is stuffed with cotton, but I force out words. "Are you joking?"

Give me the whole damn bottle, lady, I think.

She says nothing, just stares at me and holds it out again. I lick my lips. I can imagine how easy it would go down, how it would dull the hard edges of everything that's happening and protect me from getting myself hurt.

Take it, I think. *She's offering it free and clear, so take it, take it, take it.*

I clench my hands. "No."

She sets it back on the cart, and I think two things: one, since she doesn't force the issue, that it was a test...and two, that she isn't happy I passed.

I feel like puking. I wonder if that's another part of this process—what my brain waves look like just before I hurl. But I feel something else too. As if I just fought a battle (with Rita or myself, or probably both) and for the second time now, I won.

Regardless, Rita doesn't miss a beat. "Colors next," she says.

She holds up a square card that's fire-engine red. "Look at the color for thirty seconds."

"Just look at it? Nothing else?"

She nods.

I stare at the color for what seems like forever.

"Okay. Now I want you to associate. What does this color bring to mind? State each association and then hold that image in your mind for a count of fifteen seconds. Then move on to the next. Okay, begin."

"Fire engine," I say. I picture the shiny cherry pickers that used to roar through the neighborhood where Marybeth and I lived as children. I hold the image.

"Next."

"Apple." I picture the apple from earlier, remember its taste.

"Next."

"Blood."

After maybe ten associations, she sets down the red card and holds up another one, this time emerald green.

We go through blue, then orange, then purple, brown, white, black, silver, just about every color I can imagine. Just about.

Finally, after about fifty colors, she says, "We're scheduled for a break."

Which is interesting, of course, because I know damn well the one color that she didn't show me.

* * *

Yellow is Sunshine. Yellow is Sunshine. I force my mouth to form the words, pretend they're just the chorus of a song I'm singing backup on.

But I can't say it. Even though this is what I'm here for, right?

My anger is unreasonable. I know it. Nothing terrible has happened. Nobody's done anything heinous to me. They've just skipped a color.

I jam my hands into my pockets and walk.

Maybe it only bothers me because it's so blatantly manipulative.

Or maybe it's that I thought I knew how hard this would be and then, *wham*, something as stupid as a missing yellow flash card makes me realize that I have no idea how hard it's going to be after all.

I turn a corner, and then another. People pass me, and I keep my head lowered. I know they're looking at me. I'm Adam after all. Sunshine's Adam. And now I'm a freak show.

After a few minutes, I return to Memory Room A, where I stew until the break is over.

When she returns, Rita wires me in and then sits. "We'll resume with colors."

She holds up the first card and—surprise, surprise—it's yellow, the same exact shade of Sunshine's dress. Exactly. It's like they took the damn dress to a Home Depot and color-matched it. I stare at the mocking rectangle of yellow and wait thirty seconds.

"Association please," Rita says.

I swear she wears a self-satisfied smirk, as if she's some kind of emotional vampire and my pain is her lunch.

I can't say it, but I wonder if she can see it in their map of my brain.

"Lemons," I finally say. I hold tight to the image of a lemon, its thick, dimpled skin, its squashed football shape, its sour-pucker taste. But behind that, like the ghost that she is, is Marybeth, in her yellow Sunshine dress.

I don't look at Rita.

"And..."

"Finches." I force myself to picture the bird feeders from my first foster family's home, where goldfinches had flocked, scrapping over the black thistle seed. And still Marybeth is there, and I can't block her out no matter how hard I try.

"And..."

I hear the roar of my own blood.

"Parkway streetlights," I say. "Tennis balls. Yellow jackets."

Rita stares at me. Then finally, she sets down the yellow card. "That'll be it for today. We'll resume at nine a.m. tomorrow."

She disconnects me, then folds her arms and continues to look at me.

I stand and stretch. "I'll be here."

"And I'll expect you to come prepared to be honest and give everything to the process. Otherwise all this is pointless." Her voice reminds me of the jagged black lava rocks I passed on my way into the building. "Am I clear?"

I press my lips together. My pulse pounds in my temples. I nod. Then I turn and leave.

Chapter 11

"I need a drink," I tell the ceiling. "Just one. Even a beer. You don't know where I could get one around here, do you?"

The ceiling doesn't answer.

"Some friend you are. I could go find Rita. She'll be happy to give me that drink."

Great. I'm talking to myself.

I roll over and bury my face in the pillow. So much for the battle I won this afternoon. Now I want to jump out of my skin. I want to go outside and scream at the sky until I empty myself of this need.

I need a drink. I need a drink. I need a drink.

Or at least a distraction.

I sit up on the edge of the bed. For a minute, I hesitate. Then I get up and find the phone and dial 0.

"Good evening, Adam," a man's voice says. "This is Nicholas. How may I help you?"

"Can you connect me to Genevieve's room?"

"Of course. One moment please."

After a series of beeps, the phone rings…and rings. But then I hear her voice saying, "Hello?" and I let out a breath.

"Hi, Genevieve. It's Adam. I hope I'm not bugging you."

"Adam, wow. Hi. No. I'm glad you called. Looking for some company?"

Something in me loosens. "I'm…" I swallow. "If you're sure you're not busy."

"Busy? Around here?" she says. "Give me five. I'll come get you. I don't want to have to send a search party because you're wandering the halls again."

I laugh. "That's probably a good idea."

"Excellent. Be there in a bit."

I change into clean clothes and finger-comb my hair, and a few minutes later, she knocks. When I open the door, she's wearing tight jeans and a cropped T-shirt that says Beach Bum on Duty.

"I am *so* glad you called," she says.

I follow her into the hall. "I'm glad I called too."

"Food first?" she asks. "Then we could hang?"

My stomach growls. I put one hand against it and Gen smirks.

"I think my stomach is hoping for another of those amazing BLTs."

"BLTs two nights in a row?" She rolls her eyes. "Craziness. There are other delicacies to sample, Adam."

"Delicacies?" I arch my eyebrows. "Really?"

"Would I kid?"

"Well then, Miss Resident Expert, what would you recommend for tonight's dining experience?"

She turns until she's walking backward and grins. "Now I feel important. Let me think." She taps a finger against her chin. Her light blond hair curls neatly along her temples, the silver dragonfly barrette shining from one side. "Well, the hot dogs and Jay's famous macaroni salad are not to be missed."

"Sounds like real gourmet fare."

Her grin stretches. "I'm not sure if your taste buds are up for it, but it's what *this* food connoisseur recommends."

"I'll try to rise to the occasion."

In just a few turns we're at the cafeteria. I wonder how I could possibly have gotten so lost last night.

Tonight a few other people sit at the tables. In one corner, a pair of women laugh, and the laughter is something alien, a sound from a world I once lived in. I tense. From the way Gen looks at me, it must be written all over my face.

She dings the bell, and Jay comes out from the kitchen. "Hey, Genevieve, Adam. What can I get you tonight?"

"A couple of barkers and mac salad for both of us. And strawberry milk shakes." She turns to me. "You *do* like strawberry, right?"

"Sure."

"Good. Because there's nothing like a guy who doesn't like strawberry to ruin the start of a perfectly good friendship."

A friendship.

"Good choice, my dear." Jay says. "I'll have those dogs out in a jiffy."

"Make them to go, would you, Jay?" she asks.

"Where are we going?" I ask her.

She tips her head. "You'll see."

We wait without speaking. Though the conversations around me continue, I feel eyes watching me. I wish for just one day I could unzip myself from my skin and be someone else, someone who nobody looks at or whispers about or makes judgments about before they've even met him.

Eventually, Jay returns with a large paper bag, the top rolled over. Even through the sack, the hot dogs smell great. And I realize something funny (okay, really funny, after the afternoon of food sampling that I had). I've missed food.

"Mustard?" Gen asks.

Jay nods. "It's in there. Ketchup too."

Everyone in the room watches us leave, even if they're pretending not to.

We navigate the maze of hallways. Finally, Genevieve pushes

open a door, and we step out into a courtyard. Overhead, the moon is nearly full. Its light frosts the landscape, which is a really disorienting effect in the tropical heat. My body wants to shiver, but after the air-conditioning, sweat pops out along my hairline. Nearby, insects hum. Alongside the path, flowers are closed up for the night.

Near the center of the courtyard, three benches form a half-moon around a concrete fountain. At the top, an angel weeps over a fallen sun, her tears spilling along each tier. Genevieve sits on one of the benches and pats the seat beside her.

As she opens the food bag, several dark birds with markings around their eyes appear on the ground by her feet. She reaches into the bag and pulls out a couple of cookies—making me think this is some kind of routine—and tosses them to the birds.

"Mynah birds," she says. "They'll always come if you have food."

I take a cookie and crumble it. Having finished what's on the ground, the birds shuffle toward me. I toss the crumbs and they snatch them up.

When I look up, Gen's watching me. The way she looks at me, as if she's actually seeing me, the person, rather than just Sunshine's guitarist, makes me feel exposed.

I fold one arm across my stomach. "What?"

"I don't know. I guess it's just surreal that I'm sitting here with someone so famous, and you're so…"

"I'm not sure I want you to fill in that blank," I say.

"Real." She frowns. "You're so real."

"You don't stop being real when you get famous."

She hands me a hot dog, then unwraps one for herself, concentrating on slathering it in mustard from little packets.

"I guess you're just not what I expected," she says.

I flash to images of the days following Marybeth's death. The words I flung at the media. Striking the cameraman. I eat the hot dog in three big bites, toss the excess bun to the birds, and then start on the macaroni salad.

"Were you a fan?" I ask.

She shakes her head. "Being here on the island, I sort of missed the whole Sunshine craze. Dr. Elloran just said you might be uncooperative or…difficult. She said…" She hesitates. "She said you drink too much."

Pieces of macaroni salad stick in my throat. I grab a milk shake and suck some of it up through the straw. It tastes sickly sweet. By my feet, the mynah birds dance around, waiting for another handout.

"Wow," I say, though I shouldn't be surprised. I signed away my privacy a long time ago for a one-way ticket to fame with Marybeth.

Gen dips her head, hiding her face. "I'm sorry. I probably shouldn't have said that."

"It's okay." I sigh. "It's true. I think I might be an alcoholic."

Saying the words feels like coughing up guitar picks.

"Oh," she says.

"But I haven't had a drink since before I came here. It's hard as hell." I hold up my hands to show her how they shake. "But I'm done with it. I have to be."

She rubs my arm. "You'll make it."

The hairs stand up where each one of her fingers lands. For a second, I meet her eyes. "You don't know that."

"I know, but I have a feeling." She takes her hand away and looks at the ground. Her sandals scuff on the stone path. The mynah birds have disappeared back into the night. "I'm sorry if I ruined dinner. My mouth gets ahead of my brain sometimes. I think I'm out of practice talking to people my own age."

"I guess that's something we have in common."

"Really?" she asks.

I laugh. "Really."

"I can't imagine what it must have been like." She sips her milk shake and then says, "Your life, I mean. With Sunshine. Being onstage. Having so many people love you for who you are."

I drink my milk shake too, staring straight ahead. I wish it were whiskey. How can I explain that Sunshine had been so much less than what the world saw—not a superstar but only Marybeth in a new incarnation—and yet so much more than what anyone else could possibly even imagine? "They don't love you for who you are. They love you for who they *think* you are."

She nods, but I know she can't understand that. Most people can't. It's a lonely thought. Around me, the night seems too big.

It's bizarre to be having this conversation about Sunshine with... well, really a stranger. After all the time I'd refused to talk about her, even to Jack, somehow, now, the words want to come.

"She was never Sunshine to me," I finally say. "She was Marybeth. She was just a girl. She was *my* girl."

"It must have been unbearable to lose her."

Invisible hands close around my throat. Because there are words pushing up, trying to escape. Maybe it's only because now there's the promise of having her back.

"Do you want to hear about her?" I hear myself say. I hadn't meant to.

Genevieve's gaze finds mine. She's so eager she's practically humming with it. And yet her interest doesn't feel sick or wrong. It feels comforting.

"Please," she says.

I nod and take a deep breath. The night air tastes like the sea.

"She would never let me kill a spider." I don't know why this is the first thing I think of, this silly quirk of Marybeth's, but there it is.

Gen tips her head. I know she wants to hear the big things, the things that made the world love Sunshine, but she nods at me to continue.

"One time we smuggled a spider out of a concert hall in a rum bottle, because she was sure someone would kill it. Damn thing somehow survived the fumes. Probably the drunkest spider ever. She set it free in her African violet. It lived the whole rest of its spider life in that plant in our tour bus, spun this cool funnel web there."

Seriously, I'm telling this girl about our pet spider. But she only watches me, her eyes bright.

Maybe it's because these are things she won't find even in the unauthorized biographies of Sunshine. Or maybe we both know that these really *are* the big things, the things that made Marybeth uniquely Marybeth. And that's it, isn't it? I'm not telling her about *Sunshine* at all.

"She liked those ridiculous fruit candies," I start again. "The ones where the wrappers look like watermelon slices and pineapples."

"I know the ones," Gen says. "My mom used to have them in the house at Christmas."

Mom. She says it so easily, as if everyone has one.

I tell her how, when Marybeth was twelve, I sat on the side of the tub and watched her pierce her own eyebrow with a sterilized sewing needle just to piss off Mrs. Casing, her foster mom at the time.

I tell her that Marybeth wore combat boots to our middle school formal, and I tell her that Marybeth loved sea horses and that she collected antique brooches.

"She told me that when we got married…" My voice catches on the words, and I drink my milk shake until I think I can talk again. "She'd carry a bouquet made entirely of brooches."

"Why brooches?" Gen's voice is soft, thoughtful.

I try to smile but my mouth won't cooperate. "I don't know. I guess they made her feel connected to other lives, other families."

I don't mention that those brooches are in a shoebox in the back of Marybeth's closet, that they'll probably get sold someday for thousands of dollars each, and their original owners will be forgotten, eclipsed by the fact that they belonged to Sunshine.

"You're not here to resurrect Sunshine," she says then. "You're here to bring back Marybeth."

I don't answer. In the silence, I'm hyperaware of everything around me: the constellations, the moon-shadows of the palm trees, and maybe most of all, the nearness of this girl I hardly know.

"You okay?" Gen asks.

I nod, even if the nod is a lie. "Tell me about you."

She shrugs. "Compared to you and...Marybeth, what's to say?"

I smile, and this time it feels almost comfortable. "I don't believe that. So I know you work the vampire shift here. And I know you like dragonflies"—I point to her barrette—"and BLTs."

She holds up her cup. "And strawberry milk shakes."

"And strawberry milk shakes. But there must be more fascinating Genevieve factoids to share."

"Hardly." She stirs her shake with the straw. "I'm a girl who lives in the middle of nowhere with a dad who...well, who has really good intentions but doesn't always use the best judgment."

"What about your mom?"

"She's back in the States. Refer back to the dad with the good intentions but less-than-stellar judgment."

"Do you see her?"

She shakes her head. "She left a long time ago."

I think about this girl, here—as she says—in the middle of nowhere. No friends. No school dances. No real school for that matter. "You never thought of going with her?"

"Of course I have," she says. "It would be nice to be a normal girl going to a normal high school instead of being homeschooled. Maybe have a boyfriend."

She blushes. I pretend not to notice.

"But…" I say.

She sighs. "Can we just talk about something else? Like what about you? Not Adam the rock star. Just Adam the normal guy."

He's gone, I want to tell her. *Vanished a long time ago.*

I tip my head back and blow out a breath. I could have filled hours with details about Marybeth, but now I'm at a loss. Who am I without Marybeth? Who was I even *with* her?

"I'm just the guy who played guitar and drank too much," I say.

For a second, the crickets seem to get louder or maybe it's just the weird silence that drops over us.

"Oh, so no factoid for me," she says finally.

"Well…" I shrug. "I rode a camel once."

"Now we're getting somewhere," she says.

"We were in New York, at the Bronx Zoo. Marybeth dared me and…"

"You never met a dare you didn't like?"

"Something like that."

The night settles between us, heavy with the hum of insects and the weight of my own thoughts.

"Gen, what we're doing here, do you believe it?"

"The cloning?"

I wince at how casual the word sounds, but I nod. "The cloning. The memory implantation. Everything."

She looks at me directly.

"Do I believe it?" she says. "Yes. One hundred percent."

Chapter 12

"Let's try this again," Dr. E says when I enter Memory Room A. She holds up a cue card, and I don't even need to look to know it's the color yellow. I guess I don't have to ask why she's here instead of Rita.

My head pounds like I have an epic hangover, except I think it's more of an I-haven't-had-a-drink-in-days hangover. "Sunshine," I say.

She nods, her lips pressed together, and then says. "Thank you."

When she gestures to the chair, I sit, and she starts to wire me up.

"I wish I could tell you it will get easier." She jams a pad on my forehead with her thumb. "But it won't. Not before it gets harder. Sometimes we have to do things a certain way to get what we need. And that might make it seem like we're playing with you. But we're not. Lean forward, please."

She attaches two more pads at the base of my skull, and I think she's going to push them all the way through my head and out my jaw. I'll have bruises tomorrow, no doubt.

"For example, we can't just ask you to be frustrated…or angry or to feel pain the way we can ask you to look at a flash card of paisley, but we need to map those things, so we have to find ways around that. There is a lot of science behind this, Adam. We know what we're doing."

I think back to Rita handing me the shot of vodka, and though I feel chastened, there's also still a core of anger.

I stare at Dr. E, hoping I can burn a hole into her with my eyes.

"Now let's begin," she says, reaching into the cart for God knows what.

* * *

That night, in bed, with the lights off, I imagine I'm back in the tour bus. I pretend that the sound of the room's air conditioner is the hum of the motor and the rhythm of wheels on asphalt as we move from one anonymous place to another.

They were all the same. Small towns no different from cities. Concert halls and sports stadiums and state fairs. Faceless people in the audience and people-less faces in the roped-off crowds that waited for us everywhere else.

In some way, the people, the places, they were like the ocean. And Marybeth and I were drowning in them.

Chapter 13

The guitar shows up in my apartment after my session one Tuesday, leaning against the couch.

Not just a guitar. *The* guitar.

As in *the exact guitar*, as if divers had found all the pieces on the ocean floor and put them back together perfectly. Even the pattern in the wood—the thickness of the dark zebra stripes that run its length—is identical.

But hey, if they can clone a girl, why not a guitar?

I stare at it. I know the exact way the strap will fit against my shoulder blade and how the stage lights will reflect off its polished surface. I know just the sound it will make under my touch.

My fingers itch, and I close them into fists. It's like someone keeps trying to put back the pieces of my life from a year ago, one by one.

It's just a guitar, Adam. I can't tell if the voice in my head is Marybeth's or Genevieve's, and that thought tumbles around like rocks inside me.

I grab the instrument and jam it into the bedroom closet. Putting it down, my fingers accidentally hit the strings, and the discordant sound follows me out of my apartment and into the hall, although I know at some point the note is no longer real but only my memory screwing with me.

It's what everything comes back to. Memories. And now there's no alcohol to kill them dead.

I need to get out of this building.

At the front desk, I imagine myself asking, *Where's a good place for a guy to get a cocktail, buddy, somewhere they don't care if you're underage?* I imagine him gaping at me. Right before he calls Dr. E to tell her that maybe her star recruit isn't so stellar after all.

In a minute, I'm outside, and while I might have left the damn guitar back in my room, the memories that came with it follow me.

I'm tearing through shiny blue wrapping paper and ridiculous amounts of Scotch tape on a present that didn't really need to be wrapped, because with one glance I can tell what it is.

I'm sitting on the base of the slide at the kiddie playground, the hot metal burning through my jeans, strumming. Marybeth sits on one of those coiled-spring ponies nearby, her head propped on her hands, atop its enamel mane, listening.

Some fleabag motel room. LaLa and Jeddy are dead and Marybeth is lying on the bed staring out the window. I'm sitting on the stained floor and my guitar is propped against the wall and I think, *Maybe I'll never play it again.*

I'm arguing with Jack about getting something flashier for the stage. Something highly lacquered. Maybe yellow. Him: *Adam, be reasonable. No guitarist has only one guitar.* Me: *Not going to happen.*

The guitar sitting against the wall in the empty tour bus, a note woven between the strings where I'm sure to find it.

All this from a fucking replica-ghost-clone guitar in my room.

Thanks a lot, Dr. E or whoever decided it was a good idea.

The memories follow me to a narrow road, edged by a low, weathered wood fence.

I shove my hands into my pockets and pick a direction. The crumbling, uneven pavement beneath my feet feels strange after the sterility of the building. Shadows move across the ground in time with the waving palm leaves overhead.

I follow the road. At one point, it bends around in a U, and I hear the white noise of the ocean, which makes my stomach clench.

The fence curves with the road. At the bend, where the wood looks newer, a ribbon holds up a dried bouquet of flowers, a memorial to a life probably stolen in the span of a moment. A reminder that this is the real world, where asphalt crumbles and people die like flowers, and life moves forward with or without you.

A car whizzes by, so close that the wind from it flaps the bottom of my shirt. For a second, it shocks me, but I'm not sure what I expected, that we were the only people on this whole island? I wait for someone to roll down the car window and scream my name the way they do back home, like I'm still someone important.

Nobody does.

Eventually I reach town, if you could call it that, because the stores are really nothing more than shacks. A few have signs carved into pieces of wood. I squint at the language, which I don't recognize. But something tells me I was right, that we're in the Pacific.

I stop in the road in front of one of the buildings. Every place, no matter how remote, has a bar. And I know this is one, even though I can't actually read the sign. There's something about the noises of a bar. It's a universal thing: sometimes it's cue stick against pool ball, sometimes slightly too-loud laughter, sometimes just ice rattling in glasses. And the inviting darkness behind the windows. Or maybe it's just some subconscious connection between me and anything 100 proof.

I wonder if there's a drinking age here.

Don't you dare do it, I tell myself.

Then I notice the girl. Maybe eleven or twelve years old, she stands on the sidewalk staring at me.

"I know you," she says in deeply accented English.

So they do know me here. I tense and then remind myself that she's just a kid and seeing me could be epic for her. Her eyes are huge. It wouldn't kill me to be nice.

"Do you want an autograph?" I take a step toward her and mime signing my name.

She backs up with a little "Oh!"

A little voice in my head whispers that something isn't right here.

"No autograph?" I ask, stepping up onto the curb.

The little girl lets out a cry, and at the same time a woman comes running out of one of the stores.

"No!" She rushes toward the girl, pushing the child behind her, but she's looking at me.

I raise my hands to show I'm not doing anything.

"You…" Her English is broken too, and she looks up, as if trying to find the words in the sky. "Go back to your plezza of gostess."

"Plezza of…?"

She steps backward, keeping the girl behind her, her eyes focused on me. Her skin is pale against her dark hair.

Sweat drips down the back of my neck. "Lady?"

With the hand she isn't using to hold the little girl back, she traces some kind of symbol across her forehead.

Warding off evil, I think. I shiver. *Plezza of gostess.*

And then I get it. Place of ghosts.

When they've put a dozen yards between me and them, the woman turns, and they run to the nearest building. For a minute, I'm locked in place, my heart beating way too hard. Then I look at the bar again. The urge to drink is gone. I just want to go back.

To the Place of Ghosts, I think.

Jesus.

Chapter 14

The storm comes out of nowhere. One minute the day is perfectly clear, and the next, dark clouds boil in and the wind bends the palm trees in half. The rain starts, and I'm drenched in about two-point-five seconds. Miniature rivers race down the side of the road.

After the encounter in town, the weather seems appropriate.

When I finally step back into the air-conditioned compound, I shiver. My sneakers squish and squeak through the quiet hallways. I head to Gen's apartment and knock.

A puddle forms at my feet. I knock again.

Finally, the door opens and Gen's sleepy face appears. She squints out at me. "Adam? What's wrong?"

"I don't know." I feel like I'm waking from a dream.

"You don't…?" She frowns. "You're soaked. Come in. I'll get you a towel."

She leaves me alone in her living room. This is the first time I've been in her apartment. I look around, taking in the little touches of Gen. A faded green blanket draped over one arm of the couch, its satin edges worn almost completely away. A bookshelf filled with worn paperback mysteries. A framed photo of a young blond girl and a golden retriever, the dog's muzzle covered in birthday cake, the little girl laughing. On the coffee table, her dragonfly barrette sits in a clay dish. Seeing it there instead of in her hair seems weirdly intimate.

Something in my stomach flutters.

I'm glad when she returns, and yet it's like being caught snooping.

She drapes the towel around my shoulders, her hands lingering. She feels like an anchor to the real world and not a place of ghosts. I lean into her touch.

"Sit," she says.

I open my mouth to protest—I'm soaked; I'll ruin the furniture—but her arched eyebrows stop me. I sit on the couch and she sits next to me, our knees touching. A dark spot of transferred rainwater forms on her pajama pants where our legs meet. My heart beats too fast, and I'm not sure if it's from the incident in town or from her nearness.

"What on earth happened?" she asks.

I watch the wet spot on her knee grow and struggle to find words to tell her.

"I walked to town," I start. "And there was…"

I shake my head, unable to explain.

"Whatever it is, just say it, Adam." She laughs a little staccato laugh. "You're freaking me out."

I must look like a crazy person, dripping and tongue-tied and probably pale as a ghost. I force myself to take a deep breath and tell her the story.

Gen listens, barely blinking, hands folded across her chest. She looks smaller somehow, self-contained.

"It was just so…bizarre," I say when I've finished. But none of my sentences get across how unsettled it left me.

Gen doesn't quite look at me. Instead, she stares at the picture of the cake-eating dog, probably wishing she was back there with her pooch rather than here with this nut-job guy.

"Wow," she finally says.

"What do you think she meant?"

"What she meant? Jesus, Adam. How would I know?" She gets to her feet. There's a bite to her voice that I haven't heard before.

I look down at the floor. I can't blame her for being mad. Now that I'm sitting here in a bright, modern room that could as easily be in Manhattan as on some tiny island, it all seems a little ridiculous.

But then she sits back down and unfolds herself a little. "I'm sorry. That's just a little creepy."

My heart is still beating too fast, but I relax back against the couch. "I'm glad I'm not the only one who thinks so."

"Well, maybe it was some kind of freak-out-the-tourist game. Or maybe she recognized you, Adam, and…"

"I don't think so. They were both so freaked out. You never heard anything weird like that in town? Do you think they know what we're doing here?"

She frowns. "I doubt it. But we're in the middle of nowhere, Adam. I'm sure there are a million superstitions around here. Maybe something you were wearing or your lighter skin or…"

"So maybe I'm just making something out of nothing." What I don't say is that maybe my own freak-out has more to do with finding that ghost guitar in my room than with the locals. Place of ghosts is right. "Maybe they freaked *me* out more than *they* were freaked out."

"Maybe this place just has some weird kind of vibe. What we do here is pretty strange." Finally, she smiles. "Or maybe the ghosts of the girls we've resurrected are drawn here?"

Girls. The plural makes my tongue itch.

She immediately puts one hand over her lips, as if she knows she's said too much.

"So you know who the other clone is," I say.

She shakes her head, even though it's sort of late for that, and I catch her gaze.

"Uh-uh. No way. Dr. E would kill me if I told you. Not to mention my father. So do not even think about asking."

"I could guess," I say.

What other superstar is out there onstage, cloned, her memories those of someone six feet under, and nobody even knows about it, not even her?

Gen taps one foot on the rug. "You could."

Or maybe it's a politician.

Or some rich guy's girlfriend.

Or a brilliant scientist.

"I bet it's Rita," I say, although "brilliant scientist" may be a huge overstatement. "And the memory implantation went horribly wrong and that's why she's as bitchy as she is."

She smirks, but suddenly I realize that I'm talking about this as if it were some game and not the most important thing in my life. *What is* wrong *with me?*

"Why is it such a secret though, Gen?" I ask. "For the world or for the girl?"

She shrugs. "Both, probably. Can you imagine what it would do to someone knowing they were a clone and not the original? To know that all her memories were really someone else's? Fake memories?"

I shake my head. "But they're not fake memories."

"Aren't they?" Her eyes hold mine.

I do not need to think about this.

Suddenly the locals and their place of ghosts seem very far away. I just want to go back to my room and sleep for a week.

I stand up and smile at Gen in a way that hopefully makes me look less crazy. "We can pretend this never happened, right?"

She laughs. "Until I need to blackmail you for something, sure."

"Fair enough," I say. "I'll let you go back to sleep."

At the door, I hesitate. I want to squeeze Gen's hand or kiss her cheek. I want to say, *Thank you for being my friend.* But I don't.

Instead I say, "Good night," and start back toward my own apartment.

* * *

Halfway back, I turn a corner and bump into a man. He's standing in the middle of the hallway, arms folded across his chest, looking at a life-size photo of Sunshine.

"Oh, sorry," I say.

"Don't be. That's what I get for standing in the middle of the hallway." He holds out his hand. "Reggie Grayson."

Reluctantly I shake his hand. "Adam Rhodes."

"Yes," he says. "I know."

Though he's wearing blue jeans and a button-down white shirt with the sleeves rolled up to his elbows, the set of his shoulders and the easy way he speaks tells me he's somebody. He gestures to the picture of Sunshine. In it, she's sitting in a meadow, her arms wrapped around her knees.

"She sure was beautiful," he says.

I register the fact that he's speaking about her in the past tense.

He nods at me. "Looks like you got caught in the storm."

I realize, though I'm no longer dripping, that I still have Gen's towel draped across my shoulders.

"It came out of nowhere," I say.

He smiles, but something in his expression says sadness.

"That's the way it is on this island," he says. "Anyway, a pleasure to meet you, Adam Rhodes. You should go dry off before you catch your death."

Chapter 15

The stupid guitar taunts me from the closet all night. In the morning, I stumble down to Memory Room A, marveling at how this state of half-awakeness feels ridiculously like being drunk.

While Dr. E wires me up, I wait for her to mention the guitar. I'm planning to tell her that it was a shitty thing to do to me without warning. Because without that guitar, maybe I never would have walked to town and run into that little girl and her mother and then made a fool out of myself in front of Gen.

Pussy, I tell myself. *You're just tired. Get a grip.*

"Today's session will be a little different," Dr. E says. "A little more personal. We're going to touch on your memories of Sunshine."

So I guess we're not going to talk about the guitar. I blow out a breath and push back the irritation.

"This, of course, is the most important part of our calibration. All the other pieces mean nothing if we don't get this right." She presses a button and my chair turns until I'm facing the blank wall that's usually behind me. A second later a panel opens and a large monitor slides out. "So here's what will happen. First we'll look at some photographs of Sunshine. All I'm going to ask you to do is look at them. Think about them. Nothing more."

I close my eyes before the image can appear on the screen and take deep breaths.

"Adam?" Dr. E says.

"Yeah. I'm good." I open my eyes.

The first photo shows Marybeth at the age of eleven. She looks like she did the first time I saw her, that November morning at the bus stop.

She wears faded denim overalls, the kind you'd picture on a farmer's daughter. Only on Marybeth they look cool—an unconcerned kind of cool—and even at eleven she looks hard-edged. Somehow those baggy overalls, with her yellow shirt beneath them, the strap unhooked from one shoulder and dangling, make her look like a child of the streets. Her dark hair is long and a bit stringy, hanging in two low ponytails over the front of her shoulders.

How young she looks in that picture, her life—both our lives— stretched out ahead of us, even if it hadn't felt like it.

I feel so much older than eighteen.

The picture dissolves, leaving an ache so deep it nearly takes my breath away. God, I wasn't expecting that from a single image.

Dr. E watches me, her brows furrowed. "Adam, are you still with me?"

I nod, but my throat is too dry and tight to speak. This really is the place of ghosts.

But is that so bad? Aren't ghosts a way of knowing that even after death, life goes on in some way?

"Can I move on to the next image?" Dr. E asks.

"Yeah." My voice is a croak.

The next photo is from the same time period. I wonder how much her foster parents sold those pictures for. Enough to take a cruise to the Bahamas, I'll bet.

Click. A new photo winks onto the screen. This time Marybeth is maybe thirteen. She's hunched into a black hooded sweatshirt, so large it nearly swallows her, which was probably exactly the point.

She still has that street-smart look. Only in this photo she's grown into it, her clothing and razor-cut bangs matching the expression on her face. Back then only I had known the sad girl beneath that exterior.

For a minute, I'm back in the principal's office at John Glenn Middle School, Marybeth next to me, her hands jammed in her pockets, her jaw thrust out. Defiant as we await punishment for whatever stunt we've just pulled.

Yet when the principal turns away from us to answer his phone, MB looks at me and grins. And in that moment I know I love her.

I want to close my eyes and lose myself in the memory, but already the next picture comes: Marybeth sitting with her back against the oak tree in the park, reading a book.

Click. Another image. She's wearing thick black mascara and flipping off the camera.

Click-click. Clickety-click.

I force myself to keep watching. If somebody could have whipped up a torture just for me, this would be it. Watching Marybeth and knowing I can't touch her.

But you can, Adam, a voice inside my head says. *She's here somewhere. Here in this building.*

I shake the thought away and stare at the wires connecting me to the machine. I imagine digital fingers probing my brain, trying to find the places that light up, the places where the memories live. I imagine it's a pediatrician asking, *Where does it hurt, Adam?*

Here, Doctor. And here. And here. And then he pokes every place I tell him, prods and kneads and palpates.

* * *

A few photos later, Marybeth is onstage singing, the band behind her—LaLa, Jeddy, me—on the small pseudo-stage of the Hip Sip.

And though we're blurry where she's in sharp focus, I know Jeddy and I are looking at Marybeth.

In the photo, Marybeth wears a short skirt and high black leather boots—I remember the day she bought them at the Goodwill—and a simple white sweater, somewhere between angel and devil. She tried on so many roles over the years, as if she was always trying to find a comfortable place, always trying to discover who she really was, where she belonged.

With me, I think.

Then that picture, like the others, like Marybeth herself, disappears.

Click-click. Marybeth looking bored in her ninth-grade school photo.

Click. Marybeth with LaLa, their heads tipped together, wearing some kind of crazy hats with feathers at the top. Probably out shopping.

Or shoplifting, more likely.

Two girls who couldn't have been more different. They're both smiling. Thinking back, I don't think Marybeth smiled with anyone as much as she smiled with LaLa.

With each keystroke, Dr. E pushes us forward through time, as if she were some kind of god, until LaLa and Jeddy are dead and Marybeth Travers, lost girl, has officially become Sunshine, loved by all.

"We're almost through," Dr. E says finally. "Last one."

Click.

My breath catches. The image is a candid shot of Sunshine—I'm guessing it was taken by paparazzi—and in this one I'm with her.

They've caught us mid-stride on a gravel road. Between the baseball cap and the oversized dark glasses, her face is hidden, but her head rests against my shoulder and my arm is around her waist.

I try to remember when and where it was taken but can't.

Then that photograph disappears too, and the screen darkens, and I'm left hollow.

"Doing okay?" Dr. E asks.

Not really, I think.

"Yeah," I say. "Fine."

Chapter 16

"So where are we going, exactly?"

Gen holds a branch aside and turns around to look at me. "The swamp."

"The swamp?" I slap at a mosquito that's sucking on my arm. "I thought you had a chore to do."

"I do."

I'm feeling cranky, the kind of cranky that makes you want to tear off your own skin. And the humidity, which makes breathing feel like sucking on wet rags, is not helping. The whole island feels like a damn swamp.

"To do what? Dispose of bodies?" I pick my way down the slope after her.

"Something equally gross, Mr. Crabby," she says. A cloud of insects hangs around her blond hair like a dark halo. She waves them away. "But it's for extra credit. If I don't pull a B in bio, my dad is going to kill me, so Rita took pity on me."

I look around. "This definitely looks like her idea of taking pity."

"Ha!" she says and then, "You don't have to do this with me. You can go back if you want."

"Nah. I'm in. It's just been a rough week. But why are we going to a swamp?"

She continues down the steep slope. "To collect frogs."

"Of course." I grin. "To collect frogs. What else would we be doing?"

She smacks me on the arm and I try to sidestep her, but my foot skids on damp leaves. I pinwheel my arms, trying to catch my balance, but my feet go out from under me and suddenly I'm tumbling down the hill. I slide to a stop on my back in a heap of rotted plant goo.

Almost instantly, Gen is standing over me, her eyes as wide as an owl's, a horrified expression on her face. She leans in.

"Ribbit, ribbit," I say.

She clamps one hand over her mouth and giggles.

I raise my eyebrows at her. "Hilarious. Are you going to stand there and laugh or help me up?"

Looking chastened, she holds out a hand to me.

I swear I don't even think about it. It's like this weird urge overtakes me as I reach for her offered hand, and instead of letting her help me up, I pull so that she overbalances and falls forward. I mean to roll away so that she lands in the soft leaves beside me, but I'm not quick enough, and she lands partly on top of me, one hand on my chest. Her face is only inches from mine.

She's breathing hard, and her breath smells of peppermint. Her face shines with sweat. We both freeze.

I think hours pass.

Finally, she rolls off to one side until she's lying back in the muck. We don't look at each other. I can't get the picture of her face, so close to mine, out of my head.

She starts giggling again, and this time, she can't seem to stop. Her whole body shakes with it.

And then suddenly I'm giggling too. And God, it feels good.

It occurs to me that I didn't believe I'd ever laugh like this again, and though guilt stabs through me—how can I laugh when Marybeth is dead?—I feel lighter than I have in years.

Gen gasps, giggles still coming in little bursts and fits like bubbles that rise and pop in ginger ale.

"I can't breathe," she says, rolling onto her side to look at me. Half-rotted leaves hang off her shirt. One dangles from her hair, caught in her dragonfly barrette. I reach over to pick it out, and our eyes lock.

I'm the one to look away first.

* * *

We sit at the edge of the pond with our toes in the water, which is soupy-warm and honestly kind of gross. Between us, a plastic container holds two dozen small green frogs, which puff out their throats and croak their displeasure at being trapped.

I lean back, propping myself on my elbows. "What's Lemonsucker going to do with them?"

Gen wiggles her toes, stirring up silt from the bottom. "Some kind of memory experiments probably."

I look at the frogs climbing over each other in an attempt to escape. I wonder what their ultimate fate is going to be, and part of me itches to tip over the container and set them free.

Gen stares at them as if she's thinking the same thing. I'm not sure when the day turned so serious.

She touches her finger to the plastic. "I know how they feel."

"Trapped, you mean?" I ask.

"Yeah."

I sit up again and face her, but she keeps looking at the frogs.

"Sometimes," she says.

"Being on the island?"

The corners of her lips twist, and she seems to think about it.

"The island," she finally says. "My father. Collecting frogs for extra credit instead of just writing some report."

We sit in silence. Huge, metallic red dragonflies skim across the water. The color reminds me of the bicycles that children with true biological families get for birthdays or Christmas. *Great association for my calibration*, I think.

My mind wants to fly everywhere.

"I used to dance," Gen says.

I don't know if the change of subject is on account of the dragonflies, which do seem to dance, or if it isn't a change of topic at all. My brain is fuzzy from the heat.

She tips her head back to stare up at the sky. My eyes take in the lines of her throat, how the sunlight makes her hair glow. My heartbeat quickens, and even as it does, my chest squeezes at the idea that my body could be betraying Marybeth in its reaction.

I think of how close Genevieve was only an hour earlier. God, this tropical heat is killing me.

I need to stop this.

"When I was a little girl I thought I would be good enough one day to dance onstage. I imagined the spotlights and the audience, the applause. People wanting my autograph." Finally, she looks at me. "But I guess…Isn't that what all little girls want?"

She doesn't say to me, *You had that.* She doesn't tell me how lucky I was, how lucky Marybeth was.

I think about Marybeth at age eleven, all hard lines and sharp edges and barbed wire. "Not all little girls."

"Maybe not." Gen's voice is soft, her eyes unfocused. I think her mind is somewhere far away. Maybe on some stage in a soft pink dress, the ribbons of ballet shoes crisscrossed up her legs.

"I don't know when I stopped loving it though. If it was before or after."

"Before or after what?" I ask.

She looks at me sharply. "Coming to this stupid island."

"You didn't miss anything," I tell her. I think I understand the connection now. "Being onstage...having the whole world watching...You can still be trapped."

"Yeah," Gen says. "I guess so. Adam?"

"Mmm?"

"You know how you asked about my mother?"

I nod.

"I would go live with her if I could. But..." She shakes her head. "She left more than just my dad."

"I'm sorry," I say and then nothing else. What else is there to say?

I open the lid to the container that holds the frogs. Gently, I lift out two before replacing the cover.

They sit in my palm, frozen with fear. With one finger, Gen reaches over and touches each one.

I lower my hand to the ground, but the frogs stay, as if they don't know what to do. Eventually I give each one a nudge until they leap off and disappear back into the pond.

Chapter 17

Back at my apartment, I fall into bed and sleep for like a million years. Okay. So maybe more like twelve hours.

At some point, I dream there's a knock on my door. Or maybe there really is. Maybe Gen's come back to fetch me for milkburgers and cheeseshakes.

I giggle, which is so not appropriate for Adam, Guitarist of Sunshine, and World-Class Screwup. Or maybe I just dream that I giggle.

Then I'm onstage, sitting in the memory room chair, a circle of spotlights shining down, hot on my neck and face. Marybeth stands at the microphone, her back to me. Wires run from me to her, memories pumping through them. Our audience is only three people: Dr. E, Genevieve, and Rita, who cups her hands to her mouth and boos.

The spotlights flash so bright I have to close my eyes, and when I open them again I'm lying in bed in the tour bus. Marybeth, wearing overalls, sits on the edge of the bed, one leg folded beneath the other, holding my guitar.

"It's not the one I bought you." She plucks the strings. The discordant notes make me want to cover my ears. Finally, she puts it down and lies beside me, her head on my pillow. She's so warm. I taste salt at the back of my throat. "So tell me about your girlfriend."

"What?"

"Your girlfriend. Pretty blond thing."

I close my eyes and breathe in the scent of her strawberry shampoo. "She's not my girlfriend."

"If you say so." She picks up the guitar again and lays it across her stomach, strumming it, and doesn't comment.

I sit up and grab the guitar from her and slam it onto the floor so hard it cracks.

* * *

I jerk up and out of bed. For a minute, I think I really smashed the new guitar. But I'm in the compound, not the tour bus, and the room is dark except for the blue glow from the clock.

I put on yesterday's jeans and crumpled T-shirt and I walk the halls. I don't know what time it is, but it feels late. Or really, really early.

The dream—dreams—follow me around like a diseased version of the Hope-Ghost. Or maybe the Ghost of Fuckups Yet to Come. Ha-ha. I reek of sweat and nightmares.

I squeeze my hands into fists. *You know what, Marybeth? You weren't the only one who lost LaLa and Jeddy. And then you disappeared into your sadness and you left me completely alone. And as much as you needed me, I needed you too. Did you even notice?*

You left me completely alone, I think again. But the image that pops into my mind isn't Marybeth, but me, walking down the steps of the tour bus, duffle bag slung over my shoulder.

I shake it away. I think I'm coming unglued.

If I had a bottle of tequila I could make it all vanish. The dreams. The sharp edges. The pain. Swallow by swallow the world would blur until it became a perfect bubble of nothing.

And I'm dying for it. Flopping around like a fish. Suffocating.

One by one, I check the doors. I lay my palm against them, as if Marybeth 2.0's presence inside might warm them like a hidden fire.

Then I press my ear against each one, listening. Music plays in one room, not Sunshine's music but something harder, driving. In another room someone snores loudly. From the cafeteria comes the clatter of metal and the rush of running water.

I peer in to see if Gen is there, but the tables are all empty.

In my head, Marybeth says, *So who's your girlfriend?* I press the heels of my hands against my eyes to try to push the voice away.

And still I move from hallway to hallway, from door to door. Looking. Listening. Touching.

She's here somewhere. Behind one of these doors she's here, sleeping her sleep of memories, becoming Marybeth. Becoming Sunshine. And I feel her, like a heartbeat, the living center of this place of ghosts.

Once I've walked every hallway, I head back to my apartment.

I retrieve the clone-guitar from the closet, half expecting to see a crack running along the bottom, and sit back on the bed, in the spot where Dream Marybeth sat earlier. I pluck at the strings, cringing at the out-of-tune notes. Without thinking, I start to tune it by ear.

When I'm done, for the first time since Marybeth died, I play.

Chapter 18

"Today," Dr. E says, "I need you to remember Sunshine."

"Remember her?" *As if she isn't my every waking thought?*

"A specific memory," she clarifies, "a specific moment—or moments—in time. We need something extremely sensory. Think: smell, sight, taste, touch, sound, preferably speech…or singing. So you understand what we're looking for, we need to know we're matching apples with apples. If your memory takes place in an ice-cream shop, we need to know that when you're tasting vanilla we're not mismatching that with the smell of motor oil. Are you following?"

"I think so," I say, but I guess the look on my face tells her I'm not, because she tries again.

"The memories," she says, "they're like a code, and we want to make sure we've set the decoder ring properly. We need to see a coherent memory. So if our computer tells us you're seeing a plaid strawberry, we'll know something isn't right. Does that make more sense?"

My sleep-deprived brain finally catches up. "I think I get it."

"Good. It's a simple exercise, but an important one, because if we can't get this right the whole calibration will have been for naught."

Tension vibrates in her voice, and it occurs to me how easy it could be to jeopardize the project, that any little screwup—mine or theirs—could mean I don't get Marybeth back.

"Once you call up your chosen memory, I'll electronically 'poke' the part of your brain it lives in. It won't hurt, and it'll essentially allow you deeper access to the memory. It'll be like a vivid dream. Except you'll know you're dreaming."

I groan. I've had a few too many vivid dreams lately.

"Okay. Get your memory ready, please."

She rolls over a different-but-the-same machine from the corner, switching my wires so I'm plugged into the new whatsit.

I'll pick a harmless memory, I tell myself, *me and Marybeth taking an algebra test or standing in line for mystery meat at the school cafeteria.*

"It'll take us a minute to locate the memory once you tap into it, so you might get some strange mnemonic feedback initially."

I swallow, holding on to quadratic equations rather than sinking into the memory of the smell of Marybeth's shampoo.

"Sure, Dr. E. Whatever that means."

"Static. Bits and pieces of sensory stimuli. White noise. Do you have your memory, Adam?"

"I do," I start to say, but it vanished at "white noise," no more $x^2 - 3x = 12$, not even the damn strawberry shampoo. Instead, I instantly think: *Blowing sand, ocean waves, wind.*

The memory that comes—the memory of my dreams—comes without my permission, the way memories sometimes do. And it isn't a harmless cafeteria line or study session. But really, is any memory harmless when it concerns the person you loved the most and lost?

I try to retrieve the image of the numbers, the scratch of pencil on paper, the old desk carved with initials of dozens of students before me. Instead, I feel the cool darkness of a familiar tunnel, the crunch of sand beneath my feet, the...

"Great," Dr. E says, as if she can see what's in my head. "Hold the memory."

As if a memory were a real moment locked forever in a block of glass.

There's a tug low in my belly, like I'm made of string and someone's trying to unravel me. Then white light flashes behind my eyes, and I'm engulfed in blowing sand. It bites at my cheeks, blinds me. Beyond the sand, there are only shadows.

"I'll dial it down," she says. "Bear with me a second, Adam. This happens sometimes."

White noise, I think. *Or what did she call it? Mnemonic feedback?*

I grit my teeth and curl my hands around the arms of the chair. The chair that was so much—I don't know—*realer* a minute ago.

Sweat runs into my eyes. I wipe it away.

Finally, Dr. E's voice says, "Great. There," and the blowing sand disappears.

I let out a breath as the memory resolves, until it's so clear that it's as if I'm in two places at once. I'm in a white-walled room with Dr. E, but I'm also at Smitty's Point with Marybeth, her hand in mine.

The memory is so vivid that I can read the graffiti on the underpass walls—RHONDA IS A WHORE; CINDY LUVS CHRIS; JADEN WAS HERE—and hear the echo of our footsteps and Marybeth humming under her breath. I shiver in the remembered dampness.

My chest squeezes and I think my brain might burst into flame. I try to pull back from the memory, to remind myself that it's nothing more than chemicals, a sequence of electric impulses, biological code. Marybeth...me...that day at the beach, we've been transformed into digits and symbols, racing along the wires from my brain to Dr. E's computer and then to the brain of Marybeth's clone.

"Just relax into the memory," Dr. E says. And though everything inside of me clenches, the me in the memory lets Marybeth pull him to the edge of the ocean, where she sails that stupid-ass ADAM ♥ MARYBETH boat.

I want to grab that younger Adam and tell him to hold on to this, to stop thinking about Tuesday's baseball tryouts and the hell he's going to catch if his foster dad finds out he cut eighth period to go to the beach. I want to tell him to pay attention to the way Marybeth smells like strawberries and coconut and the lightness of her laugh, because one day she'll be gone and that's all he'll have.

Maybe worse than that, I want to shake her with her damn toy boat, her hope its only passenger. *When did you lose that, Marybeth? When?*

In the now, I clench my hands around the arms of the chair.

Finally, the boat vanishes from my sight. Instinctively, I wait for the memory to switch, for me to be on the toy-turned-life-size boat like in the dream version, looking at Marybeth back on shore. But of course it doesn't. I remind myself to breathe. The memory is over.

Then, in that instant, the memory wavers and splits into a series of other images. Sick, flash-forward images that come in time with my pulse.

Throb. Marybeth with dark rings around her eyes, her pupils dilated. *Throb.* The strobe lights of a club, Marybeth colored violet, aqua, a sickly green. *Throb.* A picnic basket between us on a dirty tile floor, watermelon hard candies and the crackle of a PA system. *Throb.* A raspy voice across a phone line. *Adam, come get me.*

I don't know if it's some glitch in Dr. E's high-tech gadgets, or if it's my own damn memory trying to pull me places I don't want to revisit. Ever.

Finally, though I'm left breathless and shaking, the beach resolves again. Marybeth's hand is in mine. God, she's only thirteen.

Three years after that day, she'll be famous, no longer Marybeth but Sunshine. Four years after, she'll be dead. Five years, and I'll be here in this chair, trying to bring her back from the dead.

What have I gotten myself into?

Chapter 19

"Are you okay?" Gen asks, and I realize I have no idea what she's been saying for the last three hallways.

"Huh?" I say smartly.

"I said, 'Are you okay?'"

Actually, Gen, I think, I'm this close to freaking out. A little while ago, I relived a memory. Only it was more than that. Because it was so real. And the stuff in the memory, it happened a long time ago, and yet I could feel the sting of blowing sand. But never mind the sand. I could feel Marybeth holding my hand.

And then those other things. Reminders of the bad things I'm going to have to live through again. That I'm going to make her live through again.

There's an electric current running under my skin, and if somebody touches me I might rocket through the ceiling.

I realize Gen is watching me, her eyebrows raised, waiting for an answer.

"Sorry." I try to pull myself back into the moment, the hallway, the too-bright fluorescent lights. "I'm fine."

Gen frowns. "You don't look fine."

"Yeah, well…" I try a smile. "I forgot to put on my lipstick this morning."

Instead of laughing at my pathetic joke, she sighs. "Suit yourself, Adam."

We walk the rest of the hallway and half of another. We pass a couple of technicians. Gen nods to them and they nod back. Finally, we stop at a doorway.

"Here's my stop," Gen says.

She digs out her key card and slips it into the slot. The gizmo beeps and the lock clicks open. She cracks open the door but then hesitates, and we stand there in a weird silence. And still I feel like I'm in two places at once. Here with Gen. On the beach with Marybeth. Here with Gen. On the beach with Marybeth. My head throbs. I massage my temples.

From beyond the door, I hear a soft, rhythmic thumping, and a kind of liquid bubbling like a fish tank.

"Listen," Gen says. For a second, I think she means to the sounds. But with her free hand, she touches my arm, and her words come out in a rush. "I know you're not okay. Are you sure you don't want to talk about it? I can maybe get someone to cover my shift and we can take a walk."

She waits for me, her head tipped to the side. I know she wants to help, but now she's another girl looking at me with so much expectation. My stomach squeezes, and I want to tell her not to look at me like that.

Instead, I concentrate on the sounds behind the door. *Dum-dum. Dum-dum.*

And the bubbling.

"Adam?" Genevieve says.

She's so focused on me that the door slips open a little more. I see the curve of glass, liquid inside, and lights and levers that remind me of Dr. E's equipment.

I think of the frogs we captured. There are experiments everywhere.

I shake myself out of my trance. "No. Go make some money so

you can escape this island prison. I'm good. Really."

She raises her eyebrows and considers me, like she doubts what I'm saying. But finally she plays along. "Maybe I should just find myself a rich boyfriend and forget this after-school job."

I blush a little at the implication.

She dips her head and groans. "I did not just say that."

I put one finger beneath her chin and lift it until she looks at me. "When you get off, come find me. We'll have milk shakes or something."

She watches me for a minute longer but finally says, "Deal."

Her hand lingers on my arm, and then she lets go and heads through the door.

* * *

Back at my apartment, I run the shower hot and stand beneath it long enough to make my muscles unclench, even if my mind won't stop running. Afterward, I stand, dripping, at the sink and rub a clean spot in the steam on the mirror. My own reflection surprises me, a stranger staring back from the smeared glass.

My face is fuller—I've gained weight here—and my eyes aren't bloodshot. I look older.

But that can't be right. How can time keep moving while Marybeth is six feet under the earth? How can my body be thriving when hers is rotting?

She's here though, I remind myself. Marybeth reborn.

My hands clench the edge of the sink.

God, I need to see her.

I pull myself away from the mirror and get dressed. In the bedroom, I sit down on the side of the bed and pick up the guitar.

I strum a random melody—something I heard somewhere but can't quite place, something entirely *unrelated* to anything—and the memory of the beach, the boat, Marybeth, fades a little.

Finally, I let the notes of the half-remembered song trail off and instead pluck the strings. It takes me a minute to realize I'm trying to re-create the sound coming from the room where Genevieve works.

Pluck-pluck. Pluck-pluck. Dum-dum. Dum-dum.

When I find the right sound, I close my eyes and pluck the strings over and over. I don't just listen. I feel it.

It only takes me a minute to understand what I'm hearing.

A heartbeat. Amplified maybe fifty times, but a heartbeat nonetheless.

Then all of a sudden a stuck cog slips, and I get it.

Marybeth's heartbeat.

* * *

Five minutes later I'm at the door, knocking. No, not knocking. Pounding like a crazy person. Until finally, Gen's voice on the other side of the door says, "What the hell?" Until the door opens, and the heartbeat sound spills into the hallway again.

Seeing me, her mouth forms an O.

"Adam!"

I try to look around her, but she pushes me back, joining me in the hall.

She yanks the door shut. "What are you doing?"

My own heartbeat is way too fast. "She's in there?"

She shakes her head, but her expression—her lips pressed together, her eyes wide—says I'm right. "No."

"Why didn't you tell me?"

She bristles. I can see it in the set of her shoulders and in the way she looks at me. In her, I see a trace of Marybeth's defiance, and it makes me ache.

"What good would it have done? To torture you knowing I see her every day?"

"Can't I…? See her, I mean?" I hate the need in my voice. I try to step around her, to grab the doorknob.

She blocks my way, keeps her gaze locked with mine. "Are you crazy? My father would kill me. Not to mention Dr. Elloran."

I lean back against the wall. I can't quite get a breath.

"You need to go," Gen says.

"What I need is to see her. Just for a second."

"Adam, stop!" she says. "You know this isn't up to me."

She pulls a cell phone out of the pocket of her jeans and puts her finger on a button, like she's going to speed-dial someone. "Don't make me call security."

"You'd call security on me, Gen? Really?" I think for a second. "And since when is there security here? Is there?"

She gives me a small, guilty smile, letting the hand with her phone drop to her side. "Okay, so no." Her voice softens. "I'm sorry, but I can't let you in there. So please don't get me in trouble, huh? Please."

She puts her hand on my arm, and my resistance slips. I'm so damn tired. I let her steer me away, although I look back over my shoulder until we turn the corner.

"Thank you," she says. "Adam, you're going to see her. You just need to be patient. Give me a minute to get someone to cover. We can go get something to eat. Talk."

But the need to see Marybeth is still burning a hole through my insides. I wave Gen away. "Don't bother."

Her whole body seems to wilt, and I know I've hurt her. I also know I'm kind of being an asshole. None of this is her fault. She's just a kid like me, only here because her father dragged her away from her normal high school life in the name of science. But I can't help myself. I walk away without looking back.

Chapter 20

Halfway back to my apartment, when that adrenaline rush is finally fading, a worm of an idea squirms into my brain. Maybe it's not that they don't want me to see Marybeth. Maybe what they're hiding is that there's nothing—no one—to see.

"You're losing your mind, Adam," I tell myself out loud. It doesn't seem so far-fetched.

But thinking about it, shouldn't there be security? Shouldn't there be people swarming the hallways? How many people should it take to resurrect a superstar? More than this, right?

So is this an elaborate ruse to steal my memories of Marybeth? But for what? To write some kind of bestselling tell-all? Maybe create a virtual reality *Be Sunshine for a Day* game?

Maybe I was supposed to catch a glimpse of the room where Gen works, to put two and two together and guess Marybeth was in there. To make the illusion complete?

Maybe I'm not getting her back.

My legs wobble, and I put my hand against the wall to steady myself. I have to force myself not to put my fist through the plaster instead.

Behind the first thought comes another. Is Genevieve in on it? Is that why she was so determined not to let me in the room?

I swallow the idea like a sour chaser for a tequila shot. Then I head for Dr. E's office.

* * *

There's no light on in her office; the space where the door doesn't quite meet the floor is dark. I knock anyway.

Nobody answers.

I knock again. "Dr. E, I need to talk to you."

Nothing.

Of course, dummy, I think. *It's the middle of the night. Only you have freak-outs regularly at this hour. Everyone else is sleeping.*

I take my key card out and slide it through the slot beside the door. With a buzz that seems louder than an explosion, a red light flashes. I glance around to make sure nobody witnessed my pathetic attempt at breaking and entering. Thankfully, no doors fly open, and nobody rushes toward me yelling accusations.

Still, that doesn't help me get answers. I sink down against the wall beside Dr. E's door to think.

As soon as I do, I notice light seeping out from the door across the hall. Inside, a shadow passes by, and then a second later, it passes again.

Somebody's awake.

I stand and walk across the hall.

At my knock, the door opens almost immediately and Rita steps out into the hall.

Oh crap. The last thing I need now is Miss I-Need-a-Damn-Attitude-Adjustment.

"Dr. Elloran is off duty," she says.

But even as I lift my hand to wave her off, the need to know still scorches my insides. I hesitate. And what the hell. Even if she is a bitch, Rita can answer my question as easily as Dr. E can.

"I need to see her," I say.

Standing with one hand on the open door, she frowns. "Dr. Elloran?"

Which is what I thought I meant, but when I open my mouth, I say, "Marybeth."

"Hmm," she says, helpful as ever.

I plant my feet. "I need to see her."

She looks at me as if I'm a bug. "You'll see her eventually."

"No." I shake my head. "I mean now. I need to see her now."

"And exactly why is that?"

I take a deep breath. "Because I'm starting to wonder if any of this is real, or if you guys are playing me for a sucker."

"I see," she says and then surprises me by waving me inside.

Her office is smaller than Dr. E's and has wall-to-wall bookshelves, which are probably filled with titles like *How to Be a Witch in Three Easy Steps* or *Tips for Pissing Off Everyone*. One of the bookshelves holds a huge aquarium with frogs in it.

Sorry, guys, I think.

But their new home looks kind of posh actually, a plastic pond, lots of smooth stones, crickets.

No fancy diplomas hang over Rita's desk. No awards either. Big surprise.

"Sit," she says.

I sit down at her desk, which unlike Dr. E's, is cluttered with framed pictures. I pick one up. It's one of those side-by-side frames. On one half, there's a picture of a couple. The guy has shoulder-length hair and a huge smile. The woman looks like she's maybe in her early twenties, but the red hair and the eyes tell me it's Rita. She looks heavier, almost plump, and she's smiling, a big flower tucked in her hair. The photo on the other side shows the same couple kneeling down, surrounded by at least a dozen dogs. The sign on the building behind them reads: Angels with Paws Rescue.

The photos are so out of sync with what I know of Rita that the world tips sideways. The smile alone does it, never mind the dogs or the flower in her hair or the way the guy beside her looks at her, as if she were the only person in the world.

"Are you done examining my personal effects?" she asks. She leans back against her desk and crosses her arms over her chest.

I put the frame down.

"You cannot see Sunshine because Sunshine isn't yet ready for you to see her. Nothing more. Nothing less."

Alrighty then.

"Meaning?" I ask.

"Meaning that her physical form, her corporeal body, isn't ready for you to see. She's a work in progress. And it's best for your sake and, consequently, for the success of our project, that you not see her until she's recognizable as the Sunshine you knew."

Her words bring to mind a fetus going through all those weird animallike phases—fish, lizard, claws and tail—before becoming a baby. Is she some kind of a monster? Is that what Rita's saying?

"So I'm supposed to just trust you." It isn't a question.

"Pretty much," she says.

But she tips her head back, lips pressed together, as if she's considering something.

Something's happening here, but I'm not sure what. My stomach flutters.

"You can't see her. Not now. Not up for discussion." She makes a cutting motion in the air with one hand to end the subject. "But if you're worried that we're all bluff and only out to exploit your and Sunshine's estate, I think I can do something to assuage that particular concern."

* * *

I follow her to Memory Room A. She glances over her shoulder, then unlocks the door with her key card and lets us inside. Then she closes the door behind us without putting on the light.

"Wait here," she says.

I hear her bumping around in the dark and then the creak of another door. A minute later the room behind the one-way glass fills with light.

Rita gestures for me to come.

"Now this"—she jabs a finger toward my face—"this is between you and me. You understand?"

Again, I get that feeling of something weird happening, some mix-up in the natural order. Like for this moment, ol' Lemonsucker and I are in something together.

She pushes a rolling chair toward me. I catch it and sit.

A minute later she's wallpapering me with the conductor pad thingies that Dr. E always uses, pressing them on with her thumb like she's trying to stick them right into the center of my brain.

"Ow," I say, and I swear she smiles.

When she's done, she rolls me over to the bank of computers that covers the far wall. I watch her flip switches and dial dials and punch buttons.

"What are we doing, anyway?" I try to sound calm, but the fluttering in my stomach ramps up. This is Rita. She could be preparing to turn my brain into gray-matter soup.

"You wanted to 'see' Sunshine. You wanted proof that she's here, that what we're doing is more than science fiction, right?" she says. "So I'm going to show you Sunshine. Just...not her actual body."

"You're..."

"Yes. This may be a little unorthodox. But you'll get your proof."

Before I can respond, she punches one final button and says, "Here we go."

I wipe the palms of my hands on my jeans. But...

"I don't feel anything."

She holds up one finger. "Wait."

And then a black hole opens up inside me.

Chapter 21

I wake up on the floor, my cheek pressed against the tile, one arm twisted beneath me.

A female voice says, "Shit," and then, "Adam, are you all right?"

I start to say, "Sure, Dr. E," but then I remember. Rita.

With my free arm, I push myself up. My head balloons, and I think I'm going to black out again, but I hold still and it fades to a steady pounding.

Rita offers me her hand. I hesitate, but then take it and let her pull me up.

"Sit down," she says.

I drop into the chair and press my thumbs into my eyelids, trying to push the pain back. "Jesus. What did you do to me?"

"I gave you memories," Rita says.

"Memories? You gave me a headache is what you gave me."

"Yes, well. This is a little unorthodox, so I'm not surprised."

"Great. Fabulous." Despite my pounding head I get up and start for the door. I'm done with this. Whatever I started out wanting isn't going to happen tonight.

"Adam," Rita calls to me before I reach the outer door. "This is between you and me. Don't forget."

I squint under the glare of the hallway fluorescents, and I'm grateful to reach my apartment and step into the wonderful darkness. But the door barely clicks shut behind me when my mind churns up an image of the tour bus. A place I've tried not to think about for ages.

I shove it away. Enough. Stop thinking.

In the bedroom, I flop facedown on the bed, and the image—memory—is there again, stronger. Suddenly I remember the bus's dark interior, its smell a combination of leather and conditioned air and rain, so strong I can almost breathe it right in.

The rush of the sensation comes out of nowhere.

Except it doesn't, does it?

I groan.

Rita. Crap.

I close my eyes and run through the memory: shadows from raindrops that join together and run like rivers down the windows, muffled laughter from somewhere outside, the huff of the bus's heater. Only it's like seeing the tour bus through a fun-house mirror. The windows seem higher, the furniture a little bigger, the curved ceiling farther above my head, the smells just a shade off from how I remember them.

In the memory, the bus is parked, but I still feel disoriented and slightly motion sick.

Then again, maybe I got a concussion falling out of the chair. Or maybe good ol' Rita did something to my brain.

But it's more than that. Because it's like I'm in a projector booth at a movie theater, looking through a tiny window at the movie playing on the big screen. Well, except it's a movie that isn't just a picture. It's taste, touch, and freaking scratch-n-sniff.

Goose bumps pop up on my arms.

The memory carries me forward. I'm sitting on the bed. Except I'm not me.

Finally, I get it. The "me" in the memory is Marybeth. And I feel her. As if she's part of me.

I don't mean just physically. I feel her consciousness. At least, this small piece of it. This moment in time. The fizz and sweetness of just-swallowed Cherry Coke. The soreness of her sneaker rubbing against a blister on her heel. The tickle of flyaway hair against her cheeks. The smoothness of the piece of beach glass that she worries between her fingers.

In the memory, the first notes of a song form, played on guitar. I/she looks up, through the open bedroom door. From where I/she sits, she can see down the long aisle of the bus to the dining room, where I'm playing the guitar, my head bent low.

It's a song she doesn't recognize, and she thinks it's beautiful. But there's also an ache, her ache, but in the here and now it makes my belly cramp. Because her not knowing the song is a canyon between us, and it makes her imagine a world where there is only me and no her.

Then the memory is gone. I want to follow it, to see where it goes, if she says something to me, if she walks to me and I exchange the guitar in my arms for her body. If that takes away the hurt inside of her, even for a little while.

But the memory stops short. There is no more.

I feel hollow.

PHASE II

Chapter 22

In the morning, Dr. E takes me to a new room. Instead of the antiseptic Memory Room A, this one looks more like a lounge. An overstuffed couch against one wall makes me imagine Dr. E saying, *So tell me about your mother*, in a thick German accent. There's also a pair of blue, comfy-looking armchairs and a table stacked with magazines. Photos of Sunshine on the wall. The only thing that in any way says "lab" is the MAP machine in one corner.

I still have the fragment of memory stuck in my head. *Implanted*, I think. Once in a while, I poke at it to see if it's still there, like a little kid pokes at the hole where a baby tooth once was.

"Welcome to Phase Two." Dr. E closes the door behind us. "In this phase we'll be harvesting your memories of Sunshine."

She sits in one of the chairs and gestures to the other one. I perch on the edge.

"Okay."

"Of course, we can't identify every memory missing from those recovered after Sunshine's accident, but we have enough to puzzle out where the gaps are. It'll be like a game of Memory. Did you ever play that as a child?"

Obviously she doesn't understand that my childhood wasn't the kind where you played board games or card games, but I nod, because it's easier.

"Good," she says. "So we'll take the 'cards'—aka memories— that we already have for Sunshine and find the matching 'card' in your own memory bank. All that tedious mapping, Adam, the flash cards and the vials of scents...It told us where to find what we need.

"We'll also take an extensive cross section of memories from you, to ensure that we've got everything. And, of course, we'll harvest all vital memories."

It all sounds so clinical. I have to remind myself that they're talking about a person. Someone I loved. Love. I'm starting to think that Dr. E doesn't particularly care about that.

"So if you're ready," she says, "we'll get started."

I nod. "I'm ready."

The chair spits her back out and she pulls over the MAP machine and starts to wire me up.

When she's finished, she says, "What I want you to do is visualize Sunshine. Close your eyes and picture her standing onstage. Picture her yellow dress, her bare feet on the polished stage. Picture her dark hair, how the stage lights reflect off her. As clear as you can, Adam." She pauses. "Do you have the image in your head?"

Of course I do. Doesn't she know I've spent the last year trying to drink that image away?

"Yes." I clear my throat. "I do."

"Excellent. Now hold that image. Picture her features, her lips and nose, the green of her eyes."

I hold her in my mind. Sunshine. My Sunshine with that beautiful, melancholy smile.

Not Sunshine.

Marybeth.

Dr. E says, "Now let her sing."

In my mind, Marybeth puts one hand on the microphone and lowers her gaze to the floor. When she opens her mouth, the words to "Neptune's Garden" start. She sings about soft white sand and shooting stars and a garden beneath the sea.

"Wonderful," Dr. E says. "Now keep her singing for as long as you can."

I want to tell her that I could let Marybeth sing Sunshine's entire repertoire and then do it again. Everything inside me might be cut to ribbons by the third song, but I could do it.

But finally, she says, "That's perfect, Adam. Give me two minutes and we'll move on."

I open my eyes and watch her fuss over the MAP machine.

"Okay." She returns her attention to me. "We'll ease into this. I need you to remember the first time you met Sunshine. I'll be guiding you through it, Adam, and what I need is not just the memory of Sunshine herself, but the circumstances: the setting, the weather, what you were wearing. Try to remember everything you can about that day. Hear the sounds. Smell the smells. Now close your eyes."

I close them.

"All right," Dr. E says. "Take a deep breath. Now...How old were you when you first met Sunshine?"

"I was twelve."

"And Sunshine? How old was she?"

"Eleven," I say.

"Good. Now let's set the scene."

I remind myself to breathe. These are forbidden places. Moments from another life. The past is the past and all that BS.

I say, "I was at the bus stop. My foster father was watching me from his car to make sure I got on the bus."

"Did he always?" she asks.

"No." I shake my head. "I'd tried running away a few weeks earlier. I'd made it as far as the city with money I'd stolen from my foster mother's purse, but a cop at the train station figured it out and brought me back."

"And how did Sunshine come into the picture?"

"She wasn't Sunshine then. She was Marybeth. Marybeth Travers."

"Of course. Tell me about the first time you saw her."

"She was already at the bus stop when I got there. There were a few other kids there too. She was new, but I think she would have stood out anyway."

"How so?" Dr. E asks.

I shrug. "I could tell she'd been around the block a few times. She had that look, you know, like she'd been knocked around."

"Keep going. Where was she standing?"

"By herself, beneath the old maple tree."

"And what was she wearing?"

"Denim overalls and a yellow shirt."

"Good," she says. "Keep going. What was your first impression of her?"

"I was drawn to her." *Why are you saying this, Adam?* "Everything about her said keep away. But I found myself walking toward her."

"How many kids were there?"

"Seriously? It was a long time ago, Dr. E."

"Hold that thought," she says, and then after a minute, "Okay. I've got the area of your brain pinpointed for this memory. I'm going to give it a boost. Just like before, you're not going to feel anything, but the scene is going to become a lot clearer in about five, four, three..." Her fingers fly across the keyboard. "Two..."

Then it's there.

"Three," I say. "There were three other kids: Emily and the two brothers, Josh and Luke. They both had that white-blond hair. There's a name for it."

"Towhead," Dr. E supplies.

"Right. Towhead."

And maybe her little boost did something to the rest of my mind too, because all of a sudden the words start spilling out.

"Marybeth was wearing ponytails. She always did back then. Or sometimes braids. She wore these elastic bands with yellow balls at the ends.

"I walked toward her. I could feel my foster father watching from the car, impatient to be somewhere else. But…" I completely lose the thought. I dig the heels of my hands into my eyes and press. "Sorry."

"It's okay. It's all important, Adam. Take as much time as you need. So you were walking toward her…"

"I think she noticed me, even though she pretended not to. That was classic Marybeth. Don't give anyone the satisfaction." I smile at the memory of the tough little kid who became the girl the world loved. How strangely life works.

Dr. E says, "Keep going."

I think of how I approached her, the squeak-squeak-squeak of my sneakers on the sidewalk, my hands jammed in my pockets. And I lose myself to the memory.

Chapter 23

The new girl doesn't look up when I walk toward her. Her shoulders hunch, body language that says, *Don't look, don't touch, don't dare come close.*

I get it. I perfected the same look over years of moving from one foster family to another. *Sorry,* they'd say, *it's not working out with Adam. We've tried so hard—you know we have—but he's just not manageable.* Like I'm a puppy they're returning to the pound because it peed on the carpet.

"Hey," I say.

She looks up, but doesn't say anything, just silently checks me out. Finally, she shrugs. "Hey."

"I haven't seen you before," I say.

"No." She crosses her arms over her stomach. "I guess you haven't."

Her vibe says, *Go away, go away, go away.*

I should walk away, I think. But instead I ask her, "Did you just move here?"

"Uh, yeah." She frowns as if she can't quite figure me out. "Otherwise you would have seen me, right?"

I can't help it. I grin. "Guess that's right."

For some reason, that makes her grin too.

The other kids watch us with interest. Good. Let them.

My foster father is watching us too.

"So who are you anyway?" I ask.

"Marybeth. I'm living with the Jordans down on Oakland."

Living with, I think. *So she's definitely a foster.*

"The Jordans, huh? Good luck with that," I say. "They've got a bunch of kids, right?"

"Yeah. Well. They're not the first and they won't be the last. You?"

"Adam," I say. "I'm stuck with the Androvs, just around the corner. House with the stupid ceramic gnome on the lawn."

I don't tell her that the guy sitting in the car by the curb is my foster father. I don't want to give him the satisfaction of having her even look in his direction.

I also don't tell her that I'm going to run away today, that I have a wad of money I stole from under my foster parents' mattress and I'm going to catch a train to the city. That I can't stand one more day with my foster mom, with her perfect hair and her perfect kitchen and her perfectly ugly zombie face.

Instead, I make a show of rolling my eyes and get rewarded with Marybeth's snort of laughter. I puff up. I feel like I just won some hard-fought prize. Or maybe like I've punched through a brick wall.

With that, the bus chugs down the street. It rounds the corner so fast I expect it to hit the curb and tip right the hell over. Which would be epic.

"Nice driving," Marybeth mutters.

"Oh, that ain't nothing. Just wait."

The bus bumps up to the curb. The trio of "real" kids—kids with biological families, not in foster care—board the bus nicely, their backpacks hooked over their slim shoulders. I hang back with Marybeth, long enough to look cool. Finally, my foster father lays on the horn. The bus does too.

"Nice," Marybeth says. She sounds older than eleven, which I figure is what she must be.

I shrug like none of it makes a difference and head for the bus, dragging my own battered knapsack behind. The cash in my pocket feels like it's glowing red-hot, like everyone can see it.

The second I put my foot on the first stair, my foster father's car takes off. If I turn and run now, I can be halfway to the train station before the driver even gets a call out on the radio.

But I look back at the new girl—at Marybeth—and I climb up the stairs and walk to the back of the bus and take a seat. She follows. I try hard not to grin.

When she slides into the seat next to me, I do grin, even though I know how uncool it is. Because I think maybe, for the first time in a long time, I've found a friend.

Chapter 24

The thoughts in my brain keep spinning around.

Marybeth's heartbeat coming from the room where Gen works.

The bizarre not-me-but-Marybeth memory that Rita somehow implanted into my brain.

Phase Two and the super-Technicolor memory session.

Even the leftovers of the dream Marybeth from a few nights ago that I can't quite shake.

So when Genevieve knocks at my door, the last thing I need is a fight over my trying to see Marybeth last night. But she just smiles and says (maybe a little bit shyly), "If you're not still mad about yesterday, do you want to get dinner with me?" As if she's willing to let the whole thing go. And if she's willing, I sure as hell am.

"Dinner sounds great."

Still, it's awkward. Neither of us says much as we get our food and head out behind the complex to the small picnic area. For a little while, we eat in silence. Gen sucks a strawberry milk shake through a straw, her cheeks puckering from the effort of pulling the thick liquid up the narrow tube.

Finally, I say, "We started Phase Two today."

She looks up from the drink, massaging her cheeks.

"Damn that's thick," she says and then, "Phase Two, really? How was it?"

I balance my plate on my knees. It's piled high with waffle fries slathered in melted pepper jack cheese. Real healthy stuff. One of these days I'm going to have to start watching what I eat. My jeans are finally not falling off me and pretty soon I'm going to be popping the damn button.

"Exhausting," I say.

"I'll bet." She takes the lid off her cup, holds the straw aside, and drains the last of the shake. Then she puts one hand against her stomach. "That shake was ridiculous."

She's so small; I can't help but wonder where she packs all the food away.

"Finish up and let's walk," she says. "I think we both just need to get away from this place for a while."

This place of ghosts, I think.

I take one last cheese-drowned fry and pop it into my mouth. Then I get up and dump my plate in the trash.

The air smells damp. It's starting to drizzle, and the cool rain helps clear my head.

Now that we don't have the food to keep us busy, I don't know what to say. My brain is on a carousel, going around and around and around.

I stop walking and look at her. "You could have told me."

She doesn't stop, and after a second, I jog to catch up.

"That I work with Sunshine?" she says. "Yeah, sure. I could have. But why? So you could give me grief like you did last night?"

I don't know what to say to that.

"I'm sorry if I was harsh, Adam. It's just…Things aren't always that easy, you know?"

"I know," I say. Of course I know. When has anything in my life been easy?

We turn off the path onto the road. Stones crunch beneath our feet. The sun dips all the way to the horizon.

"Do you?" she asks, which seems a weird thing to ask me, but before I can answer, she waves the question away. "So what was the memory retrieval process like? I've heard the scientific staff talk about it, but I've never talked to someone who's actually been through it."

"It was strange. It started off as nothing more than me remembering the first time I met Marybeth, but then they give your brain some weird kind of—I don't know—superbooster. And then it's like you're *in* the memory."

"What do you mean, '*in* it'?" she asks.

"Like—I don't know how to explain it, Gen—I knew it was a memory. It's not that I was having a hallucination, but it was so real that it was like reliving it, only *knowing* that I was reliving it, all at the same time. I know that doesn't make any sense."

She scrunches up her lips like she's considering it. "A lot of things around here don't make sense. But you're okay?"

"I'm…" I blow out a breath. "It was hard."

Her hand creeps into mine, squeezes.

I flinch. I don't mean to. It's just automatic. But she yanks away as if I've stuck her with a pin.

For a minute, we walk in uncomfortable silence. I want to tell her I'm sorry, that it's not her. It's me. I can't do this with her right now, not when I'm so close to having Marybeth back. But I can't find any words.

She steps off the path onto the dark, narrow road I walked a few weeks ago. The sun is down now, and she switches on a flashlight I didn't know she had. The rain has stopped, and in the humid heat, sweat pastes my hair to my forehead. Gen seems unbothered by any of it.

"We're not going to town, are we?"

She shakes her head.

"My dad doesn't like me coming out here," she finally says. "But what he doesn't know won't hurt him…or me, right?"

"You talk about your dad. Who is he, anyway?" I ask. "Someone important?"

She laughs. "You could say that."

"Why's that funny?"

"You don't know?"

I shake my head and then realize she can't see me in the dark. "No."

"My dad *is* Project Orpheus, Adam. This is his baby."

"Wow." I whistle. "I didn't see that coming. His name isn't Reggie Grayson by any chance?"

"You've met him?"

"Briefly."

"You know what?" She waves her hands, the flashlight beam zigzagging across the pavement. "I *so* don't want to be talking about my dad."

The road twists around. At times I feel as if I'm on the edge of a wide open space. From somewhere below, I can hear the ocean. Not even a single car passes.

"Where are we going, anyway?"

"Nowhere, really."

Except something about her voice tells me that's not exactly the case.

"Nowhere? Well, that's a fun night out."

She sighs. "Just a place I'm drawn to. You'll see in a sec."

A little farther on, where the road bends around on itself, Gen's flashlight reflects off the low wooden fence.

"Here, hold this." She hands the flashlight to me and kneels beside the fence. I train the light on her. Where she kneels, the bouquet of flowers still hangs on the crossbeam, dried out now, fastened by a purple ribbon, faded from the sun.

The roadside memorial.

Gen traces the ribbon with her finger. She seems thoughtful and maybe a little sad, and for a minute I'm reminded of Marybeth. I feel like there's something big that I'm missing.

"Who died here?" I ask.

Gen shrugs. "Some girl, I think."

She busies herself untying the ribbon. Once she frees the bouquet, she holds it against her chest, the dried flowers with their drooping heads like a bouquet for some undead bride.

"So you're stealing some random dead girl's flowers?" I try to make light of it, but looking at her like that, I shiver.

"Dead person, dead flowers. No one will care."

She climbs over the low fence. I start to say something else, but I give up and follow. Just beyond is a cliff. Far below, the ocean roars, but all I see are stars and sky and dark.

Gen stands with her toes out over the edge, and for just a second, a crazy fucked-up second, I think she's going to spread her arms and try to fly.

Fall, she's going to fall, she's going to…

I want to grab her but I'm frozen. I can't breathe.

Then she tosses the bouquet over the edge. There's no sound to tell us when it hits the water.

Finally, Gen steps back from the edge and I can breathe.

"It's funny." She glances back at me. "As many times as I take the old ones down, there are always new flowers. But no matter how many times I come here, Adam, I never see who leaves them."

We climb back over the fence. As I do, the flashlight beam hits the ground and reflects off of a familiar metallic rectangle. Gen's key card.

My heart jumps.

I look at Gen and realize she hasn't noticed that she dropped it. *Don't do it, Adam.*

Before I can stop myself, I grab the key card and shove it in my pocket.

Chapter 25

We don't talk on the way back. When we get to my apartment, I want to reach out and touch her, but she keeps her hands in her pockets.

"Do you have to go to…" I hesitate. "Work now?"

She looks down at the floor. "Not tonight. I'm tired. I think I'm just going to go to sleep."

For a minute, she doesn't leave, and I stand in the open doorway, wanting to say something else but not knowing what.

Something has changed. I wish I understood what…or why. I think it's probably something I did.

Finally, she takes her hands out of her pockets and touches my cheek. This time I don't flinch.

She smiles, but it feels heavy, sad. "Good night, Adam."

"Good night, Gen."

Inside, I drop down onto my couch. The heaviness is inside me too. Or maybe it's just everywhere. Maybe the laws of gravity changed when I wasn't paying attention.

Then abruptly, the world shifts.

It only takes me a second to realize what's happening this time.

Oh crap, I think. *Is this supposed to happen again, Rita?*

The velvet curtains feel like some kind of undersea forest, I/she thinks as we walk through the folds away from the stage. The roar of the crowd follows us, the silence of the hypnotized audience having given way to mad applause and whistles and screams. We swim through the curtains, away from it. There is no adrenaline from being onstage. There is only the feeling of obligation, of commitment, of emptiness that even the adoration of millions will never fill.

Here in the stage curtains, this is an in-between place, she thinks, and I am her.

She holds back, wanting to stay here in the dark for as long as possible, wanting to become it, maybe. But people are waiting, people who won contests and people who paid big bucks to have a moment with Sunshine after the show.

She looks back at me. She reaches for my hand. She aches for some connection.

But someone, a stagehand or a backstage manager or maybe Jack pulls her forward, hurrying her along.

Save me, Adam, she thinks. And even as she thinks it, there's a second thought. Darker. That I can't save her. That nobody can.

* * *

I emerge from the memory—Marybeth's memory—panting and sweaty. I stumble to the kitchen and then the bathroom and open every cabinet, hoping there's something. Cooking wine, cough syrup, mouthwash. Something to burn away the pain. But there's nothing, so I fill a glass with water. My hand shakes. Every part of me shakes. I gulp it down and then gulp a second.

Rita, what did you do to me?

I rummage through the few kitchen drawers until I find a flashlight. I need to walk this off.

Outside, I'm so lost in the memory of the memory—oh God, I'm really going crazy—that I don't realize where I'm heading until I reach the bend in the road where Genevieve pulled down the flowers.

Someone's standing by the fence. My heart nearly stops beating. I half expect the figure to dissolve into smoke. Maybe this is what the woman meant by "place of ghosts."

Instead, the person turns and lifts one hand to shield his eyes from the light.

I move the beam from his face to the fence—where, sure enough, there's a new bouquet of lilies and orchids tied with a bright purple ribbon—and then back to his face.

I know who it is immediately.

"Reggie Grayson," I say.

He smiles, a tight smile, and his eyes crinkle. It's Gen's smile. Gen's eyes. It's why he looked so familiar the first time I met him, I realize now.

"Adam," he says. "It's good to see you."

And even as he speaks, even as my eyes move from him to the fresh bouquet on the fence and then back, even as my mind replays Gen telling me that she's drawn here, even as my mind recalls Dr. E saying, *We've done this before,* the dark truth of it forms in my brain.

Oh no. Oh no, no, no, no.

Black spots crowd the edges of my vision. I have to remind myself to exhale and then inhale again, because I keep forgetting.

"Out for a walk tonight?" he asks.

But maybe he sees from my face that I'm putting it all together, because his smile falls. He sighs and nods, as if in acknowledgment.

"Let me buy you a cup of coffee, Adam." His tone says that it's really not up for discussion. "We'll talk."

* * *

We reenter the building through an entrance I didn't know existed. Mr. Grayson leads me down a short hallway with several doors—for a minute I think I hear the heartbeat sound again, faintly, and then it's gone—and into an apartment that makes mine look like a hole in the wall.

"Have a seat," he says. "I'll call for coffee."

I sit in a high-backed leather chair and wait while he disappears into another room.

The girl who brings the coffee is one of the regulars at the cafeteria. When she sees me she ducks her head, a blush creeping across her cheeks as if she's caught us doing something pervy. She sets the coffee mugs on the table and then hurries back out.

Once the door closes behind her, Mr. Grayson smiles. "I don't know which one of us makes her more nervous, me or you."

I take one of the mugs. "Maybe both of us together."

"Could be." Then for a minute he doesn't say anything.

I sip at my coffee.

"Mr. Grayson…" I start.

He holds up a hand. "Adam, my Genevieve, she doesn't know. She thinks our first project was a British pop star, a girl who is, and has always been, very much alive. And I'd like to keep it a secret. Hopefully forever. For her sake. The staff is sworn to secrecy, and if they value their careers and their bank accounts, they'll hold their tongues. And so will you."

I think I'm going to hyperventilate. "So I'm right then?"

"You are, I'm afraid. Genevieve was our first. In fact, she's the reason for Project Orpheus. Except, of course, it wasn't Project Orpheus back then. It was…Well, it didn't need a name because it wasn't a business, you understand."

I don't understand anything, but I nod anyway.

"How did she…" The word catches in my throat because it's just so damn wrong, and for a few seconds I can't shake it free. "Die?"

Breathe, Adam, I tell myself. *Breathe, breathe, breathe.*

"Hang on," Mr. Grayson says. "I'm going to need something a little stronger than coffee for this."

He disappears and then returns carrying a silver flask, which he empties into his coffee cup. As he pours it, it smells sweet and rich and golden.

Brandy, I think. *The good stuff. The kind that goes down as smooth as velvet.*

As if he knows what I'm thinking, he says, "I'd offer you some, but we both know that isn't a good idea."

On the contrary, I think it's a very good idea. Maybe the only way I'm going to get through this.

He takes a long swallow, and I wet my lips.

"She was struck by a car," Grayson finally says. "Right at that blind curve. She was walking into town for a shaved ice, Adam. A shaved ice. And just like that, she was gone."

He looks away from me. My own brandy-less coffee churns in my stomach.

That's how we always lose the people we love. Just like that. Gone in a heartbeat.

"I was sick with grief, Adam. But I'm sure you know all about that. Awful thing. Awful. Makes you desperate. To have all this money, but not be able to bring back my little girl. But, of course, if you look at what we're doing here, that's not true."

I don't respond, and he keeps talking. He talks about some cloned sheep called Dolly, about MAP machines and memories and jellyfish DNA, and about how South Korean scientists engineered cats that glow in the dark, ridiculously random things that sit in the shadow of his daughter's death, of the Big Secret. And at some point, I stop hearing him.

I don't mean to. It's kind of like that old cartoon about what you say and what your dog hears. *Blah, blah, Rover, blah, blah, blah.* Only what I hear is, *Blah, blah, Genevieve-died-and-was-cloned-and-my-life-just-keeps-getting-more-and-more-fucked-up, blah, blah, blah.*

But I understand. Because that's how we cope with these things, isn't it? By looking away.

Though the Gen I know—the only Gen I've ever met—is down the hall sleeping, I think I'm going to puke. Because my mind keeps drawing a picture of pretty Gen lying in a satin-lined box, her blond curls dried like straw against her fleshless skull. I want to scrub the image away, want to tell her dad to go get the whole bottle of brandy and hand it over.

Because somehow, somewhere, I've stopped being able to look away.

But there's one question sweeping away everything else in my mind. I'm terrified of the answer, but I need to know.

"Is she the same?"

Mr. Grayson looks at me. I want him to smile. I want him to reassure me. But his eyes look a little wet.

"Is she ashes-to-ashes made whole, flesh and blood, Lazarus risen from the grave?" He puts down his coffee and leans forward. "She's the same in so many ways it's like a miracle. Utterly identical. Her likes, dislikes. The way she laughs. The things she laughs *at*. She can tell the story of how she fell off the stage during her second-grade play. In perfect detail. And it's real for her."

I'm listening now. I lean forward too.

"To everyone else, Adam, this will be a perfect resurrection. They will have Sunshine back exactly as she was."

The switch—from talking about Genevieve to talking about Marybeth—takes my breath away. My whole body vibrates like a just-strummed guitar string.

"And you will too. Except…" He takes the flask from the table and turns it completely upside down, shaking the last few beautiful caramel-colored drops into his empty coffee mug. There's kindness in his voice, but there's something bitter too. "There will still be a beautiful young girl in the ground, and nothing will ever change that. But no matter what, you can't look back."

Chapter 26

"Can you give me a hand, Adam?" Genevieve asks, sitting up in her coffin.

I'm sitting in the front pew of the church. Except it isn't a church. It's Memory Room A. Okay—and it isn't really a pew. Just a row of folding chairs facing the coffin, which rests on a wooden platform.

I get up to help, but Dr. Elloran pushes past me—I don't know where she came from; I thought I was alone—and helps Genevieve climb down.

"Success," Dr. E says.

Beside me, someone claps, and I realize it's Marybeth. Only she's still eleven, dressed in her usual overalls and yellow T-shirt. On one arm, she has a dragonfly tattoo.

"When did you get here?" I ask her.

She shrugs. "I've been here the whole time, Adam."

When I turn back to Genevieve, she's standing with her hands on her hips. She's dressed all in yellow.

"What do you think?" she asks.

I start to ask, "About what?" but then I see the glowing cat ears poking out from beneath her blond hair.

"I don't...I..." I shake my head.

"Jellyfish DNA," Marybeth says from beside me, quite matter-of-factly. Except her voice isn't her voice. It's Mr. Grayson's. "It's the newest trend in cloning."

...And I jolt awake.

The bedside clock says 2:00 a.m. I lie there in the dark, breathing heavily, sweat collecting behind my neck. The sheets feel soaked. Cold air blowing from the overhead vent hits me, and I shiver.

I turn over, away from the obnoxious blue numbers, and press my face into the cool pillow.

I test the word: *Cloning.*

Cloned.

Clone.

Genevieve, the girl I've gotten to know so well—ha!—is a clone. Genevieve, my friend, with her love of unhealthy food and especially strawberry milk shakes, is the clone of a dead girl.

My brain can't process it. Any of it.

When I flip over again to check, the clock says 2:13.

Chapter 27

In the memory, I'm walking through the middle school hallway on my way to social studies.

I still can't get used to how real this feels. I know I'm remembering. I *know* it. I can feel the cushions of the couch I'm sitting on in Memory Room B. I can hear the hum of the MAP machine. If I open my eyes, I can see Dr. E.

But I can also feel hair on the back of my neck—hair that I chopped off a long time ago and smell Eau de Mystery Meat as I pass the cafeteria. I can feel the stickiness of the hallway floor and hear the sucking noise my sneakers make when I walk.

And I know it's a damn memory, but it's sure better than the here and now—I can't shake the image of Genevieve in her grave—and I give myself completely to today's memory retrieval session.

In the memory, I slouch past the vending machines that sell stupid crap like apples and bottled water and all that so-called healthy stuff the PTA decided should replace our Pepsi and Reese's. Except the apples do nothing but rot, and only the rich-bitch girls buy the water.

Something whacks me in the back of the head.

I whip around, but nobody's there.

When I look down, there's a paper airplane on the ground. Whoever threw it must have done so and run.

I pick up the plane. Words stretch along one wing: MEET ME AT THE BASEBALL FIELD. MB.

MB?

It takes me a minute. Then I grin. MB...Marybeth.

And I know, I just know, that she doesn't mean after school.

I don't hesitate. I make sure nobody is watching and then duck out the side door.

The memory fades until it's just a normal memory, no more super-booster.

I remember walking out to the baseball diamond, seeing her standing at home plate, her toe kicking the dirt. I remember grinning like an idiot, imagining her tossing the plane at my head and then running as fast as she could to get there before me and try to look cool.

"Let's fast-forward a little," Dr. E says.

My mouth is too dry. I swallow, trying to find some spit.

"What happened after you met her there?" she asks.

"We..." No spit. No spit at all. "We left the school grounds."

"Where did you go?" she asks. Then, "Don't tell me. Remember."

And once again, I'm back there. This time, I'm sitting at a wobbly wooden table in a dark little coffee shop called Java Bean, where it smells more like spice than coffee, pretending I'm at least twenty and not thirteen. Pretending I belong there. Pretending the girl sitting across from me, looking for all the world like she is in her element, isn't the coolest thing that's happened to me in forever.

* * *

Across from me, Marybeth props her elbows on the table, her chin resting in her hands. She stares out the grimy glass storefront at the thunderclouds rolling in, radiating boredom. I sip the coffee. It's dark and bitter and, honestly, disgusting.

"You don't say much," I finally say.

She shrugs and then a second later one side of her mouth tips up in a half-grin, as if she realizes how ironic her response was.

"So what's your story?" I ask.

She keeps looking out the window for so long I think she isn't going to answer.

She looks at me, her eyes an intense shade of green. "Dead mother," she says matter-of-factly. "Drugs. Father…unknown. Not as in don't know *where* he is, but more like don't know *who* he is. You?"

I shrug. This is the way we have to speak of such things. Like name, rank, and serial number.

"Parental units declared unfit, capital Un, capital Fit."

"Mmm," she says.

Outside, the clouds open and fat raindrops pour from the sky.

"Well," I say, "I guess we're stuck here for a while."

Marybeth's half-smile blooms into something so bright it might as well be the sun. Inside me, something hard begins to crumble.

Then it's all gone and, once again, she's just bones in a grave.

Stop it. Stop doing that, I tell myself. She's not just bones in a grave anymore. She's here too. Alive somewhere. Except now all I can hear in my mind is Mr. Grayson's words. *There will still be a beautiful young girl in the ground, and nothing will ever change that.*

"Excellent," Dr. E says. "You're doing great."

I put one hand across my stomach to stop everything inside me from spilling out. "It doesn't feel great."

All these things I haven't allowed myself to think about for so long, suddenly they're all I'm thinking about.

"I know," she says. "I'm sorry for that."

She doesn't sound sorry.

"I'd forgotten that day. How could I have forgotten so much?"

Why am I saying all this to her?

"We all do." Dr. E's voice has that gentle tone that I'm starting to recognize as fake. "Forgetting is a natural thing. It's one of the ways the brain protects us. We cope. That's what the human mind is built to do."

I shrug. I am so incredibly tired.

"But physically"—Dr. E rolls her chair around to face me—"physically, Adam, while the human *mind* forgets, the human *brain* remembers. Those memories, they aren't available for immediate recall, but they still exist. We just have to find them and activate them."

She stops as if she's waiting for something, and I realize that I'm starting to doze off.

I clear my throat. "Sorry."

"Are you having trouble sleeping?" she asks.

Well, Dr. E, I think. *You see, Rita implanted me with Marybeth's memories, and they come out of nowhere sometimes. Oh, and I found out about Gen being the clone of a dead girl, and it's all a little overwhelming.*

"We can give you something to help," she says, before I can say anything stupid.

A drink, I think. *A drink would help. Some of Reggie Grayson's brandy, maybe.*

"No," I say. "No sleeping pills."

"Shall we continue then?"

I'm so exhausted that I can hardly keep my eyes open. And worse, I think if I have to relive another memory today, I'll run screaming through the hallways.

"I..." All of a sudden I'm not sure I trust my voice to answer.

Dr. E nods as if she gets it. "It's okay. Get some food in you and get some sleep. We'll pick up again tomorrow."

Chapter 28

I stand at the bend in the road by the fence, staring at the bouquet and at the scatter of old, dried-out flower petals in the grass. I have to concentrate to keep from gagging.

I try to imagine Gen, vibrant Gen, dying here.

Like Sunshine. Marybeth.

I can't grieve for another girl.

I hop over the fence like Gen did last night and look down over the edge of the cliff. How easy it would be to disappear, to just fall to the ocean that rushes in and out below. Nobody would stop me.

Is this how you felt, Marybeth?

When the world starts to swim and I think I really might fall, I step back and sit down on a tree stump. As soon as I do, something sharp digs into the corner of my butt cheek.

I get up and brush aside some leaves. Beneath them, the trunk is hollow, hiding a metal box nested inside.

As I lift it from its hiding spot, my heart starts pounding. It can't be a coincidence that there's a box here, directly behind the place where Genevieve died.

In my head, a voice—not MB's this time, not even my own better judgment, but one that sounds suspiciously like Gen—says, *Don't open it, don't open it, don't you dare open it.*

I undo the latch and open the box. Inside, a single barrette sits on top of some papers and a small book. The barrette is bent and stained with either dirt or old blood, the metal rusted as if it sat out in the rain for a long time, but I can make out the familiar dragonfly.

I push it aside, shuddering when I touch it. Beneath it is the book, gold letters on the cover that spell JOURNAL, and a newspaper clipping—or rather, a printout of a news story. The headline reads: BILLIONAIRE'S DAUGHTER KILLED ON TROPICAL VACATION. To the side, a blurry black-and-white photograph shows a smiling girl, maybe twelve. Though her hair is much longer, she's easily recognizable.

Oh, Gen.

Chapter 29

I can't go back to the compound, not with all the thoughts spinning around in my brain. Plus even the possibility of bumping into Genevieve right now is unbearable, so I walk, her journal like lead in my pocket.

The sun drops toward the tree line, and finally the air starts to cool. A steady breeze blows from the west. It smells like coconut and sea salt. I breathe it in.

Marybeth would have loved this place.

A few cars pass me on the road. I can't help but wonder if one of these drivers killed Genevieve.

The sun is just about down when I reach town. From the grocery store, light pours out around the signs in the window. In front of it, a dark-haired couple shares a bench, the girl's leg draped over the guy's knee. Inside me, something pinches, squeezes, shifts. Before it can freeze me in place, I look away and walk past them.

Life goes on, right? Fair or not. Marybeth died. Gen died. Probably no more than two miles away, scientists are resurrecting the dead. And life keeps going and going, with no regard for the people left bleeding on the ground.

Up ahead, music drifts out from one the buildings. I'm drawn to the rhythmic beat of drums, the brightness of a fast guitar, the fact that I can tell instantly that it isn't one of Sunshine's songs.

The sound leads me to the bar I found the first time I came to town. Now, at night, tiki torches light the path to an open door.

Walking between them, sweat beads on my forehead.

I hesitate. *Don't do it*, I tell myself. *Do not do it.*

In my head, Dr. E says, *Stay sober. That is nonnegotiable.*

But my feet don't listen to either of us.

The interior is small and dark, the music loud. It's not a touristy place; there are no shellacked marlins hanging on the wall. It's just the kind of place you go to lose yourself.

I hoist myself onto a stool. Gen's journal is a dead weight in my pocket.

"English?" I ask the woman behind the bar.

She holds up one finger and disappears into another room. Suddenly the need for a drink is so strong that my knees buckle.

A minute later a thirtysomething guy comes out from the back. I wait for him to ask for my ID, to tell me, *Get the hell out of here, kid.* Instead, he says, "What'll it be?" in surprisingly good English.

"Tequila, straight," I say.

When it comes, I don't hesitate. I swallow it down. It burns like hell. And nothing has ever tasted better.

Chapter 30

Go back now, I tell myself. *Go back now and get your act together. It's just one slip. One burning, numbing, familiar slip.*

Except it isn't. Because when the bartender comes my way, I signal for another.

Around the room, people eat and drink and talk and laugh as if the whole world hasn't gone batshit crazy.

The place of ghosts.

Cheers to that.

Bartender!

After the third round, I set Gen's journal on the bar and stare at it.

After the fourth, I flip open the cover and run my fingers across the paper.

Then finally, after the fifth, I turn the page and read about a girl trying to remember the details of her own death.

* * *

I don't know how much time has passed or how many drinks I've had, but when I get up from the stool my head balloons and I nearly face-plant.

"Fuck me," I say, catching myself against the bar.

I fumble in my back pocket for my wallet and slap way too many bills on the counter. American dollars, but it's triple digits more than enough.

I salute the bartender, whose expression is equal parts amusement and concern. "Enjoy it, buddy. It did shit for me."

Outside the bar, the world is too quiet. Or my thoughts are too loud. I'm not really sure. I stumble down the path between the tiki torches, out to the road, and back toward the compound.

I should call Jack, I think. *He'll send someone to pick me up. He might be my manager, but at least he gives a shit.*

I fumble for my cell phone. And then I remember where I am.

A car blows by, so close that the hot, reeking air from its exhaust blasts my face. A kid my age leans halfway out the backseat window and shouts something at me. Even in another language I know they're obscenities.

Something like a miniature star cracks open inside my brain, spilling its white-hot guts through me, and suddenly I'm running after the car, screaming, wordless. I want to grab it and force it to stop, to pull the kid through the window and pound him. When it disappears around a curve in the road, I can still hear laughter. I slow and grab a handful of gravel from the side of the road and throw it as far as I can, but it only bounces in the road.

The adrenaline stays. I walk toward Project Orpheus, the press of Gen's journal an unwelcome touch, every word I read like a pinprick. I want to shred it. I want to unsee it. I want it not to *be.*

I wait for the tequila to make it all at least stop hurting, but instead it's like jet fuel in my veins, scorching, moving my feet toward the complex, and then when I'm inside, moving them toward Genevieve's room.

Toward the clone's room.

My heartbeat pulses in my temples with every step, just the white noise of my own body, until I start to hear words in it. *Gen. Dead. Gen. Dead. Clone. Clone. Clone.*

I pound on her door until I hear rushing footsteps inside the apartment.

The door opens, and Gen squints at me from inside, her hair sticking up like she's been sleeping. "What? Adam, do you know what time it is? This is getting to be a habit."

"You know." I spit the words at her, accusing. "You know!"

She stares at me, her mouth open slightly. "Know what?"

"You took me to that place. The fence. The dead flowers. You fed me all that crap." I make my voice go high and girly. "Oh Adam, I never see who leaves them. Oh Adam, I have no idea who died there."

Gen stands there, staring at me like she doesn't know me. Which is pretty goddamn ironic.

"You told me I'd have to ask Dr. E about the first clone," I shout. "You *lied* to me!"

My alcohol-clumsy fingers fumble the journal from the back pocket of my jeans and open the cover. The words won't quite come into focus, but I remember them.

"I try to remember dying," I recite. "I try to remember the moment the car hit me. Or is it, 'the moment the car hit her'?"

Gen's whole face changes. Her lips twist. Her forehead wrinkles up.

She looks ugly.

She looks dead.

Jesus.

She rushes at me, so quick she's like a cobra. I stumble backward, expecting a slap across the face, but she just grabs the journal. "What's in there is none of your business."

She turns her back on me, stepping toward her apartment, but when she starts to shut the door I push it open, making her jump.

"Isn't it?" I follow her inside. "I think it's absolutely my business."

"What's the matter with you?" She reaches around me and slams the door shut behind us. "Are you drunk?"

"So what if I am? This is all part of Dr. E's grand experiment, right? Let the clone girl make friends with Adam? Make sure he believes she's human to see whether the process needs to be tweaked?"

"Not everything's an experiment, Adam. You think I'm not human? You want to cut me open, see if I bleed? Go ahead then." She's all anger now, her cheeks blotchy and red. She hurls the journal onto the floor and holds out her arms. "This is my life, Adam. I didn't choose this."

"*You* don't have a life. This is *her* life. The girl who died." I grab the photo off the bookshelf, the one with the little blond girl and the dog. I thrust it toward Gen and then smash it against the top of the shelf, shattering the glass. Gen flinches. "This is a goddamn lie."

Genevieve—*the clone*, I think, *the clone*—folds her arms across her stomach and nods. Her eyes are wet now. "So I don't matter? Is that what you're saying?"

I stare at her. The room spins a little. I can hear the rush of my own blood or maybe it's the whirl of my thoughts that's making so much noise.

"You're just a damn trial run for the experiment that really matters," I say.

She nods again but doesn't look away. "I feel sorry for you, Adam," she says. "Because you don't know anything. At least I liked you for who you are. That *experiment* that really matters...She's only going to love you because she's programmed to."

Experiment, I think. The tequila churns in my stomach like it's trying to turn itself into butter.

"Like your father only loves you because he's pretending you're somebody else." I launch the words at her like weapons.

She only nods. "Right back at you, buddy. You're so angry, Adam.

So who are you really mad at? Me or Marybeth? I get it. She left you. But I'm not your punching bag."

Then in a heartbeat Genevieve runs at me, smacking me in the chest with both of her hands. I stagger backward.

"Get out, Adam," she says. "Just get out."

It's not until I'm out in the hallway, with the locked door between us, that I hear the sounds of her sobbing.

Chapter 31

Maybe it's the alcohol, or maybe it's like aftershocks from an earthquake, but just outside the compound it happens again. I'm in Marybeth's memory.

It's worse with the tequila in my system. I'm Marybeth looking at me, and the paradox of it, the fun-house effect, makes me hurl against the side of building.

I lean there, breathing hard, my mouth sour, and let it come until I'm doing nothing more than dry-heaving.

In the memory, I'm holding a bottle of prescription antidepressants. Me, Adam. Marybeth is looking at me, her stomach sinking as I shake the full bottle.

I should have hidden them better, she thinks. *Maybe he would have forgotten about them.*

"You're not taking them," I say.

And even as the memory spins out from Marybeth's point of view, I can remember that day too, my anger at finding the bottle full when it should have been nearly empty.

She doesn't look at me. She wants to be as angry as I am, wants to feel that blue flame inside of her. Maybe it will burn her so completely that there will be nothing left but ashes. But there's nothing left to kindle the flame in the hollow that she's become.

She shakes her head and tries to concentrate on the motion of the tour bus as it transports us to another place where she'll take the stage as Sunshine and sing the songs that seem to touch everyone.

Maybe because Sunshine is not happiness. Sunshine is sorrow. And sorrow is something we all understand. It's what made her who she is. She thinks about these things rather than thinking about what I'm saying. It's easier to think about the happiness she can give to millions of strangers than it is to think about the happiness she can't seem to give to me.

"They might help," I say.

She hears the high note of desperation in my voice and finally looks at me.

"They won't," she says. There's a tiny spark of anger, and she tries to hold on to it. But behind it is an ocean of tiredness. "They never do. They never have. They only make me foggy. They make it so that I can't even cry."

"But that's just it." I drop to my knees in front of her and take one of her hands in mine. She puts her free hand on top of my head. "You don't cry, Marybeth. You don't laugh and you don't smile and you don't scream and you don't cry and you won't take the medicine that might help."

I say this even though part of me understands that she's been taking some version of these antidepressants since she was fourteen and so far none of them have made a damn bit of difference.

In the memory, I lay my head in her lap and she strokes my hair. Inside her something twists, and she realizes there is something she still feels. Love. And regret.

You should leave me, Adam, she thinks. *You should run far away from here.*

And the sincerity of her thought, the depth of it, knocks me right out of the memory.

* * *

I want to run to Rita's office and ask, *What did you do to me?* But I can't in the shape I'm in, so instead I let the night swallow me.

She wanted me to leave?

Two stone cairns mark a path that's labeled Beach Access. I turn down it, and trees immediately close in from either side, squat palms that curve and meet overhead, forming a claustrophobic tunnel. Filtered moonlight reflects off a maze of spiderwebs in the underbrush. They shimmer and ripple. I can imagine I'm walking into a forest of spirits.

Marybeth, are you watching?

The white noise of the ocean reaches me. I hurry toward it, but a few steps later, my foot catches on a tree root and I face-plant so hard my teeth rattle.

One more fail in a night of epic fails. Or never mind night. It's been a life of epic fails. Lying there with my cheek in the dirt, I start to giggle.

Finally, I get back up.

Eventually, the path angles downward. I leave the trees behind and step out onto sand. Starlight reflects on the whitecaps of the waves.

I kick off my sneakers, nearly knocking myself on my ass again, and walk barefoot to the water's edge. The surf crawls in over my feet, splashing up and soaking my jeans. I shiver at the cold, though it's nowhere near as frigid as the water off the Mid-Atlantic coast.

The sea rushes in and back out again, sucking the sand from under my feet. That's about right too, because that's how the whole world has been for me and Marybeth, nothing ever stable, nothing ever permanent. Except for each other.

Or so I thought.

I stretch out my arms to keep my balance. The undertow is strong, and I think the moon is making a tide of the tequila in my blood. I teeter backward and sit down hard.

The ocean rushes up around me, and I just sit there getting soaked and cold and sober. I suppose I should get up and go back, get myself in the shower and to bed. But I'm just so damn tired.

I scoot back out of the water's reach and then lie back in the sand, working myself down into it until it molds against my neck and skull and shoulders. Overhead, the stars glow bright against the black sky. The constellations look different so far from home. I feel small, the distance between me and the rest of the world swelling, the distance between me and Marybeth—between me and Gen now too—until it's a huge, dark chasm.

But maybe Marybeth is up there, in some kind of cosmic heaven looking down on what a fuckup I've become.

Is she watching them construct another version of her, or is she—God, I want to believe this so damn bad—being drawn back by the re-creation of her body, her memories, ready to take this second chance at life? Or is she somewhere shaking her head no, trying to tell me she's finally in a happier place?

"MB," I say, and the sound of my voice makes me cringe. "MB, what am I doing? I'm screwing everything up."

I think about Gen, about the vibrant, beautiful girl who sucked milk shakes through a straw until her cheeks ached and who made me feel at home. I think about the things I said to her. The stolen journal. The broken picture frame.

In my head, Gen's voice repeats, *I feel sorry for you, Adam.*

All of a sudden I want to cry. But I don't. Instead, I close my eyes and listen to the surf.

Chapter 32

I wake up, shivering and wet. Light bleeds through my eyelids until the whole world is red.

For a minute, I'm five years old again and still with my parents—my real parents, before I was taken away from them—in the double-wide trailer with the hole in the roof. I've wet the bed and I'm lying in my own cold piss.

But that isn't right, because my arms and legs and hands and feet feel stretched out like I'm Plastic Man and my head is gummy and someone stuffed gauze in my mouth. And I think I hear the ocean, which makes no sense at all, unless…

I open my eyes. They're crusty and dry and the sun nearly burns them out of my head.

Oh. Shit.

I sit up, brush sand from my arms and cheeks, and give my hair a good shake, which makes some dark thing inside my head pulse so hard that black spots flood my vision. Every time I move, my wet clothes rub against raw skin, and half the sand on the beach is having a party in my ass crack.

And then I remember. The journal, the bar in town, knocking on Gen's door and saying…

Oh crap.

I lean over and puke onto the sand. Then I do it a second time. And a third. Until there can't be anything left in me, including my stomach lining.

When I can get my breath, I crawl to the water and wash my face. Pathetic. Then I stand up and tip my head back and let the sun beat down on my skin, warming me.

The sun.

Something about that nibbles at me, but I don't quite know why. Then it hits me. The sun is too high in the sky.

It's late. Really late.

* * *

My hope: I can sneak back to my room, call Dr. E, and tell her I'm sick—*cough, cough*—and slept through my wake-up call. I'll tell her I need the day off, then crawl into bed and sleep until my head stops pretending to be a bongo drum.

But when I turn the corner into the hallway leading to my apartment, Dr. E is leaning against my door. Buh-bye, hope.

I can see her taking it all—'it all' meaning me—in, adding everything up, her eyebrows arched. Finally, she holds up one finger and says, "I'm going to give you one chance to explain. And it had better not involve alcohol."

I feel like every bone in my body disconnects and falls down to my feet. Any minute now the rest of me will go down too.

Say something brilliant here, Adam. Now's the time.

I stand there with my mouth open and shake my head like the dumbass that I am. "I'm sorry." It's all I have to give.

Dr. E nods and meets my eyes. I want to look away but force myself not to, to soak in her disappointment. I deserve it.

"That's all you have to say?"

I look down at my feet. For the second time in one morning, I feel like I'm five.

"Are you drunk?" she asks.

I clear my throat. Standing here wet and sandy and hungover, probably looking like the son of Swamp Thing, there's no point in denying the obvious. Maybe honesty will be my ticket to a second chance. "I was."

She nods. "I see."

My stomach cramps. This cannot be happening.

I need this, Dr. E, I think at her. *Without this, I have nothing.*

"It won't happen again, Dr. E." I swallow hard. "I swear it."

She seems to consider that. Then she says, "You're right. It won't happen again. We're done here, Adam."

"Done?"

"Done. Clean yourself up and pack your bags. I won't be jeopardizing this entire project because you can't manage to stay sober. We'll have to make do with what we have."

Without another word, she stalks down the hall and disappears, and I'm left alone. I lean against the wall, waiting for my heart to start beating again, or maybe for it to just stop beating for good.

I can't go home. I can't go back to that empty house with the reporters outside and the dark spots on the wall where pictures used to hang. I can't...

Fuck that. What I can't do is stand here and just let this happen.

I take a deep breath and then run after Dr. E, catching up with her as she turns a second corner.

I catch her sleeve. "Dr. E, please."

"Adam." Her tone is all business. "Enough. It's done."

Enough?

Cold air blasts from the vent overhead, and I shiver in my damp clothes. But my neck burns, my cheeks. I clench my hands into fists and step in front of her.

"No. It's not enough. If you want to tell me how bad I fucked up, go ahead. If you want to tell me I'm pathetic, worthless, nothing, do it. You won't be telling me anything I don't know."

"Adam." Her voice stays even, although I must look like a crazy person.

"But don't send me away."

She sighs. "I'm sorry, Adam. I know you tried your best."

She puts one hand on my arm, squeezes. But this show of sympathy, I know it's all fake. I picture the awards over her desk, the diplomas. That's what she cares about. Not Marybeth and sure as hell not me. The understanding hardens something inside me, something I didn't know was still there. For the first time in a long time, I want to fight *for* something and not against.

I take a breath. "I'm sorry too. Because if you put me on a plane home, Dr. Elloran, the minute I get off it I will call every news station and talk show and tabloid, every last person who's wanted a piece of me since Sunshine died, and I will tell them quite the story. By tomorrow your little island here will be swarmed with reporters."

But she only smiles at me, and it's a cold smile, as if the real Dr. E has finally shown up for the party. "And you're going to tell them to go where, Adam?"

My heart pounds. She's calling my bluff. Because I have no fucking clue where I am, and of course she knows that. Stupid.

She has me. She knows she has me. And in a few hours that plane is going to fly me out over the Pacific, away from Marybeth, away from Genevieve, away from hope.

And then I know. I hate it, but I know.

I square my shoulders and meet her eyes. "To the island where a billionaire's daughter died in a car accident six years ago. The name is Grayson. They should be able to find it, no problem. If you put me on that plane."

She stares at me. Her lips work, like she's going to say something, except she doesn't.

"I see," she finally says, nothing more, but I know I've won.

I should feel happy, but all I feel is defeated.

Chapter 33

"Sit," Dr. E says, stepping aside and letting me into Memory Room B.

It's morning again, but this time I'm showered and I've slept and I'm not hungover. I sit on the couch and she props herself against the arm of the chair, facing me.

"Before we get started, I need to say one thing. Another stunt like yesterday and you're out. I will not jeopardize the integrity of this project. Threats or not, I will put you on that plane and ship you back home and cut our losses if I so much as *think* you've taken a drink. Understood?"

I've played my cards. Now I just want to make things right. I nod. "Understood."

She stares at me for a minute more and then lets out a breath. "Then we'll consider it over and done. So where is it you think we should go from here?"

"Forward, I hope."

"Okay then. Let's do it. I need you to remember a time that…"

* * *

In the memory…

I'm standing at the front door of my foster home when Marybeth says, "Adam," her voice barely a hiss.

I lean over the porch rail to find her crouched between the bushes and the concrete stairs. "What are you doing down there?"

She ducks out from the bushes, leaves stuck in her hair. I jog down to meet her. Even now that she's fully out from her hiding spot, she doesn't stand up quite straight.

"MB?" I ask.

She coughs, one hand over her stomach. Her face scrunches up. My own stomach flutters, though I couldn't say why.

I try again. "Marybeth?"

She pulls up the bottom of her T-shirt. Seeing the ribbon of pale skin makes me shiver all the way down to my toes, but that stops instantly when I spy the purple-black of a bruise. There's a long red scratch too, that skips across her belly button.

She shrugs and tries to smile. "You should see the other guy."

I don't laugh. My hands clench into fists. "Who did this? If it was James Whitmore I swear I'll..."

She shakes her head and bites her lower lip, blinking fast like she's trying not to cry. I think of all the other times, the long sleeves in July, the black eyes and the burn marks, and in that instant I know.

"Mr. Jordan did this," I say.

She looks away. It's answer enough.

"Never this bad," she whispers.

"You have to tell someone. Tell your caseworker."

"At the useless BUM?" I would smile like I always do at her nickname for the Bureau of Unparented Minors, except seeing her like this makes it impossible to smile. And now her tears do fall. "I can't. If I tell, they'll take me away."

"Marybeth, he's hurting you."

"Adam, stop." Her voice is shrill. I look around to make sure nobody is listening. "I can't tell! If they take me away, I won't even have you."

For the first time, she puts her arms around me, her hands

clutching the back of my shirt, her whole body shaking. And I don't hesitate. I put my arms around her too.

In the memory...

Sunshine says, "I need to get out today." She isn't wearing her yellow dress, but those old familiar overalls, one strap undone. For that moment, she's Marybeth again.

Rain pelts the windows of the tour bus and runs in rivers down the glass. Shadows of the raindrops darken her cheeks and the backs of her hands.

I watch her. I ache with her. We've both lost so much.

"Okay, MB."

The use of her name, her real name and not the name of this persona she's become, gets me a small smile.

Her sadness is like a seed floating through the air, and I breathe it in until it grows and blooms inside me too. I see what she sees: the low ceiling of clouds with their swollen dark bellies, the puddles along the curb, people passing by, their faces hidden beneath umbrellas. And I need to get out too, to be away from this claustrophobic space, breathing air that moves and not the tinny taste and smell of the bus's air-conditioning.

I help her into her coat as if she's a child, rolling up the sleeves that hang too low over her fingers. Then I open the back door of the bus and lead her down the stairs. She turns her face into my shoulder and I shelter her from the flash of cameras as we run for the car.

The reporters follow, but the driver knows what he's doing, and while he navigates out of the private parking area and out of the city, into the streets of the countryside, Marybeth hunches low in the seat and puts on her wig, and in that moment her mood lifts the tiniest bit, as she begins the process of leaving herself behind.

In the memory...

I push through the spaces between throbbing, dancing bodies. Every few feet, I stretch up on my toes and scan the mass of people, searching for her. The whole place smells like stale beer and old vomit and body odor, and the music rattles my teeth and bones.

Heat radiates from everywhere, or maybe it's just radiating from me.

When the strobe lights fire, everything freeze-frames briefly, then shifts into some weird, staccato stop-motion. In that second, I see her. She's dancing with some beanpole of a guy who's probably at least twenty-one, her dark hair flying out behind her. His hands crawl all over her.

I shove some kid who dances into my path and he nearly goes down.

"Hey, asshole," he shouts, his words smothered by the bass beat of the song.

I ignore him and grab for Marybeth, pull her away from the guy, who just waves as if to say, *It's all cool, dude.*

MB puts her hands on my shoulders and starts to sway, rocking her hips and then grinding against me as if I'm just an extension of the other guy.

I grab her wrists and hold her away from me. The lights change the color of her face: violet, aqua, a sickly green. Dark rings surround her eyes, circles over circles, a ring of smeared black eyeliner, her eyes dark circles themselves, the pupils dilated so that only a sliver of green surrounds them.

"What did you take?" I shake her just enough so that she looks at me. "Marybeth, dammit, what did you take?"

She blinks, fast, finally seeming to register me. "I don't...I..."

Then she shakes free from me and digs in the pocket of her jeans. They're so tight I don't know how she fits her hand inside, but when she holds her hand out again, three tiny heart-shaped orange pills sit on her palm.

I slap them out of her hand, and instantly I regret it. What if they're bad? What if the hospital needs to examine the pills to be able to help her?

"Shit!"

I drop to my knees and try to find them, scanning the floor each time the light strobes, trying not to get my hands stomped on by dancing feet.

Then Marybeth is pulling at me saying, "Adam, let's just go. Let's just go!"

In the memory...

Ambulance lights spin across the lawn: red, dark, red, dark, red.

I race toward the stretcher. There's red there too. Darker. Blood. There's blood everywhere.

Marybeth lies limp on the stretcher, her eyes closed. Her skin is nearly as white as the sheets.

If I could tear open my wrist with my teeth, send my blood coursing into her to fill her up, I would do it in a heartbeat.

"Marybeth!"

I need to reach her. Other than medics, there's no one with her. She's thirteen years old and she's alone. I can't let that happen.

But there is a blue wall blocking me, or not a wall but a policeman so large he might as well be a wall. I struggle to get past him.

"Son," he says, his big, fleshy hands restraining me. "You need to stay back. She's a very troubled girl, but she's going to be taken care of now. You should go on home."

But she's a foster rat, and the word "care" is not part of our vocabulary, at least not for me and Marybeth.

In the memory...

I'm seventeen and sitting in the empty tour bus, listening to the time tick by and wondering where Marybeth went. My cell phone rings and I answer, because only she and our manager, Jack, have this number, but there's an unfamiliar voice at the end of the phone.

"Adam Rhodes?" the woman says.

I swallow. "Yeah. Who is this?"

There's a pause. It's thick and deep and I feel it down to my toes. Then she says, "I'm so sorry to have to tell you this."

In the memory...

"We could run away," I tell her.

It's night, and the tour bus is rolling along a stretch of highway in the middle of nowhere. Outside the window, the only light comes from the moon and the headlights of the occasional car going the other direction.

Marybeth looks out the window rather than at me. I don't think she's seeing nothing, though. I think she's seeing a thousand things passing by: foster families and old friends and the duck with the broken wing that she brought to the all-night animal ER, ringing their buzzer and then hiding and waiting to make sure someone came to take it in.

"We could, MB," I say. "We'll have Jack arrange new identities. 'Sunshine' can disappear forever, and we can go somewhere—maybe leave the country—and just be us."

She smiles, and something uncoils from my chest. She's going to say yes, and I'll tell the driver to stop at the first train station and we'll put on disguises and...

"Adam, we can't."

I nod. I'm tired of asking.

I sit on the bed, guitar across my knees, bottle of vodka on the nightstand. I stole it from the backstage cabinet at the last concert, and it's been sitting here ever since.

I trace the patterns of the zebrawood instrument and imagine that we're somewhere else, rather than on this bus that's going to become our tomb.

In my imagination, I randomly plug us into alternate universes where, rather than forming a band, Marybeth gets adopted by a couple out in the country. I imagine her rushing home from school to brush down the horses, sneaking them sugar cubes and carrots. Sometimes I picture her falling asleep in the hay beside the stall, dreaming of the next time I visit from the city and the engagement ring I'll bring, even though her parents protest that she's too young.

Useless, I tell myself.

But I can still escape, can't I?

I pick up the bottle for the first time and take a long drink. Heat shoots down to my stomach, and my throat threatens to close up. I gasp a breath and cough. But already the warmth is spreading through me. Warmth and something else that fills me in a way that nothing else has. Because it fills me with a wonderful, merciful nothingness.

I try to take a breath. I try not to scream. I think I'm going to shake apart.

In the memory...

In the memory...

In the memory...

The memories come in no order. One day I'm seventeen, the next twelve. But in every one there's pain. Did a single jab of a pin in the calibration phase give them the road map to all the places where they can find memories of pain?

Her pain. My pain. Because really, they were one and the same. *And this*, I think, *is my punishment.*

Chapter 34

"Want a drink?" Marybeth asks. She holds up a bottle, wagging it at me.

I sit up in bed. The covers fall off me and the air-conditioning hits my bare chest. I shiver.

Yes, MB. Of course I want a drink.

"No," I say. "I can't. Dr. E's rule. If I slip again, she'll send me home."

"You're getting tame, Adam. When did a rule ever stop you from doing anything?"

"It's called growing up," I say. I don't know why I feel so cross.

"I wouldn't know about that," she says. "I'm always going to be almost-seventeen."

"Besides…" I let my voice soften. "I promised *you*."

"Hmm. Which me? Dead me or dream me or cloned me?"

Without waiting for me to answer her impossible question, she plops down on the bed beside me, the bottle still in her hand. She twirls it so the liquid sloshes around inside.

Her shirt slips to one side, baring her shoulder. My fingers trace the curve of skin and then I press my lips into the warm spots my fingers leave behind.

She leans into my touch, tipping her neck back so I can kiss the soft hollow of her throat. "Mmm," she says, and then, "Are you sure you don't want some? I mean, hey, you made it, Adam."

I stop kissing her. "What do you mean I made it?"

She waves at the far corner of the bedroom. Beside the dresser, there's a still there, the kind moonshiners have, all looping tubes and bubbling, sunshine-yellow liquid.

Wires lead from the machine to the bed. I pat my head, finding the spots where the wires disappear into my skin.

"Suit yourself. It's not very good anyway." She drinks from the bottle and screws up her face. Inside the bottle, the liquid is no longer yellow but black and thick, tarry. "Bitter."

"My memories usually are," I say.

When I look over at the still, the liquid there has also turned black and sludgy. My stomach rolls.

Marybeth only smiles. "So are mine. Just ask Rita. You should taste them."

I nod. "I already did."

"Barely. There's so much more to learn about this." She taps her temple. "I know you want to know."

I press the heels of my hands into my eyes until I see swirls of red and orange that stay even after I let up the pressure. When my sight fades back in, Marybeth is gone, and in the corner, where the still was, there's only my clone-guitar.

I sit up for real, fully awake, aching with the stretched-out, empty feeling that comes after these dreams. I have to pee, so I get up.

The bathroom mirror reflects pale skin and eyes with dark bags underneath.

What it should really show is jagged edges, layers of my skin and bone chipping away with each memory.

I pee and wash my hands, then go out and stare at the phone and think about the horrible things I said to Genevieve.

The clone, I think. But without the tequila, the thought doesn't have quite the same edge.

Ten minutes later I'm standing outside the doorway to the place where Genevieve works.

Maybe it's my imagination, but I swear the sound of Marybeth's heartbeat reaches me even through the closed door. I know it's weird, but it's comforting, and all of a sudden I feel incredibly sleepy.

I look up and down the hallway, but the place is as dead quiet as it always is this late.

I pull Gen's stolen key card from the pocket of my jeans, take another look up and down the hall, and then hold it up to the reader. Someone is probably inside—maybe Gen herself—but at least for a second, before they'd pull me away, I'd see Marybeth.

But in my head, Dr. E's voice says, *Another stunt and you're out.*

I return the key card to my pocket and press my hand to the door.

"Marybeth, are you in there?" I whisper. My words still sound too loud. I imagine even now someone telling Dr. E that Adam is screwing up again.

I lay my cheek against the door. It's cold. Metal. "I think I can feel you here. Am I crazy?"

I sink down until I'm sitting on the floor, my head still against the door. Somebody's bound to find me here, but for just this minute I'm so tired.

"I'm scared, MB." I close my eyes. "I don't know what I'm doing. And I miss you so much."

* * *

I wake up when something nudges me in the leg. I blink, disoriented and blinded by the fluorescents.

Then two purple sneakers walk into my field of vision.

"What...?"

When my eyes adjust to the light, I look up to see Gen standing over me, unsmiling.

"Get up." Her voice is blank. "Go back to bed, Adam."

Without another word she goes back inside, leaving only the sound of Marybeth's heartbeat spilling out into the hallway behind her.

Chapter 35

I brace myself for the morning's memories, clench my stomach against the first moments of pain and punishment and whatever pieces of myself Dr. E is planning on scraping raw in this session.

In the memory—*thwap*—the stone hits the window.

Thwap thwap.

Grayish light creeps in around the dark curtains. I kick off the covers and step into the pair of jeans crumpled beside the bed.

Thwap.

I place the memory immediately as the home of the Sutters, my newest in a long line of fosters, so far not so bad. I remember being grateful for once that BUM had kept me in the same school so I could have some stability, keep the friends I'd made, socialize properly to become a better member of society. Oh yeah—insert eye roll.

I pull back the curtains and look down. Marybeth stands in the grass below. Behind her, the sun is just starting to come up.

In the now, my stomach unclenches. This memory is…This memory is okay.

Better than okay.

I give myself over to it.

Grinning, she gestures for me to come down. I mouth, *Hang on*, and grab a sweatshirt.

After a listen at the Sutters' bedroom door to make sure nobody's up for an early morning bathroom run, I tiptoe downstairs and out the side door.

"Come on," Marybeth whispers.

When her hand slides into mine and squeezes, I shiver. Together, we run away from the eyes that might be watching from inside the house and don't stop until we're out of breath.

"Where are we going so early?" I ask after I can breathe again.

She smiles. There's a brightness about her this morning. "You'll see. We have to hurry. The sun is almost up."

We run again, down to the trailer park on Oakland and through it to the main drag, where she ducks beneath a chain barring access to an abandoned construction site.

Oh great, I think. *I can see it now, some busybody at the trailer park calling the cops. I just got settled with the Sutters.*

"This better be good, MB," I say.

She only grins and motions for me to follow. God help me, I do.

We hike up the dusty, gravelly construction road. On one side is a low hill covered in tall grass and wildflowers. A bulldozer stands off to the side, forgotten.

"Seriously?" I say. "I am not going to steal a bulldozer for a joyride."

She laughs and sits down on a boulder facing the hillside. "Be patient." She pats the flat part of the rock beside her and I sit too, paying attention to every inch where our bodies touch.

God help me if the Sutters wake up and find me gone, I think. *God help me if BUM can't find me another home near Marybeth.*

Behind me, the sun begins to bake through my sweatshirt. A line of new daylight creeps across the road.

When the sunlight reaches the hill, Marybeth bumps my shoulder with hers, "Watch."

Then it happens.

At first I think someone took Christmas tinsel and sprinkled it all over the slope, because the entire hill shimmers. Silvery, iridescent threads stretch between the wildflowers and the tall grasses. They twist through fallen branches and run across stones. With every small breeze they sway and ripple and gleam, all reflected sunlight and morning dew.

Spiderwebs, I realize.

My mouth drops open. It should be creepy, some weird kingdom of the spiders, but instead it's...amazing.

"Wow," I say.

I tear my eyes away from the sight to look at Marybeth and find that she's not looking at the hillside. She's looking at me, her eyes shining. Her hair is loose and strands blow across her face, catching in her eyelashes and on her lips.

With my free hand, I brush them back. My thumb catches her lip, which is full and soft and a tiny bit moist.

Her eyes never leave mine, even as I lean in close, and her breath is a soft rhythm against my cheek.

My heart pounds.

We're both breathing too hard.

My lips touch hers for the first time.

Then it's gone.

The hillside.

Marybeth.

The kiss.

Maybe I was wrong. Maybe this is the most painful memory of all.

Chapter 36

In the cafeteria, Jay makes me a burger and doesn't comment that it's been almost a week and a half since I've been here with Genevieve. He also doesn't comment when I take the tray of food with hands that shake hard enough to register on the Richter scale.

He doesn't even comment when I sit at a table in the corner, rather than taking the food to go, although I do feel him watching me.

I sit facing the door and pretend like I'm enjoying my burger and I'm not just interested in watching the people who come in. Each time it isn't Gen, I feel a surprising stab of disappointment.

And what brilliant thing are you going to say to her if she does come in? I wonder.

Which is a mighty good question. Because "I'm sorry" isn't going to come close to doing it.

When the other two tables of people finish up, leaving me alone in the room, Jay finally says, "She hasn't been in here all week, Adam. She's been ordering food delivered to her room."

I swivel to look at Jay. "Was it that obvious?"

"Nah." He smiles. "I'm just incredibly insightful."

I try to smile back but can't quite manage it. I return my tray to the counter.

"Hey, Jay," I say. "Can you do me a favor?"

He props his elbows on the counter. "Name it."

"Make me a strawberry milk shake to go."

With a grin, he flashes me a double thumbs-up. "You got it, kid."

* * *

Standing outside of Genevieve's apartment with the milk shake freezing my hand, I don't know quite what to do.

Not rocket science, Marybeth's voice says in my head.

Easy for her to say. She doesn't know the horrible things I said.

I take a deep breath and then knock. Behind the door, footsteps approach. I wait for the door to open, but instead, Gen calls out, "Oh, you're back for another round? Want to knock me around a little more?"

Standing there, holding the melting shake, I feel like an idiot.

"No. I..." I tip my forehead against the door. "I'm sorry, Gen. I really am. I was drunk and horrible, and the things I said were inexcusable. I know. And I'm sorry."

She's silent, but I feel her there listening.

"Please let me in, Gen. Just for a minute."

Nothing.

"What can I do to make it right?" I sigh. "Name it and I'll do it."

For the longest time, there's no answer. Finally, she says, "Go away, Adam. I have nothing to say to you."

I miss you, I think. *I'm falling apart, Gen. This week has been absolute hell, and I don't think I can get through this without you.*

In my head, Marybeth says, *Well, then say it.*

But the words won't come and the door stays closed. I set the milk shake on the floor and walk away.

Chapter 37

My days become the story of me and Marybeth. I live between two worlds. In the "then," I relive our initial, fumbling kisses and hear her sing for the first time. I watch Java Bean change to the Hip Sip, watch Marybeth hack off her beautiful long hair and smear her eyelids with thick, black eyeliner. I watch Marybeth's body grow curves.

In the now, I look back at the first of her many downward spirals and wonder why I didn't ask the right questions. *What happened at home that you were out exploring abandoned construction sites at sunrise instead of being in bed? How did you go from our first kiss to slicing up your arms in such a short time?*

What didn't you tell me, Marybeth? What didn't I ask?

How could there be so much I didn't know about you?

I imagine the memories they're retrieving traveling along the wires, no longer bits and bytes, ones and zeros, but a yellow (black?) liquid that bubbles through a moonshiner's still. I imagine Dr. E and Rita pouring it into cups and feeding it to the new Marybeth, tipping her head back and pouring it down her throat until she gags and chokes.

I imagine another moonshine still in Rita's office, one with Marybeth's memories instead of mine, artifacts from a lost life captured in the MAP machine, bubbling away.

"You should taste them," the dream Marybeth says to me, and this time it's me they put the liquid into, pouring it down my throat until I choke.

I should taste them, I think.

I should taste them.

Chapter 38

"I want to talk about the band today," Dr. E says, moving equipment into place. She doesn't say our name, Constellation. Just "the Band."

"Those were formative years for Sunshine, and I want to make sure we get everything."

I've known this was coming. For whatever good it may do, I've done my best to anchor the parts of me that might come unmoored when I think of them: LaLa and Jeddy, our band members, our friends. Our family.

"Sure," I say. "Okay." Because it's what I always say, right, even when it's not the truth? Because it's what I said when Marybeth wanted to go onstage after they died, and it's what I said back when Marybeth wanted the damn band in the first place. Because it's what I said when Dr. E originally came to me with this crazy, mad-scientist idea.

Sure. Okay. Yes. I'm in.

And why not? After all, I'm the only one left.

"Let's talk first about Larissa Laramie," Dr. E says, and just hearing her name calls up an image of her olive skin and pink apple cheeks, her hair so short that most girls wouldn't be able to pull it off. "When was the first time Marybeth met her?"

"I don't know," I say. "LaLa was always just there, someone we saw but didn't talk to or hang out with."

Dr. E adjusts something on the machine. "Okay. Then I want

you to think about how you became friends."

"The school accidentally assigned Marybeth and LaLa the same locker."

"Don't tell," Dr. E says. "Just remember."

"What the fuck," Marybeth says in the memory, turning the corner. She stops so unexpectedly that I nearly smash my nose on the back of her head.

"What, what the fuck?" I ask, but I see it almost instantly. Her locker is open, and there's a girl putting something inside.

"Umm...Hello," Marybeth says in her don't-screw-with-me voice, moving toward the girl, who I recognize from English class.

The girl closes the locker and turns. She has torn jeans and short-short black hair and too much eyeliner. She smiles.

"Oh! Is this your locker, Pumpkin?" she asks.

I look at Marybeth and Marybeth looks at me. *Pumpkin?* And I think being called a large orange vegetable—or is pumpkin a fruit?—throws her off, because when she answers, the don't-screw-with-me voice is gone.

"Umm...Yes?" she says, sounding more like a question.

"Okay," the girl says. "Well, I think they sort of assigned us both this locker. At least until they fix the door on my other one. I'm LaLa by the way. Nice meeting you."

And then she's gone.

"Pumpkin?" Marybeth says.

LaLa never did end up switching back to her locker. I still believe it was the Pumpkin thing. (LaLa had this weird habit of calling people by strange nicknames.) But it was so unexpected that it sort of stopped Marybeth before she could even put her wall up, I guess.

"Great," Dr. E says, yanking me from the memory. As if she has all she needs and that's all the time she's giving LaLa. "And Jedidiah Price."

And as soon as she says it, I hear his voice in my head. "Jeddy—*please*. 'Jedidiah' makes me sound like I should be spouting biblical things like *thou art* and *begat*."

And even though there's a familiar stab when I think of him, I smile, because...

Marybeth and I are sitting outside the principal's office again after cutting the first three periods to hang out at Java Bean. I'm imagining the reaming out that waits for me when my foster dad gets here, when the boy walks in, followed by one of the janitors. The kid is carrying a toilet seat.

Marybeth looks at me and I look at Marybeth, and judging from the way her mouth is contorting, she's trying hard not to burst out laughing.

"Hey," the kid says to me, and then, "Hey," again to Marybeth. He sits in the last unoccupied chair. "Busy day in Miller's office, eh?" His gaze lingers a little too long on Marybeth, and my cheeks warm.

"Guess so," I say.

Behind us, the janitor is talking to the admin.

"So what are you doing time for?" the kid asks. He has the toilet seat propped on his lap. A necktie—I think it has tiny giraffes all over it—hangs loosely from his neck, draping over it.

"Cutting class," Marybeth says and then, "Nice tie," with a little giggle that I know is less about the tie and more about the toilet seat.

"Yeah." He grins. "I'm great at accessorizing."

He holds the toilet seat up and I see instantly that he isn't actually holding it. It's stuck to him.

"How'd that happen?" I ask.

"I was gluing the lids down on the shitters in the staff bathroom and sort of…" He shrugs. "Glued myself instead."

"Good," Dr. E says. "Excellent."

Two people who have become no more than bits and bytes, I think, as Dr. E guides me through the memories.

* * *

I push open the cafeteria door, freed from Mr. Solomon's epic review-the-entire-US-history-from-Columbus-to-putting-on-your-kicks-this-morning tutoring session, and see Jeddy there.

He sits in the farthest corner of the school cafeteria, hunched over his tablet. He has his hood up, and I only know it's Jeddy from the crazy curls sticking out around his face like alien tentacles. That and the keyboard-print scarf that's become his newest favorite accessory. Earbud wires trail from the hood, and his head bobs in time with music I can't hear.

I see Marybeth next to him too, picking raisins out of a cookie and pegging them at the wall, where there's already a connect-the-dots of the nasty things.

I can't help myself. I stop to watch them, alone at the table in the nearly empty cafeteria, where only a few other free-breakfast kids like us are sitting before first bell.

MB chews a piece of her now raisin-less cookie, and then she plucks out one of Jeddy's earbuds and leans over to whisper something in his ear. He laughs.

Heat pushes up from some oven inside of me, firing all the way up to the tips of my ears.

But then Marybeth looks up and sees me, and her face changes and I know, without a doubt, that she is my girl forever.

In between memories, while Dr. E taps frantically at her keyboard, creating her Cliffs Notes of my life, I let myself think about Jedidiah Price and Larissa Laramie for the first time in forever.

LaLa was from a street where people tended their flower gardens on Saturday afternoons and kids set up lemonade stands over the summer. Jeddy was from the complete opposite side of town, where you locked all your doors, even during the day, and looked over your shoulder when you walked. And then there was us, me and Marybeth. All four of us so different, and yet there were these moments when it felt like everything coming together.

I don't realize Dr. E has stopped typing until I pull up from my thoughts and find her watching me.

She's probably looking for cracks in me. I think everyone is these days, myself included.

"Shall we continue?" she asks.

Marybeth sits across from me at a small corner table at Java Bean. She looks like her mind is somewhere far away. She's definitely thinking about something. She always is.

"Earth to MB," I say.

She looks up. "Adam, do you ever want something all your own?"

I give her a shrug/grunt combo. But she knows my answer anyway, because isn't that what every foster rat wants?

She sighs. "I guess I just want something that's mine, that can't be taken away."

Something. Some Thing.

In the now, I think, *Everything can be taken away, MB. Especially the things that mean the most to you. Even beautiful, quirky LaLa, and Jeddy, goofy but thoughtful, Jeddy who could write the most beautiful songs you ever heard.*

I sip my coffee. "Like this band business?"

Her eyebrows scrunch. "Are you mad?"

In front of her, her tea sits, getting cold. She's been on a tea kick lately, which LaLa started.

I shake my head. It isn't the first crazy scheme of hers I've gone along with. "So what kind of band?"

She shrugs. "Rock, I guess. Maybe folk. I don't even care what kind, Adam. I just want..."

She shakes her head to dismiss whatever she was about to say.

A family, I think. I don't say it. But it hangs there between us.

Marybeth looks at me, her eyes bright. And I see how much she wants this.

This band.

Then the memory is gone, replaced by another: LaLa and Marybeth sprawled on the floor in Jeddy's garage, painting silver stars on black T-shirts, the name CONSTELLATION on the back. LaLa's tongue is hanging out slightly, pinched between her teeth in concentration.

And another: Marybeth wobbling down LaLa's steps in red spike heels, a tight black T-shirt and leopard or snake or some kind of animal-print jeans.

Where did the girl in the faded overalls go? I wonder.

Jeddy whistling. "Looking hot, MaryBee." And me elbowing him in the ribs.

And another memory. And another.

Two lives on fast-forward.

Four, really.

Please, I want to say, *please stop.*

"Doing great," Dr. E says.

But of course she doesn't know that this—the band—is the

beginning of the end. The end of Marybeth. The end of me. The end of everything.

PHASE III

Chapter 39

"Here we are." Dr. E opens a door marked Sim. "Our home for Phase Three."

Phase III. The last phase.

Letting that sink in, I follow Dr. E into a room the size of an auditorium, painted a mind-fuck electric blue. Not just the walls but the ceiling and the floor too. The only objects in the room are a few lumpy bean-bag-looking blobs in that same obnoxious color.

I whistle. "Did someone forget to pay for furniture delivery?"

Dr. E smiles. It's a small smile, but it's more than I've gotten from her for the last few weeks. Maybe my good behavior finally scored. If only I could say the same for Gen, who still hasn't spoken to me since that night.

"Something like that," she says. "This is the simulation room. Every surface in this room, every wall and structure, functions as a high-resolution, three-dimensional monitor. During sessions, a sort of electronic fog will be pumped in. You won't see it. You won't feel it. But it'll allow every square inch of this room to become an advanced hologram. We can simulate pretty much anything here, including weather, with the help of that little box you're wired to."

Instinctively, I feel for it in my pocket. It's still there.

"And everything will integrate with the memory maps and with your own mind," she continues, "so what you see here will seem one hundred percent real."

"Wow."

"Wow is right." Her voice practically hums with excitement. "Nothing like this has ever been done before. The applications are endless. But more importantly, Adam, this is where you'll be meeting Sunshine."

Marybeth, I want to say. *Why can't you ever just call her Marybeth?*

"Our *reborn* Sunshine," Dr. E says, as if she needs to clarify. Her whole face brightens. As if she could possibly understand what this means. Immediately I start to shake. Damn body. I look around at the wall-to-wall blue, trying to ground myself in something.

"This is the part you've been waiting for, Adam." She touches my arm, her false sympathy on full blast. "Are you okay?"

If you're looking for cracks, Dr. E, I'm full of them. I'm a damn eggshell after someone dropped the egg.

I nod.

"Good. Now before you can meet our Sunshine, I need you to get acclimated to the room."

"Okay," I say.

"For Sunshine, this will be an actual experience. She will be living life, building memories, just as she's been doing for the whole of her new existence. No different, really, from how the original Sunshine experienced life. Here, in the simulation room, her physical form will also engage in the memory-building, body and mind working in concert to cement vital memories so they'll indeed be real for her."

"So she'll believe them?" I ask. "So that her past will feel like her own?"

She nods. "Exactly. But for you, it will be different."

"Because I'll know that it's a simulation."

"Right. Essentially, you'll be an actor in a play of your own life… and hers, of course. You'll see what I mean in a second. Are you ready?"

"I think so."

"Good." She reaches into her lab-coat pocket and pulls out some kind of weird-looking phone. "Ready Test Simulation One."

Rita's voice responds, "Readying."

I feel something strange, like an electrical current running through the room. The hairs on my arms stand up. My teeth chatter.

"Test Simulation One ready on your word," Rita says.

"Proceed," Dr. E says.

The change is instant and dizzying. One second I'm in a bizarre blue room in the center of Project Orpheus's headquarters. The next, it's like I took a time machine back four years, because I'm standing in a memory brought to life.

Except somehow I've brought Dr. Elloran with me.

We're standing on a sidewalk that I know instantly. It's the bus stop where I first met Marybeth.

My legs turn to rubber. Dr. E holds my arm.

"Give yourself a minute to adjust," she says, which makes things even worse, because her voice has no place in this world that belongs to me and to Marybeth.

When my legs decide to firm up, I turn in a circle. Everything's here. Every goddamn detail.

"Are you okay?" Dr. E asks.

"I'm…" I shake my head. "I don't know what I am. This is un-freaking-believable. This is taken from my memory?"

"Yes, your memory and those salvaged from Sunshine. Go ahead and walk around. Interact with the objects. A tree is going to feel like a tree."

I walk toward the maple tree. Polynoses spiral down from it, just as I remember. I hold out my hand and catch one, peel it open, stick it on my nose. I want to laugh at the sheer impossibility of it.

I run to the mailbox of the blue house on the corner and kneel down to look underneath. Sure enough, the bottom is covered with hard little dots of gum that I stuck there over the years.

I realize that, for a minute, I've forgotten how full of cracks I am. It feels good.

When I turn back to Dr. E, she's beaming.

"But how will I know what to do?" I ask.

She nods. "Well, you know those super-boosts you got when we harvested your memories, Adam? How real the memories felt? This will be similar. We'll stimulate the appropriate areas of your brain so that, effectively, you're living the memory. It's like singing along with a song on the radio. Only the radio in this case is a memory, that kind of vivid, enhanced memory that you experienced in the memory retrieval sessions. We're asking you to reenact it as you remember it. Everything will be synchronized. You just have to, well, sing along."

I nod and walk past Dr. E, down the sidewalk. Sure enough, there's my foster father, sitting in his car waiting for me to hurry up and get on the bus. What would happen if I walked over and slugged him, told him what an asshole he was to me, that I hadn't deserved it? Would the room's illusion hold?

When I turn back, the other bus-stop kids are there, standing in their group. I look past them, for the young girl who'd stood beneath the elm tree by herself.

Dr. E apparently sees where I'm looking. "You're not going to see Sunshine here, Adam."

"Why not?"

She smiles. "Because she's going to be part of the memory re-creation itself. She's going to be acting it out with you, playing the role of herself."

"Oh," I say.

Dr. E lifts the phone and says, "End simulation."

"Simulation ending," Rita says.

A second later I'm back in the blue room. The scene is gone.

"A bit disconcerting, right?" Dr. E asks.

"No lie." My mind still boggles from the exactness of the simulation, from the unshakeable feeling of actually stepping into the past.

"You'll get used to it. That's why you need this orientation before we bring in Sunshine. We can smooth out the bumps, so when we go live it'll all happen the way it's supposed to." She looks at me, her stare so intense that it's hard not to look away. "It's vital to get this right."

I nod. "I understand."

"Good."

I clear my throat. "What will she be like, Dr. E? I mean, will she…"
I don't even know what I mean.

"As you know, Sunshine has been undergoing an artificial aging process driven by synthetic hormones, Adam, with us controlling the rate at which she ages. Here in the simulation, you'll see her as you remember her in each memory through a little bit of optical illusion—and that will be her *emotional* age, thanks to the memory implants—but we'll age her physical body in steps."

"And how will she see me?"

"The same," she says. "She'll see you as the appropriate age for each memory implant. The most important thing is just to stay with the memory at all times."

I blow out a breath. "I think I've got it."

"I know it's a lot to take in. But let's not worry about that for now. Today is just for practice, and I'll be playing the part of Sunshine today."

"Okay."

"You'll have free will during the simulations. We can't force you to follow the memory, Adam, but I cannot stress enough how important it is that you do so. The fewer deviations from the original event the better, for the success of the project and for our ultimate goal of returning Sunshine, exactly as she was, to the world."

"In other words, don't screw it up," I interpret.

"In other words," Dr. E confirms.

"Understood," I say. "But I'll know what to do?"

"You will. It'll be like an internal script."

"Okay."

She claps her hands together. "So let's do it."

To her phone she says, "Ready Test Simulation Seven with full integration."

Rita's voice answers, "Test Simulation Seven with full integration ready to initiate. Just say the word, Trixie."

Dr. E lifts her eyebrows in question, and I nod that I'm ready.

"Go ahead with TS-Seven," she says.

Again, it happens instantly. The blue room becomes the exterior of the hole-in-the-wall coffee shop called the Hip Sip, once Java Bean.

I imagine the sim room walls sliding into place on tracks, objects moving. But I don't hear or see any of it. All I see is the dingy front window where the store's name forms a half-moon across the glass, a steaming mug of coffee stenciled below the lettering.

It's hard to explain, but even as I see those things, I'm remembering them. My stomach rolls.

"Go on," Dr. E prompts.

I startle. I'd forgotten her.

Where she stands is where I remember Marybeth standing. And

I see Dr. Elloran, but I also see MB, one over the other. But that's not quite it. It's more like they're both in exactly the same place at exactly the same time. That makes no sense, but that's how it is.

My stomach really lurches, as if I were on a roller coaster that just started a loop-the-loop. I press my knuckles against my mouth.

"Just go with it, Adam." Dr. E/Marybeth says. "Your brain will adjust."

In the memory, I walk through the door with Marybeth. She's wearing a plum-colored sweater. The bell (which I know is not really there in the now, but is just some blue lump of stuff) jingles. Cold air from outside follows us in.

Inside, tables and chairs are squished together, so close that you have to turn sideways to squeeze between them. A small, sad stage made of old pallets and plywood takes up one corner. The band, all of us jammed together, barely fit on it. *Togetherness*, Marybeth always joked.

I head toward the counter, past tables occupied by people: old men playing chess and students pecking away at laptops. We join the line of customers waiting for their hot ciders and lattes and for the hot cocoa with steamed milk that was Marybeth's favorite that winter. She would find a new favorite periodically and drink it constantly, until she got so sick of it that she'd never drink it again. Literally, never.

We wait our turn, until a girl with glittery purple eye shadow and multiple piercings smiles at us. "The usual, Marybeth?"

"Yes. Don't forget the steamed milk," Dr. E/Marybeth says.

I think I'm going to hurl.

"And for you, Adam?" the girl asks.

I swallow hard. "Double espresso."

I feel a hand on my shoulder that, for a second, splits the memory from reality. Dr. E says, "It'll get easier. It's like learning to ride a bike, Adam. You need training wheels to start, and it takes practice, but once you have it down, it'll become second nature. We'll do mock run-throughs until you get the hang of it."

"Okay." But as my own actions and those of Dr. E break away from the course of the memory running through my head, everything starts to spin.

"It'll be easier when you actually have Sunshine here with you, rather than me."

I try to breathe slowly through my mouth as the girl behind the counter hands over the tiny mug of espresso. I take it, half expecting it to be solid and half expecting it to dissolve into nothing more than mist when I touch it.

But it is solid, and I can smell the bitter steam rising up from it. I want to taste it, to see just how complete this memory is, but I know I'm not going to be able to put anything into my stomach, even if it is only some jacked-up illusion.

Acid rises in my throat. I put the imaginary cup down on the imaginary counter as the imaginary clerk hands Marybeth/Dr. E her beloved hot cocoa and moves on to the next set of imaginary customers.

"I'm going to be sick, Dr. E."

I close my eyes and, again, I feel Dr. E's hand on my arm, steadying.

"End simulation immediately," she says. Then, "You can open your eyes, Adam."

Even as she says it, it's over, the sounds vanishing, the vivid memory blinking off in my mind as if someone flipped a switch. I breathe in through my mouth.

"We can take a break and try again in a little while."

But my lunch tumbles around and around in my stomach.

"I'm going to be sick," I say again.

I open my eyes and cover my mouth and run for the door, out into the waiting room and into the adjoining bathroom, where I drop down in front of the toilet and puke up what's left of my ham sandwich and fries.

Chapter 40

"Gen?"

I stand outside her door for like the thirtieth day in a row, strawberry milk shake melting onto my hands. Every day Jay makes them fancier. Strawberry whipped cream. Double cherries on top. Today the whipped cream is pimped out with purple sprinkles.

"I wish you'd open the door."

The only answer is silence. The only answer is always silence.

In my pocket, her stolen key card burns. I could pull it out and slide it in the slot and open the door myself. Maybe if she saw my face she would know how sorry I am.

Or maybe she'd just know that I stole her key card on top of all the other shitty things I've done.

"I don't give up easily. You could ask Marybeth." I hesitate. "Well, I guess you really could ask Marybeth, right?"

I laugh to let her know I'm joking. Then I lean my forehead against her door. She's in there, right on the other side. I know because the shadow of her feet bleeds through the crack beneath it.

"I did the simulation room for the first time today. It's so surreal, Gen. I think I puked up a lung afterward. Dr. E says I'll see Marybeth in a few days." My throat tightens. "Is it stupid that I'm scared to death?"

From inside comes a thump, and I think she's going to open the door, that maybe she's going to take pity on the resident screwup. But she doesn't, and I know she isn't going to, not ever.

"I don't blame you for hating me. I would hate me too." I sigh. "I didn't mean any of it. You matter. You matter to me. I just want you to know I'm sorry. If I could undo it I would. But I can't. And I'm sorry."

I set the milk shake down by the door like I do every day and think about Mr. Grayson leaving flowers on the fence. Maybe this is my shrine to our lost friendship.

I wipe my hands on my jeans. Then I head out to the courtyard and feed cookie crumbs to the mynah birds. At least they're glad to see me.

Because otherwise I'm alone.

* * *

This is what alone feels like:

Fluorescent lights and the everywhere-smell of antiseptic. White hospital sheets and blue curtains hung on U-shaped rods, drawn closed to shelter everyone but you from the reality of what is actually happening.

Vending-machine coffee and too-bright smiles that promise hope when there is none, hope that you cling to anyway, because you're scared and you're desperate and you're pathetic.

Monitors with squiggly lines that you can't stop looking at and machines that hum and beep and buzz, making their own kind of music because the girl they're hooked up to no longer can.

Heads that shake and tongues that cluck-cluck and voices that whisper when they think you can't hear them.

It's a private waiting room where the chairs are soft leather instead of orange plastic, where there's a minifridge filled with tiny bottles of soda and water, where the doctor can shut the door when he says, "I'm sorry to have to tell you…"

Alone is when the doctor leaves, and the hands on the wall clock still move forward, even though your whole world has become something alien and terrifying.

And now I can add to that, because alone is also a door that stays closed, no matter how much you want the person inside to open it.

Chapter 41

"We'll do Sim Four today," Dr. E says, and just at the mention of another sim session, my stomach lurches. "I won't be playing the role of Marybeth this time. She'll be a simulation today, for the sake of easing you into this."

I nod. "Good."

"Okay then. You have your earpiece and your throat piece and your box, so you're all set. Let's do it." Into her phone, she says, "Initiate Four with full integration."

She pats my arm and leaves the blue room, and I'm alone.

The simulation begins, the memory spooling out.

Marybeth sits on a bench, her breath fogging in the cold air. Every detail is so perfect—how she bites her lower lip, the way she cups her hands around the mug of hot cocoa—that even though I know she's not real, my throat aches.

My hands shake from the effort to stay with the memory, to not just reach out and touch her, hold her so she can never leave me again.

When she lifts her mug to drink, the whipped cream topping leaves a moustache above her perfect mouth.

"Your birthday's coming up," she says. "Just a few weeks."

I kick at a stone on the ground. Words form in my mind, and it's weird because not only do I know what I'm supposed to say, but the urge to say it is almost irresistible.

"I know."

"You're going to be fifteen. You know what that means."

She looks out over the park, watching people walking and laughing.

Back then, we would sometimes play a game where we invented stories for people we saw on the street. The man in the navy-blue peacoat and horn-rimmed glasses, he was thinking about robbing a bank in order to buy his wife a Mercedes. The teenager in the pink knee-high socks was on her way to donate a kidney to a boy she'd never met. The woman window-shopping at the jewelry store had made her millions designing diamond collars for cats of the rich and famous. Kooky stuff like that.

But the memory of the game is from my now and not my then, and it fights with the memory-movie that's playing in my head. If I could look in a mirror, I think my face would be Kermit green.

"What's going to happen then?" she asks, her voice tight.

I know what she's worried about. I knew it then too. With the new laws, fifteen meant the end of formal foster care. They'd lowered the age again with the latest budget cuts. Group homes were cheaper than paying families to take in kids.

It meant that I would be more or less on my own once my fifteenth birthday came.

"Go with the memory," Dr. E says in my ear, as if she knows that she's losing me to my out-of-control thoughts.

I try to pull myself back to the then.

Sitting there on the bench, she's worried for me, I know, worried about what will happen when I move to one of the group homes. Worried for herself too.

"What happens if they assign you to a home in another county? Or worse."

I concentrate on breathing as I start to speak my scripted lines. "Well, I've talked about it with the Bureau of Unparented Minors."

"Useless BUM?" She raises her eyebrows, probably annoyed that I haven't told her before now, totally oblivious to the fact that, in the now, I'm so close to hurling.

Because there is no now *for her. She isn't real. She's a memory, dumbass. Just go with it,* I tell myself. *Just breathe and go with it.*

"And I've been saving money," I say. "I'll get my own place. Right near here. Doesn't even have to be an apartment. Just a room is fine. BUM will help me find something."

"Really?" She looks at me, her cheeks rosy with cold and maybe with hope.

I swallow. The truth is I haven't talked to anyone, haven't saved squat. I have no clue where I'm going to end up and I'm scared shitless. But with her looking at me for answers, how can I tell her that?

"Really."

My memory tells me that this is when I'm supposed to touch her. I reach for her, but when my fingers touch her skin, skin that my brain knows isn't really there, I feel my lunch coming up.

"End simulation," I say.

The Marybeth in the sim just sits on the bench sipping her hot cocoa, thinking about what I've just said, oblivious to the fact that I've stopped playing my part in the memory.

Oblivious because she's not real.

"Please," I beg, "end simulation."

Chapter 42

In the cafeteria, Jay wipes his hands on a dishrag and comes to the counter.

"Just noodle soup and crackers to go." I dip my head. "Don't bother with the milk shake."

Usually he makes small talk and then takes my order, but today, he stands there looking at me with that squinty, I'm-sorry-your-life-is-so-fucked-up look.

"You okay, kid?" he asks finally.

I shrug. "Living and breathing."

He keeps looking at me. I study the rack of chips so I don't have to look back. Then he leans across the counter toward me.

"Well, you keep doing that, you hear me? I know this probably isn't my place, Adam, but here's what I think." He whistles. "I know nobody ever talks about Sunshine's past, but I get the feeling that you and Sunshine, your lives were maybe not what kids' lives should be. And the loss of your band…your friends—"

"Jay, don't." The words catch in my throat. Maybe it's from being so sick for the last few days, or maybe it's all finally taking its toll, but I can't hear this right now.

"No." He holds up a hand. "Let me say this, Adam. Because you're a good guy, no matter what you believe, and there are people here—like Genevieve, even if she is mad at you—who genuinely care about you. About Adam the person, and not just the superstar. So don't you ever give up, like I'm pretty sure Sunshine did."

And there it is. The thing I haven't let myself think this whole time.

* * *

Outside Gen's door I clutch my takeout bag to keep my hands from shaking. My stomach is empty and queasy and I don't know if I'm even going to be able to eat at all.

"Today was rough, Gen," I tell the door. The silence of the hallway jitters through me. "I don't know if I can get through this without you." It's hard to speak the words, but they're there, choking me, and I have to get them out. "All that other stuff, it doesn't matter to me. You're the same Gen I met when I got here."

Please open the door.

"'So what,' right? I get it. It's so stupid. You're the first friend I've made in so long, and I screwed up everything. I always screw up everything. Even with Marybeth I screwed up everything."

The door rattles slightly. As always, she's there, listening, and I'm grateful for that much.

"I know it's selfish, and I'm the last person right now who has the right to ask you anything. But I really need you."

I think, stupidly, that she'll open the door now and hug me. It's been so long since anyone but Dr. E has touched me at all. But the door stays closed.

"I understand why you won't forgive me. I just came to say that I'm not going to bug you anymore, and that I'm sorry for everything."

Then I reach into my pocket and put my hand on her key card, the one I took before everything went to shit. Do I or don't I? Because now she'll know for sure that I stole it. But I hope she'll take it the way I mean it. As a gesture of honesty. Of complete confession.

I hesitate.

"For *everything*," I say. "And I'm asking you to please forgive me."

Then I slip the key card beneath her door.

Chapter 43

I carry my pathetic dinner to a bench in the courtyard and set my noodle soup and saltines beside me. My stomach is still churning, so instead of eating I watch the sky turn gold and then purple as the sun sets, and I try not to remember the simulation room or the way the memories pile, one on top of the other, like a stack of pancakes.

Finally, I open the lid and attempt a spoonful of soup. It rumbles around in my belly, not quite sure if it's ready to call it home. Thankfully, it stays down. The saltiness is heavenly.

I try not to think about what Jay said. I try not to think about what it means. Because if he knows, then how can Dr. E, who's like the Raider of the Lost Memories, not know?

I'm halfway done with the soup when I feel someone standing next to me. I don't have to look to know it's Gen. I smell her familiar scent, a combination of roses and mint. I push my dinner aside so there's room for her to sit.

"Hi," she says.

"Hi," I say.

I want to look at her, but I can't just yet.

"I don't want to talk about it," she says. "Any of it. Okay, Adam?"

I don't even want to breathe, for fear she'll disappear. "Okay."

She sits next to me, and when I finally bring myself to look at her, she's staring at my dinner.

"So is Jay starving you or can't you manage to feed yourself without my culinary ordering expertise?"

There's tension behind her words, pain. *I did that*, I think.

"It's not my fault you've made yourself indispensable," I say.

She rewards me with a small smile, and something in me loosens. Then her smile fades. "You're getting way too thin. Are you sick?"

"I've been in the simulation room for the last few days."

She peels open a sleeve of saltines and hands me one. "And it makes you sick?"

"Shoot-me-in-the-head-and-put-me-out-of-my-misery sick."

"Eesh." She shakes her head. I wonder suddenly if someone suffered the simulation room for her, so she could be who she is. Her dad maybe or her mom. *Or maybe*, I think, *that's why her mom left.* "It doesn't get better?"

"Oh, it does…If 'better' means puking up only two lungs instead of all my vital organs, and then one lung instead of two. Dr. E says it just takes practice, like I have to retrain my brain to *accept* what's happening and not *think* about it."

"Good luck with that," she says.

I nod. "No joke."

She hands me another cracker. "Eat, please."

I dutifully chew and swallow. We don't talk for a minute.

Gen looks up at the sky. Night has officially arrived, and overhead, the moon is a bright sliver.

I think about Marybeth, about Genevieve, even LaLa, the only girls I've ever really cared about, dead in the ground, and me, still here—living, breathing, screwing things up.

But Genevieve is here, right next to me, and soon Marybeth will be too. So why do I have to keep reminding myself of that?

"Thanks for the milk shakes, by the way," she says finally. "I think I've gained twenty pounds."

That she drank them makes me ridiculously pleased.

I drink her in with my eyes. I can't help it. "Milk. Does a body good."

"The comedian is back," she says.

"No." I meet her eyes. "I mean it. You look great."

She sighs. "Great for a dead girl, right?"

"I thought we weren't going to talk about it."

"We weren't. I wasn't. It's just…"

"What? Tell me."

"It's just…I was *so* mad at you, Adam, but…I don't know. It wasn't even because you found and *read*"—she pokes me hard in the chest—"my journal, or even all the horrible things you said, because I think them too. It's that you were the one person in this whole godforsaken place who looked at me like I was a girl and not some freak. And you're never going to look at me like that again."

I bow my head. I want to tell her that she's wrong, but I can't. So instead I say, "I'm glad you're here."

She nods. "Thank you for not lying to me."

After all the times I've shied away from her touch, I reach for her hand. I twine my fingers in hers, and she's solid and warm, not a ghost or a monster but a real girl, no matter how she came to exist.

She leans against me, her body molding to mine, and she sighs as she lays her head against my shoulder.

"I've missed you so much," I say.

I move my head so I can see her. Only the top of her head is visible, her blond hair so soft beneath my chin. So close, I can see that every strand is a different color, from pure white to deep, honey gold. Then she shifts to look up at me, and when she does, our lips are only inches apart.

Her breath quickens. So close, I can hear it. Too close.

I tell myself to move away, but I'm frozen there, so near to this girl who's meant so much to me.

"Adam." She says my name like a breath.

I lean in. I don't mean to. But then my lips touch hers, which are full and moist and alive, and I think I do mean to. I do mean to very, very much.

The kiss is gentle and tentative, and I slip one hand against Gen's head as the kiss deepens. But she sighs and puts one hand against my chest, pushing herself up and away.

She smiles, but she doesn't meet my eyes.

"You need to think about this first," she says.

Her hand lingers on my chest for a minute, and then she says, "Good night, Adam." And she's gone.

Chapter 44

In the dark, I lie in bed and stare up at the ceiling. My lips burn where they touched Genevieve's.

How could I have done that? Worse, how can my heart still race when I think about it?

How many times can one person fuck things up? I wonder. Apparently, my purpose on earth is to find out.

Then there's a knock on my door. I get up and throw on jeans and a T-shirt and open it.

Gen stands there, hands clasped behind her back. Though she blushes, she meets my eyes. "May I come in?"

It crosses my mind to tell her that maybe that isn't such a good idea, after what happened earlier, that if I was weak then, I'll be weak now. And this time it might not be just a kiss. But I nod.

She's careful not to let her body touch mine as she steps into the apartment, but still, all the hairs on my arms stand up. I shut the door and motion for her to sit on the couch. She shakes her head and stays standing.

"I know I told *you* to think about it, but I've been thinking about it." She sighs. "What happened...I know it was wrong. I think about Marybeth, everything she's been through, everything she still has to go through. And you came here and I met you and for a little while I think I forgot who I was, and just thought about who I could be. But I know you can't...We can't...I'm sorry."

I dip my head. "This is on me, Gen. Not you."

Her stare burns into me long enough that I finally raise my eyes to look at her again.

"No. I didn't stop you from kissing me. I didn't want to stop you. Even if I knew it could only be just that once. It was just that once, Adam, wasn't it?"

My mouth is dry. The uncertainty in her voice, the wistfulness, is too much to bear. I press the heels of my hands against my eyes.

Then I square my shoulders. "I love Marybeth," I say.

She smiles, even if it's a sad smile, and she squeezes my hand. "I know you do."

"I'm sorry," I say.

"I know." She lets go of my hand, and I feel suddenly afloat. "I should go."

I sigh. "Okay."

She opens the door but hesitates, one hand on the knob as if she doesn't want to go. And I don't want her to.

"Adam?" Her voice is soft.

"Mmm?"

Her eyes shine. "Promise me we won't let this come between us. Not after everything else."

I want to take her hand the way she took mine, but I resist. Instead, I smile at her. "I promise."

Chapter 45

On Simulation Day Eight, I manage three complete thirty-minute sessions without a single pilgrimage to the altar of the porcelain god. By the twelfth day, I get through it without turning green from the inside out.

When we hit the two-week mark, Dr. E asks me to meet her in her office.

"Have a seat," she says. "I wanted to talk to you about where we are in the process, and where we'll be going."

I sit.

She studies me. "How are you feeling about the process, Adam?"

"Like I've had the world's worst stomach bug."

I don't tell her that I punched another hole in my belt yesterday to keep my jeans from slipping low enough to show my ass crack. I also don't tell her that for most of the last two weeks I've eaten nothing but soup and saltines and ginger ale.

"I know it's rough. But you appear to be adjusting to the process," Dr. E says. "Is that fair to say?"

I guess it's true. Two days ago I graduated to toast and scrambled eggs. I nod.

"Good. Now what I'm about to ask you is very important, so please answer me honestly."

I nod again. My mouth is dry.

"Are you ready for us to bring in Sunshine?"

She sits at her desk, letting me digest her words before she continues.

"I know how long you've waited to see her, Adam, and how much you want this. But I need you to give this the consideration that it merits. Don't answer me now. I want you to go into one more session, keeping the question in mind. Then I want you to get yourself some dinner, something a little more substantial than soup and crackers—yes, I check up on you—and get a good night's sleep. Tomorrow afternoon I'll ask for your answer. Can you do that?"

There's a roaring in my ears. I'm going to see Marybeth.

I swallow and hope my voice doesn't crack. "I can do that."

"I don't want an answer that comes purely from emotion, Adam. I want you to think critically about your ability to cope—physically and mentally—within the context of the simulation, because it's vital that we do this right. A misstep at this stage could destroy everything we've done."

I shiver, but I square my shoulders. "I understand. I won't let you down."

What I mean is I won't let *her* down.

Marybeth.

Not again.

Chapter 46

I bring my guitar to the courtyard. Maybe it's knowing that I'll see Marybeth soon, but I crave the comfort of its wooden curves, the tension of its strings. My fingers find familiar chords.

Genevieve settles beside me on the bench, the way she has every day since she forgave my screwup. I feel her intensity as she watches me play. There's energy between us, even if we're both ignoring it. We haven't talked about the kiss since the night it happened.

The afternoon is humid and heavy. It's like a slow-motion kind of heat. Even the mynah birds seem to have fled from it, and only the neon-green geckos flash up and down the thick trunks of the palm trees with any amount of energy.

When I strum the opening notes of a song, it sounds equally lazy, as if the heaviness of the day is contagious.

"I don't know that one," Gen says. "It's different."

"It's one of our first songs. It was never recorded."

She angles toward me, careful to keep distance between us. "It's nice to hear you play. You're very good."

I look up and smile. "You sound surprised. Rumor has it I once made it big."

She blushes. "Do you want to play some more or eat?"

I want to play, but after my conversation with Dr. E, I know I should eat. "Eat, I guess."

I set the instrument on the ground. Gen opens one of the brown paper bags that Jay—who hasn't been able to stop grinning since the two of us appeared in the cafeteria together—packed for us. She takes out thick sandwiches—roast beef for me and turkey for her—on huge slices of freshly baked white bread.

I take a tentative bite. My stomach rumbles, but it's a good rumble, a feed-me rumble rather than a don't-you-dare one. The roast beef tastes delicious. There's a hint of garlic and plenty of salt, which my body is craving like nobody's business.

Genevieve watches me instead of eating.

"What?" I ask.

"Are you doing okay, Adam? Really?"

That she worries about me despite her own circumstances makes me want to hug her.

"I…" I start to tell her I'm doing fine, better, great. Instead, I say, "I'm going to see Marybeth soon."

The skin around her eyes crinkles. "Are you ready for that?"

"That's the question of the day apparently."

"And…"

I shrug. "I don't know."

"This is what you've been waiting for, isn't it?"

There's something funny in her voice. Like an off-key note that gets buried in the rest of a song.

"Of course it is." I set my sandwich down on my leg. "But what if I screw it up like everything else I touch?"

"You won't."

"I don't know how you can be so sure. I'm a world-class fuckup."

"You're not though." She puts one hand on my arm. It's the first time she's touched me since…

I take another bite of sandwich, but my throat is suddenly too tight to swallow. Finally, I get the roast beef and bread to go down. "Aren't I?"

"No. You're not." She trails off, and I see tears in her eyes. I want to tell her to stop, to please don't, because I don't think I can handle it. But then she blinks and her eyes clear and she smiles. "Don't sell yourself short, Adam. You're an amazing, amazing guy."

I rub my knuckles across her cheek. She shivers, but doesn't pull away.

Don't start something you can't control, Adam, I warn myself. I pull back.

"Thank you," I say.

Chapter 47

"I'm as ready as I'm going to be," I tell Dr. E. In the polished wood surface of her desk, my reflection looks ghostly. "I'd like to tell you I'm rock steady. But I can't. This is as good as it gets."

It's the most honest answer I have. I'm sure I can handle the sim physically, no puking. The part I'll never be sure about is that I won't freak out seeing Marybeth. And part of it is that, when I finally see her, maybe I'll know for sure if this is a true resurrection or just a reconstruction, if she'll have the same soul, drawn back from some version of heaven—or hell—for this second chance.

Dr. E's expression is unreadable, and I wonder if I've said the wrong thing.

"That's the kind of thoughtful answer I needed to hear from you," she finally says. "And I think it's accurate. You are as ready as you're going to be."

I blow out a breath.

She smiles, and it's that gentle smile that she used to have. Maybe these are all good omens. My return to grace with Genevieve. My return to grace with Dr. Elloran. Maybe she really does care.

"So what happens now?" I ask.

Her smile broadens. "Now, Adam, you meet Sunshine."

My heart beats so hard I can hardly hear over it. "Right now?"

"Pretty much, yes."

She holds up one finger to me, then picks up the phone. "Prep Sunshine for Memory-Lock Sim One."

Now. I'm going to see her now.

Dr. E turns her attention back to me. "She'll be in the simulation chamber with the episode already running when you get there. The process will be seamless for her. But you will be walking into the memory. Okay?"

I muster up some spit. "Okay."

"Good," she says. "You're going to be fine. So shall we?"

I take a deep breath and nod then follow her to the waiting room outside the simulation chamber. Inside my head, something balloon-like pulses, and the edges of my vision darken. I think I'm hyperventilating.

"Take a seat, Adam. Someone will be in to wire you up shortly. I'll be in the observation room the whole time, watching."

"She's in there now?" I gesture to the sim room. My voice sounds like it's coming from down a long tunnel.

"She's in there. She's already beginning the memory."

With that, Dr. E disappears. I pace until a technician comes in to wire me up.

"Won't she see the receptors?" I ask as he sticks the pads at the base of my skull and along my temples and tucks the small device they're hooked to into my pocket. As a last touch, he hands me a small earpiece, which I slip into my left ear.

The tech shakes his head. "Sunshine will be in a deep, hypnotic state for the duration. She'll see only you."

The rubber ball that's been bouncing around in my chest rises up, blocking my throat. Unlike Dr. E, this guy seems to see that I'm ready to completely freak.

"Breathe, kid," he says. "The hard part is over."

No, I want to tell him. *The hard part hasn't even begun.*

But a light over the simulation-room door changes from red to green and the door clicks open. Before I can say anything more, he nods toward it.

"It's time," he says. "Go on in."

Chapter 48

I step into the memory. Instantly, the weight of my guitar pulls at my shirt, the strap biting into my neck, even though I don't have an actual guitar with me. It's just an illusion, but so incredibly real.

If I look behind me, I know I'll see the sliver of light from the waiting room as the door closes. But I don't. I walk forward. Toward Marybeth.

The simulation room has become an outdoor space. I shiver in the cold, which is bright and clear and completely different from the compound's normal air-conditioning. When I was still in foster care, I always refused to wear a jacket, even during the coldest part of winter. It had been one small rebellion in a lifetime of small rebellions.

My teeth chatter. Or maybe it's just because I'm scared shitless.

In my earpiece, Dr. E says, "You're doing fine."

I walk down a narrow, rutted road through small patches of snow left from the weekend's storm. All the houses I pass are falling apart, porches rotting, paint peeling, windows dirty. It's the kind of road where rusted cars sit on cement blocks in the front yards. I find the mailbox numbered thirty-nine and walk up the driveway.

Part of my brain says I should have walked right out the other end of the compound by now. But the illusion remains as perfect as ever.

I follow the driveway up past the house—which can't decide

if it wants to be blue or purple—to where the pavement ends at a stand-alone garage.

I remind myself to breathe.

This is Jeddy's house. His parents are "patrons of the arts," as Jeddy always says with finger quotes (adding with a grin, "That means they're unemployed"), so he permanently volunteered their garage as a rehearsal area.

If this whole band thing even lasts.

Even as I think it, the guilt comes. *Marybeth wants this so bad.*

I crunch through dirty, packed-down snow around to the side door and look in through the small, dirty window.

Something boils up inside me, trying to pop me right out of the memory. *Marybeth is in there. Marybeth is in there.* My brain starts the chant.

I try to push it aside, because as soon as I let myself think about it, as soon as I give myself a minute to remember that this isn't real, that today isn't really that long-ago day, that Jeddy and LaLa are nothing more than holograms in the simulator, not even real ghosts but only electronic ones, my stomach begins to roll. I hold on to the side of the building, aware even as I do that it isn't really a building but probably only a sliding wall or a blue block.

Stop it. Stop it. Stop it.

In my ear, Dr. E says, "Let the memory carry you, Adam. Don't think about it."

Get it together, Adam, I warn myself. *Breathe through it.*

I let go of the wall. Then I walk through the door and into a world of people I thought I'd never see again.

LaLa, behind her drums, which her parents had carted over for her in their pickup truck, is the first one I see. The sight of her familiar torn denim jacket nearly undoes me completely. She stops picking out a soft trial beat long enough to wave, and as the memory urges, I do the same.

My "then" thought: *Her parents must have had a shit-fit when they dropped her off and saw the neighborhood. Ten to one there's a can of pepper spray in her purse.*

"Hey, Adam," she says.

"Hey, LaLa," I return as I'd done that day all those years ago. Only now I struggle to keep my voice from shaking. "How go things?"

"Oh they go, Cookie Crumb. They go."

No, LaLa. They're gone, I think. *They're all gone. You're gone.*

My chest aches.

And so, I want to dash around her and see Marybeth.

But Dr. E's warning sticks in my brain, and I pull myself back to the memory. It has to play out.

"Hey, close the door, will you?" LaLa shivers.

I close the door. In the garage, an ancient space heater blasts air so hot it threatens to burn the skin right off my cheeks. Over the door, a hand-painted banner—part of a torn bedsheet—in black with silver lettering says: CONSTELLATION.

Jeddy sits at the stool behind his keyboards, swiveling aimlessly. His knit, keyboard-patterned scarf trails on the garage floor, the fringe gray with dust.

"Hey, Jeddy," I say, following the memory exactly, even though black spots push in at the edges of my vision and I'm afraid I might be starting to hyperventilate again.

I study them both—LaLa with her short-short hair and her pretty face and the light of a thousand candles inside her, and Jeddy, who grins at me like we're at the heart of a conspiracy—and it's hard to believe they aren't real.

I look around, and for a second the memory and the now come together as I ask, "Where's MB?"

"In the house, grabbing us some drinks."

I lean my guitar against the wall then hoist myself up to sit at the wooden counter. My heartbeats and LaLa's drumbeats count down the seconds until Marybeth arrives.

I can't do this. I can't do this. I can't want this so badly and be so damn afraid at the same time. I'll explode.

Another heartbeat. Another drumbeat. Two. Three. LaLa drums. Jeddy spins.

Then, exactly the moment the memory says she will, the side door opens and Marybeth walks in.

Chapter 49

Marybeth stops just inside the door, four cans of ginger ale cradled in her arms, a bag of tortilla chips balanced on top. She kicks the door closed with one foot.

And I feel it, that this is really her. It's like everything has been floating away, and now someone turned on gravity, like she's somehow brighter than Jeddy or LaLa or anything else in the room. Brighter. Sturdier. *Realer.* I try to see through the illusion that I know is there to help the memory along. I try to find the clone beneath, the Marybeth who could be any age. But all I see is the Marybeth I know from the memory.

"All I could find," she announces, and then, seeing me, "Jeez, Adam, about time you showed."

Instantly, tears sting my eyes. I blink hard to keep them back. *Stay with the memory. Stay with the memory.* But overriding everything else is the knowledge, the feeling, that this girl, this clone, this version of Marybeth, even if she looks exactly—*exactly*—like she did that day, isn't just memory but real, flesh and blood and bones, thought and emotion and, well, everything.

"Whatever, MB," I force the words out, words I'd once spoken so casually, as if she'd always be there to hear them.

I won't ever take you for granted again, I want to say. *I won't ever let you down again.*

A year's worth of regret and grief and anger wants to come rushing out all at once.

"Stay in the memory, Adam," Dr. E says in my ear. I want to shake her, to ask her if *she* could stay in the damn memory if she were me.

Marybeth smiles to let me know she isn't *really* mad that I'm late, and I want to pull her close, to crush that bag of chips and those stupid soda cans between us. But I can't. And maybe that's the hardest thing of all, to play along as if this were reality, when all I want is to hold her and tell her to never, never, never leave me again.

"Anyways," she says, her face breaking out into that wide Marybeth grin that I'd seen less and less over the last few years. "We're all here now. *The band!*"

She drops the chips and soda onto the counter.

"Enough with the gushing," Jeddy says, still spinning. "Let's jam."

I grab my guitar and let Marybeth direct me to a stool. I'm grateful when we start, because it lets me bury myself in the music, no matter that the music is awkward and painful, with our lack of experience.

But sitting here with people who've been dead for years, sitting so close to Marybeth who is alive and real and breathing and warm, my fingers shake so badly they trip over the chords.

I want to panic, because I'm changing the memory, aren't I? With each chord I screw up, I'm changing the memory. Maybe Marybeth will think I'm a screwup. Maybe she'll rethink the whole band. Or worse, maybe she'll have some kind of seizure because I'm changing things that can't be changed.

Then another little voice speaks up in my head. And for once, it's my own.

It says: *Maybe it wouldn't be so bad to change things.*

Stay with the memory, I warn myself. *Just stay with the memory.*

And beside me, tentatively, Marybeth begins to sing.

The memory re-creation lasts forever and ends too quickly.

"We should go," MB says with a dramatic sigh. "My 'mom and dad'"—she makes finger quotes around the words—"will be waiting. Do you believe they make me call them that? We're on for Thursday night, right?"

"You got it, Mary-Bee," Jeddy says, wagging his eyebrows. "Your place or mine?"

She swats him. I half expect her hand to go right through him or for him to dissolve into a million pixels. But the illusion holds.

Jeddy grins. "Mmm-mmm, feisty. You'd better watch out, Adam. This girl is H-O-T for Jed."

"Yeah, yeah," I say.

Marybeth waves to LaLa and Jeddy. *Good-bye, my friends,* I think. I wonder if the memory simulation will ever bring me together with them again. I miss them already, the ache from their deaths suddenly sharp and bright and new again. The air is too thick to breathe.

Then Marybeth and I walk out the door and we're alone. It's flurrying, and snowflakes settle on her dark hair. It's hard to believe that we're really indoors, deep in the tropics, that the night and the street and the snow are all products of science and electronics and our memories.

We crunch down the driveway. Marybeth is flying high. I can feel it in the way she bounces as she walks beside me. Her happiness fills me.

At the road, she reaches for my arm. The world goes black at her touch, and for a second I'm in another memory, a later memory. In it, she's no longer Marybeth but Sunshine, and we're in our room after a concert, the quiet—after the white noise of the crowd—as deep as the ocean, and I'm slipping off her dress, my lips traveling along her bare shoulder—

Her hand curls around my arm and I'm back in the now. Or the then that is the now at this moment. This is so damn confusing.

But God! She's real. Warm and soft and electric. The muskiness of her perfume rises off her, a stolen squirt of her foster mom's expensive stuff. And most of all, she's Marybeth in a way that a simulation could never be, no matter how believable the illusion they can create.

Again, the disconnect between the memory and the now hits me. And this time it isn't nausea that rises up, but grief and relief and love, and I'm grateful for Marybeth's high from the music, and for the darkness hiding the tears she'd see in my eyes if she looked at me now.

My throat aches.

At the turnoff for her house, we stop. Though I know I need to finish the memory before I fall apart completely, I hate to leave her now that I've finally gotten her back, hate to feel her hand slip away from my arm, hate the still-chaste kiss that means good-bye. Even as I watch her walk up the driveway I want to call out to her, to grab her hand and run far away from this place.

"Good night, Adam," she calls.

I swallow hard. "Good night, MB."

Then she's gone, and the night and the snow and the street and the sharpness of the memory vanish, and I'm once again standing in the blue simulation room.

I can't breathe. I can't see.

Dr. E appears through a door, hurrying toward me, saying, "You did beautifully, Adam. Let's get you unhooked."

I need to get out of here. I need air.

I pull away from Dr. E and yank at the receiver pads myself, throwing them onto the floor, shoving the expensive little box that they're attached to at her as I stumble toward the door and out through the waiting room to the hallway, where the fluorescent lights seem surreal and somehow disrespectful. Mr. Grayson is there, his hand extended for a shake, as if this moment were something to celebrate, but I can't stop. I can't breathe.

Then Gen is there, her smile too bright. Over the buzzing in my ears I hear her say, "Oh, Adam, I was just coming to see if..."

She breaks off and her smile falls when she sees me. I wave one hand toward her but I can't stop because I'm suffocating...or drowning. Yes, drowning. This was how Marybeth felt.

I need air. I need the humidity and warmth of the tropical day to erase the cold and the snow and the dark.

How I find my way to the back door when I can hardly see is something of a miracle. But, then again, this is a place of miracles, right? I want to laugh. Can't.

The sun hits my face, my arms, my hands, but I feel the chill of the night, the snow, Marybeth's hand on my arm, her lips against mine. My own lips still tingle with the taste of the ginger ale she'd been drinking.

I hear Genevieve's voice saying, "Wait," and I open my mouth to tell her I'm sorry, really, really sorry, but I need to be alone for a while. Only no words come out.

"Adam," she says, "Adam, stop."

And maybe it's her voice or the sound of my name, but the dark thing that lives inside me rises up, up, and up, and finally I can't push it down any more.

I drop to my knees and cry.

Chapter 50

Genevieve kneels beside me, her arms around me, her head against mine. I resist for a minute, then I lean into her.

Once I start, I can't stop. It's as if everything that's been festering inside me all these months is trying to escape, and I cry until every muscle in my body aches and I'm totally emptied out.

Eventually, I sit up. Gen rocks back, keeping one hand on my shoulder, but doesn't say anything. I don't look at her, just wipe my nose and eyes on the sleeve of my T-shirt.

I nod, hoping she'll understand all the things I can't say. She stands up and takes my hand, helping me to my feet. I wobble, nod again. I still can't bring myself to look at her.

"Better?" she asks, pushing my damp bangs away from my forehead.

My breath hitches. Shoot me now. I clear my throat and hope my voice will come. "I'm sorry you had to see that."

"You shouldn't be," she says. "Come on. Let's walk a little."

We wander down the path. It feels like days have passed, instead of maybe an hour or so, since my session with Marybeth.

She's alive. I touched her. She touched me.

All around, birds chirp and flowers bloom, and suddenly the sim, the winter night, the snow, the band, all seem surreal and very, very far away. My head swims.

"Do you want to talk about it?" Gen asks.

When I think I'll be able to speak without falling apart, I ask the question I never thought I'd ask out loud. "Am I doing the right thing, Gen? Bringing her back? Or am I making her relive all this pain just to lose her all over again?"

She stops walking and turns me to face her. The frowny way she looks at me scrapes me raw. "Lose her all over again? Why would you..."

Her expression changes. She understands what I'm saying.

"Then Sunshine's death wasn't an accident," she says.

Like razors, the words cut my throat and tongue as they come up. "She killed herself."

But afterward I feel relieved to have spoken the horrible secret I've carried for so long.

See, Gen? We all have our secrets.

Gen sinks down into the nearest bench, as if all the air has gone out of her. I sit beside her. But for me, all the air is suddenly rushing back in, and it's feeding a white-hot flame of anger that I didn't even know was there.

"She didn't get caught in an undertow and pulled out to sea. She swam to her death. She took her antidepressants because they made her sluggish and sleepy, and then she went for a swim."

"God! Adam, are you sure?"

"She knew that shoreline, Gen." I pound my fist into my other palm. In my mind, I can see that little red boat all those years ago, getting pulled on the rip farther and farther from shore. "She knew those currents, and even if she was somehow—*somehow*—stupid enough to get caught in a rip current, she *knew* how to get out of it. She knew and..."

Gen stares at me, her mouth hanging open. The words are jagged rocks. They'll cut me if I speak them. But I do.

"She knew that *I* would know. And they found antidepressants in her bloodstream, the ones she was supposed to have been taking but never did."

"So maybe she was really trying. Maybe she just gave the meds one more try and then…" Gen dips her head and looks at her hands. "So…What? The way she died was her way of telling you she took her own life?"

"I think so." My words sound too small.

"She didn't leave you a…" In her pause, the way her eyebrows crinkle up, I can hear the omitted word: *suicide.* "Letter?"

I shake my head. She didn't. Not even a few words to tell me that she forgave me.

"I thought she did. I found a paper woven into the strings of my guitar, but it wasn't a note. It was just the music for a new song."

"But why wouldn't she at least say good-bye?"

I shrug. Even the anger is leaving. I have no energy left for emotion. Suddenly all I want is to go back to my room and sleep for a month.

"I don't know. Maybe so nobody but me would know, and I wouldn't have to live with everybody looking at me like I was to blame, like I should have watched her closer, like I should have done something."

Gen puts one hand over her mouth, not looking at me.

"It didn't matter though. I look at myself that way every day."

She still doesn't say anything, just tips her head against mine and holds my hand, and we sit that way for a long time.

Chapter 51

Back at my apartment, we stand in the doorway. Gen shuffles her feet. "Let me order us some food."

I shake my head. "I'm not really hungry."

"Then humor me, okay, because I'm starving."

I give her a small smile. I understand. She doesn't want to leave me alone. "Okay. I could use something to drink."

She raises her eyebrows.

"I mean like a soda," I clarify. "Believe me. The last thing I want is that kind of drink."

Inside, she heads for the phone. I hear her ordering. When she returns, she sits on the arm of the couch, but doesn't say anything. I think she's digesting everything that happened today almost as much as I am.

Finally, she says, "The world was always watching her, Adam. How could nobody have known?"

I shrug. "There was speculation. A few of the tabloids tried to run with it, but it didn't fly. The coroner ruled it an accident. I think Jack paid dearly for that lie."

"Who's Jack?" she asks.

"Our manager," I say. "He wouldn't have wanted that for Marybeth."

She nods and doesn't ask anything else, and finally our food comes. There are mashed potatoes with gobs of gravy; macaroni and cheese with crumbles of bacon; soft, sweet buttered rolls; and like seven desserts. Gen doesn't try to force it on me, just hands me a bottle of lemonade and tucks into her own food. Now and then she silently holds out her fork with something for me to taste, and I find myself taking it.

We don't say much.

Later, when we both know it's time for her to leave, she hesitates. "Adam…" she starts.

"I think I'll be okay," I say, knowing it's what she needs to hear. But more than that, even though I'm empty of everything and exhausted to the core, I think, for the first time in a long time, it might actually be true.

Chapter 52

I don't know if it's because the first time is behind me, or if it's because I've started to come to terms with all this, or if it's only that I'm totally drained, but I don't feel like a complete head case entering the sim room on Day Two.

Dr. E wires me up herself, and although she watches me more closely than usual, I think I can pass inspection. Apparently she does too, because she says, "If you're ready, let's do it."

She nods toward the door. "On green."

I take a deep breath, which isn't as steady as I'd like—so okay, maybe I'm a partial head case—and when the light over the door turns green, I open it and walk in.

I step onto a sidewalk that's such a perfect re-creation that I can make out cracks in the concrete and a single paw print from a dog that's probably graying around the muzzle now.

I shiver at the thought.

Instantly, the memory starts, propelling me toward a blue-and-white house that I'd lived in for a few years.

Marybeth sits on the front stairs, her eyes closed. She's singing softly. My heart starts to pound. I wipe my wet palms on my jeans.

Okay, so maybe I'm a complete head case after all.

I stop to watch her like I did all those years ago

In my ear, Dr. E recites her now familiar mantra. "Go with the memory, Adam."

So as best as I can, I do.

I stand on the sidewalk, my hands in my pockets, listening, watching her. The angles on her face soften when she sings, and her eyelashes glow where the sun touches them. She's not wearing makeup, but her cheeks are pink from the wind, and she's so beautiful I think my heart might forget to keep beating.

The words belong to a new song that Jeddy wrote for the band, a ballad that everyone knows he wrote for Marybeth...Well, everyone except for Marybeth, who is completely oblivious to such things. Not that anything would come of it. Marybeth is mine and I'm Marybeth's and everyone—including Jeddy, despite his song—knows this.

We're rehearsing tonight, and Marybeth, being Marybeth, wants to make sure she has the words memorized perfectly. Guilt jabs me like a needle. Instead of practicing, I've been at the field tossing around a baseball with a few of the guys from school.

Maybe my thoughts are loud enough for her to hear, because she stops singing and opens her eyes. She tips her head and smiles. "What?"

"Don't stop," I say, which makes her blush. She starts to sing again, this time looking down at the steps, her hair falling so I can't see her face. "I'll be right back."

I dash inside, past the door to the kitchen, where my foster mother and her bestie are cackling over something they think is funny, and I take the stairs two at a time up to my room, where I retrieve the guitar.

In the now, I have no desire to hesitate, to look around at this place where I lived, to look at my foster mother or the pictures on the wall that don't include me. As I had then, I just want to get back to Marybeth.

Outside again, I sit beside her, close enough that our knees touch, and set the guitar on my lap. She doesn't stop singing, so I close my eyes and listen until I find my place in the song and my fingers find the right chords.

I play.

Marybeth lays her head on my shoulder, the sweetness of her voice in my ear, her breath on my cheek and neck.

There is nothing, I think, *that will ever take her away from me.*

This time, when the session is over, I manage to get all the way back to my apartment before I cry.

Chapter 53

"How are you?" Gen asks.

"Better. Thanks." Which is sort of true, I guess.

"Good." She holds up a big brown bag. "Hungry? I thought we could go on a picnic."

"A picnic?" Just the word makes my stomach churn.

"What? Heat? Humidity? Bugs the size of cats? I *know* you want to." She grabs my hand. "Because what you need is to get away from this place and these sims."

She keeps my hand firmly in hers. I know I should tell her that it's not right, especially now that I'm so close to having Marybeth back, but I can't, not to this girl who has been through so much herself. Not to this girl who maybe, in another lifetime, I could have loved.

Did I just think that? Something in me squeezes and won't let go.

"Come on." She tips her head toward the door. "None of Jay's famous homemade potato chips unless you come."

I sigh. "When you put it that way..."

We go out the back, heading toward the airstrip we landed on when I first got here. Past the airstrip is another path, which brings us to a small, abandoned marina. If I can even call it that. There's a falling-down dock and several boat slips, empty except for a busted-up dinghy pulled halfway onto the dirt.

"Project Orpheus used to use this," Gen says, "but for the most part, the airstrip is easier now. Nobody bothers with the place much, but I like it."

The dock groans when we step onto it.

"Are you sure this will hold us?" I ask.

Gen shrugs. "If not, you can swim, right?"

"Ha-ha. Funny." But with the late afternoon sun beating down on my face, I find myself smiling. She was right. I needed this.

We take off our shoes and sit down on the dock, legs dangling over the side, our feet inches above the water, which is so incredibly blue. I can see fish swimming down there, bright spots of color.

She opens the brown bag for today's grand reveal.

"Voilà! Fish tacos," she announces. "I thought the setting would be appropriate."

I look down at the fish. "Or morbid."

"Or morbid," she agrees. "But here at Project Orpheus, where we deal in resurrecting the dead, morbidity is a way of life, no?"

I know she means to make light of it, but I hear something bitter in her tone. She hands me a taco and takes a bite of her own.

I don't eat right away. Instead, I watch her chew.

"Your father doesn't know that you know," I say.

She looks up sharply. "You talked to my father?"

I nod and wait for her anger, but instead she swallows another bite of fish taco and shrugs. "My father is an idiot. How could I not know? I live here in the middle of this. The first time I went into town, the woman at the ice-cream shop fainted and some old man made the sign of the cross. It was a good clue. And there's your 'place of ghosts.'"

"It's still a leap," I say.

"Well, after the initial debacle in town, I sort of put two and two together. My father was already working on Project Orpheus and I knew what it was all about. So the idea was like this weird little itch in my head, and all I had to do was pay someone enough to send me some old newspaper files, and there was my picture—sorry, *her* picture—staring back at me."

She takes another bite of her taco as if this is just any old conversation.

After a minute, she continues. "It was sort of terrifying. Kind of like finding out you're a ghost who hasn't moved on to heaven or something. But not exactly. It's hard to describe."

She grins as if it could possibly be funny. I imagine Marybeth 2.0 finding out she's a clone. I can't even imagine how she would react, how she would feel.

Gen watches me and I wonder if she can see the gears turning in my brain.

"So how was it today?" she asks.

"I don't know. Fucked up?"

"That good?"

I crumble a piece of taco shell into the water. The fish swarm around it until the water near my feet boils. We both watch them as if they were the most amazing things on the whole fucking planet.

"I guess seeing Marybeth with the band…I mean seeing her *now*, after so much time has passed, I'm realizing that it was the only time she was really happy."

"She had a hard life."

"All she wanted was a family. And that band was her only real family."

"You're still her family, Adam."

"But it wasn't enough, was it?" I stare down at the fish, which are starting to disperse. "*I* wasn't enough. I mean, what if it's just genetically wired into her."

"You can't believe that," she says. "It could be different this time."

"Maybe." I lean toward her. "Maybe I could make it different."

"I don't understand," Gen says.

The idea wiggles around in my brain. "I can try to change it."

I could change what happened, what, for Marybeth at least, hasn't *yet* happened. I just have to figure out what to change. And how.

I get up and pace the length of the falling-down dock, which groans beneath me, threatening to give way. But I can't help myself. I'm full of nervous energy.

"I could break up the band," I say.

Gen squint-frowns at me like I've completely lost it. "What?"

"LaLa and Jeddy wouldn't have died if it weren't for the band. They'd be..." I wave my hand. "Somewhere out there now. Alive. *Alive.*"

Gen shifts to watch me as I walk another lap along the water.

"Or maybe I can make it so that Marybeth isn't so attached to LaLa and Jeddy. So that their deaths, if I can't stop them, will be sad but won't shatter her."

"But you're not creating some kind of alternate reality," Gen says. "You're not reinventing what happened. You're just re-creating it. Adam, the things that happened, happened. You can't change them."

I stop pacing. "Can't I? At least as far as Marybeth is concerned. I mean, aren't we going to do that anyway? Dr. E is going to implant a false memory into her brain at some point, the idea that she faked her own death. So if we can do that, why not something else?"

"But that's different, isn't it? Only a few people know the truth about what happened that day, right? But that's not the case with the band. What about the world out there? Even if you can change it in Marybeth's memory, what happens the first time she hears about it in the real world? You can't change it in the memory of everybody."

I shake my head. "I don't know. I'll figure it out."

But could I do this without shaking apart the whole sim? And what would happen to Marybeth? Would she shake apart too?

"Adam." Gen gets up and walks over to me, putting one hand on each of my arms. "If you even try it, Dr. E is going to throw you out. And that's not going to do Marybeth any good."

"What am I supposed to do then? I wish I could talk to her. Outside the simulations, you know? Ask her…"

"But ask her what? Even if you could see her"—she holds up one finger as if to stop me from running with what she's saying—"which you can't. But even if you *could* see her, you can't just have a conversation with her. She's reliving her life now, full time."

I tip back my head and stare at the sky. "I know."

"You just need to breathe. She's happy now, right?"

I nod.

"Then let her be happy," Gen says. "You still have time."

Chapter 54

The simulation room is in its natural screaming-blue mode when Dr. E sends me into a claustrophobic arrangement of walls and blocks and lumps that might have come from the Oompa-Loompa School of Design. Still, something about it seems vaguely familiar.

It's Day Something-in-the-Double-Digits, and still my heart pounds.

In an instant, everything transforms and I'm standing in the apartment—if you can call a tiny room with a single bed, a chair, a hot plate, and a minifridge an apartment—I lived in after foster care. Simultaneously the memory clicks into place.

I fall backward so that I'm lying diagonally on the bed, my arms folded beneath my head until the me in the now matches the me in the then.

Three...two...

Marybeth knocks at the door.

"If you're a Jehovah's Witness, I've already found God," I call out.

"You have not," she yells from the hallway. "You are a godless sinner and proud of it."

I laugh. "Then come sin with me, baby."

I get up and open the door, watching her reaction as she walks into my brand-freaking-new, post-foster-care home. It's still almost bare. I realized moving in how few things I own. Some clothes, some books. The guitar MB gave me.

From the floor above, a bass beat pulses down through the ceiling.

Through the walls I can smell stale beer and puke. Marybeth's lips are pursed but otherwise she's expressionless. I wait, my heart pounding, for her opinion.

She looks at me and grins that ridiculous shit-eating grin of hers that I love. "So where do I sign up for one of these?"

I guess she doesn't hear the mice scratching in the walls or see the stains in the carpet that I don't even want to try to identify. She just sees my freedom and the fact that I'm still here—only one town over—and not in Utah or New Mexico or someplace else half a world away.

"A few more months for you," I say, running my finger down the bridge of her nose, "and then maybe we'll be next-door neighbors."

She sits on the bed and then falls back, looking up at the water-marked ceiling. I pull her hair out from under her and spread it out until it's a dark sunburst against the threadbare sheets. Then I climb onto the bed beside her and lie facing her. Her eyes shine.

"Next-door neighbors," she says. "I think I'd like that."

"Is that so?"

"Or maybe we could even be"—she wags her eyebrows and then giggles—"roomies. Save the state some money."

"That's very generous of you," I say. "Or maybe you're saying you're just a sinner too. Interesting."

I try to stay with the memory, with the familiar banter. But I'm shaking in a way I never did that time because...

I cup her chin in one hand and kiss her.

And unlike the quick kisses we shared in other memories, this one is full and deep and promises a lifetime of the same.

She pulls back for a breath. And while I can still taste her on my lips, can still feel the stir of her breath on my neck and my body's response to it, something in me breaks. The words slip out, even though they're *now* words and not *then* words and I know I shouldn't say them, I know I shouldn't dare.

"I love you so much, MB."

She sits up and looks at me and I think, *She knows; she knows something isn't right.*

"Are you okay, Adam?" she asks, her eyebrows squinched up. She's not supposed to say that in this memory. None of this is supposed to happen.

All of a sudden Marybeth's eyes jitter, a weird little side-to-side motion.

"Stay with the memory," Dr. E warns in my earpiece.

I swallow hard. "I'm okay."

Again that little jitter. Back and forth. Back and forth.

Dr. E is going to kill me.

Before I can do any more damage, I go with the memory and kiss her again, and her lips are full and soft and perfect. They're *Marybeth's* lips.

A little while later, she kisses me one last time and then leaves to go shopping with LaLa. The simulation ends.

"Do. Not. Deviate. Again," Dr. E says when I come out of the blue room. Her tone is severe. No gold stars for me today.

"I won't," I promise. "I swear I won't."

Chapter 55

The simulations move along. Random moments of our lives, sometimes days apart, sometimes weeks. Nights playing at the Hip Sip.
The afternoon we signed the contract for a gig at the club in the
city, a huge step up for Constellation. The day Marybeth turned
fifteen and LaLa threw a party, more a celebration of her freedom
than her birthday. Marybeth lying beside me in my apartment or
hers, writing songs and singing them for me. As if our whole lives
had revolved around the band.

And hadn't they?

So I play my role. I recite my lines. I feel the things I felt back
then, even as I feel new things now, sometimes unwanted things,
regrets and whys and hows. I have my then thoughts and my now
thoughts and the thoughts stuck in some kind of limbo in between.

Sometimes at night before I fall into an exhausted sleep, I imagine Marybeth in between sessions, sleeping her sleep of memories,
time passing differently for her, quicker, moving through a dead
girl's life in fast-forward, becoming Marybeth for real.

And still, I want to prolong this, to keep Marybeth—and myself—
here in this all-too-short time of happiness and hope and promise.

That she can *not* know that none of this is real sometimes doesn't
seem possible, and I wonder time and time again what would happen if I slipped, if I did something to let her know this is all just a
replay for her benefit, that she's only following in the footsteps of
one who came before her.

Will there come a day when I find her journal hidden some-where, a page that begins: *I try to remember dying?* Maybe she'll tuck away a box of artifacts from a girl long gone, a faded yellow dress, or a hairbrush with strands of dark hair from a dead girl, the locket LaLa gave her at that birthday party with a picture of us all onstage.

Sometimes at night when I lie in bed, I think of Marybeth and I think of Genevieve and their faces overlap.

Let her be happy, I think.

Let them both be happy.

Still, I find myself dreading the day that will soon come with a knot in my stomach that feels like a ball of rubber bands getting bigger and bigger, until it can't possibly fit inside me.

I once had an English teacher—Mrs. Barker—who said the best books are the ones where the ending feels inevitable. It's like that now, the sensation that we're in a barrel, hurtling toward the edge of the falls, and at the end we'll go over, no matter what anyone says or does.

Chapter 56

"New York City!" Marybeth announces. She plows through the door of my apartment, waving her cell phone.

"Hello to you too," I say.

But hearing those three words, I shiver and I can't stop shivering. This is the simulation I've been dreading. Because this is when the clock starts ticking, a final countdown to the moment our lives will shatter. Did shatter.

My mouth has no spit, but I recite my lines.

"New York City? Smog. Taxicabs. Subway. Sirens. Am I missing something?"

She punches my arm, hard.

The ache spreads up into my shoulder and deeper, into my chest. At some point, it stops being physical.

"Hey! Ow!" I say.

I want to say, *Fuck New York. Fuck the band. We're all that matters. You and me, MB.*

I want to take her hand and pull her out of the simulation and out of this building and into another life.

"The club. Pluck. They want us to play." She twirls, her eyes bright, almost manic. "They want Constellation, Adam. They want the freaking band!"

She flops back on my unmade bed, and she's the most beautiful thing I've ever seen. *Later*, I think, *later that same night she'll be lying there again and she'll draw my T-shirt up over my head and kiss the bare skin of my chest and belly and...*

And suddenly I'm angry. Not in the then but in the now. In the part of me that can't just let myself go with the memory no matter what. I don't know where it comes from. It's just all of a sudden there, and I'm so damn angry that I can't even stand it. I want to take the word "band" and banish it from her vocabulary.

Because they're dead. LaLa and Jeddy are dead and no matter what I do I can't change that.

Let her be happy.

But what if I can't?

And then the thought creeps back in.

Sure I can.

I think I have an idea that just might work.

* * *

The door to Dr. E's office is open a crack. I knock and push it open without waiting. Even before I'm in the office, I say, "I can't do this to her again. I want to resurrect LaLa and Jeddy."

There. I've said it.

But Dr. E isn't alone.

"Adam," she says, "You remember Rita."

Then to Rita, she says, "You'll excuse us."

Rita gets up and gives me a look, her eyebrows raised. She smiles, and I want to scrub it off her stupid face. "Always a pleasure, Adam."

After she leaves, Dr. E says, "Now would you like to sit down and tell me what this is about?"

"I want to resurrect LaLa and Jeddy," I say, but I don't sit.

Dr. E studies me. Then she says, "You know we can't do that."

"Why not? We're doing it with Sunshine."

"For one, we don't have their DNA."

For just a second, in the corner of Dr. E's office, I think I see my Hope-Ghost shimmer to life. "Their DNA? We can get that though. Right? A hairbrush maybe. Marybeth had some stuff of LaLa's and I've never gone through it. We can…"

We can dig up their graves, I think, even as I hate myself for it. *We can do whatever we need to do, if only we can bring them back.*

Dr. E holds up one hand. "And their memories, Adam? They both died in the crash. Neither was hooked up to a MAP machine."

"But we could re-create them maybe. I remember so much. And there are memories from Sunshine's MAP machine that you could use. And their families, other friends, teachers." I know I sound desperate, but I don't care. "If it's about the money, Dr. E, I was the beneficiary of Sunshine's entire estate. I'll sign it over right now. Just give me a pen."

"Adam!" Her sharp tone cuts through my words. "Stop."

"So then, stop Marybeth's memories before they die. Please, Dr. E. Don't make her go through this again."

"What do you think would happen once we finish the simulations? When she comes out to join the world only to find that there is no more band?"

I hate that her words are the same as Gen's words, because that might mean they make sense.

"I don't know." I shake my head. "We can tell her that LaLa and Jeddy got married, ended up as missionaries in freaking Zimbabwe or something. I bet you could even simulate a wedding, let her attend. You're planning on implanting a false memory into her anyway, right? The whole faked-death thing. Why not this one?"

From across the desk, she looks at me. "You and I both know that can't happen, Adam. We can't undo what's been done. The tragedy, the grief, that's part of what transformed the girl, Marybeth, into the superstar, Sunshine. Without it, she might have stayed Marybeth forever. Surely you, of all people, realize that."

"What I realize is that I don't give a shit if she ever becomes Sunshine. I just want Marybeth back. That's all." The words keep coming even though I know I should stop, that any minute she could tell me I'll be on the next flight out. "And without the tragedy, she might still be here. She might not have killed herself."

I expect Dr. E to gasp in shock, but her expression doesn't change.

She sighs. "You're not telling us anything we don't know, Adam. We've mapped your memories, remember?"

I finally sink down into the chair. "You've known?"

"Yes. We've known." She smiles reassuringly at me. "But that's a good thing."

I'm not reassured. "A good thing?"

"If we know, Adam, we can keep it from happening again."

"How? Drug her up? Been there, done that. Didn't work. Send her to a therapist? You think that's going to change what's inside her?"

"We don't want to change what's inside her, Adam, because it's what made her special. But we can monitor her, keep her in our sight at all times. We can keep her from trying it again. She'll get past it, Adam. She's not the first kid to make a terrible, terrible decision. She's just the first kid to get to take that decision back."

"So you don't care if she's miserable, only that she's alive."

She meets my eyes. "This project isn't about happiness, I'm afraid."

"It isn't about Marybeth either, obviously," I say. "It's about Sunshine, right? Because Sunshine wasn't really a person, was she? She was a brand."

"Your words, not mine," she says, her voice tight. "I couldn't care less about her 'brand.' What I care about is the science, getting this right. We've already discussed this, Adam. Sunshine provides us with the ultimate platform to prove our technology. If we can re-create Sunshine exactly as she was and have the world believe it—"

"Then you can sell your damn technology. I get it." But I remember the awards hanging in her office and I think I know. It's not about Marybeth. It's not about Sunshine. I don't even know if it's really about science for the sake of science or science for the sake of business. I fire the words at her. "It's about the glory of doing something that nobody else can do. It's about playing God."

She leans forward. "Science isn't about glory, Adam. It's about precision. It's about repeatable results. Playing God? If we can perfect this, we won't *need* any God. We can cheat death all on our own."

Wow, I think. My mind can't even form words.

"If you want out, Adam, that's fine. We can call your part in this done. We'll say thank you for your time and effort and send you home. If you want to chance having a damaged Sunshine."

"That's not..." Frustration bubbles up inside me until I could scream. "All I'm asking you is that we take a chance with her. Not to make her relive that tragedy with the band. See what happens. Maybe she'll still end up becoming Sunshine, and you'll still have your precious award to hang with the others and—"

"All you're asking?" She laughs as if that's funny. "This is black and white, Adam. You're with us or you're not."

My head swims, and I do the whole open-close-open-close fish-mouth thing.

"You are with us, Adam, aren't you?" she prompts. Then she nods as if answering for me. "You're doing the right thing, you know?"

Finally, I nod back at her.

Dr. E smiles. "There. Now that's better."

Chapter 57

In the simulation, I'm at LaLa's house. It's a whole different world there. The couch is the color of eggshells and we take off our shoes at the front door, and if we're there on Sunday, Mrs. Laramie—who also has short-short hair—makes us French toast.

LaLa, I think in the now, *shouldn't have died.* Her life was *right.* She should have grown up and gone to college and gotten married in a big, ridiculous, poofy-dress-and-cake-smeared-on-the-face wedding to some guy who was as pretty and as nice as she was. She should have had two kids and a dog and a house with geraniums in the garden and all those stupid, pointless things that everybody seems to want.

Jeddy and I are hanging out in the furnished basement, playing the newest first-person shooter video game while we wait for the girls to come back from their shopping trip (which should have been like an hour and a half ago). So typical of Marybeth and LaLa.

Finally, we hear footsteps rushing down the stairs and Marybeth pops her head in, wearing a huge grin and carrying a bag. Both in the then and in the now I see the difference in her, as if someone has taken sandpaper and smoothed out her edges.

"Hey," LaLa says, coming down behind Marybeth and dropping her own bags onto the floor.

Marybeth is already opening hers and pulling out something the color of the summer sun. "Look what LaLa got me for my early birthday present."

I raise my eyebrows. "Did that come with sunglasses?"

She punches me lightly on the arm. "Adam!"

Then she holds it up. And there it is, the dress the whole world knows.

I swallow, hard. The clock in my head continues its endless countdown.

Chapter 58

"All you can do is wait and see what happens," Gen says.

"Right. Meaning let LaLa and Jeddy die again." I kick at the dirt. "So much for letting her be happy."

Gen stares at me, her lips pressed together. I refuse to look at her. I know I'm being a shit, but I can't seem to help myself.

"It sucks. I get it. But if she seems to be heading down that same path, you know the signs now. You can get her the help she needs."

"Now you sound like Dr. E," I say.

She arches her eyebrows. "I'm trying, Adam. Okay?"

I sigh. "I know."

We walk. I know where we're heading. To the place where Gen died. I want to ask her if she even realizes it, or if there's some kind of whacked-out compass inside her that brings her here without her even thinking about it.

"What if it isn't enough? Do you see what I'm saying? There are all these questions. How could I never have thought of them before?"

She looks at me, her gaze steady and straight. "You wanted her back so badly, Adam. Your heart didn't want you to be asking questions."

"I guess." I jam my hands into my jeans' pockets before the urge to reach out and hold Gen's hand gets too strong. "I mean I've been telling myself that if we brought her back, if we managed to pull this off, then everything would be okay, that she'd be so grateful for this second chance. But what if she isn't, Gen? You know, she tried to kill herself one other time."

I didn't mean to say it, but there it is. Gen jerks around to look at me, but she doesn't say anything. In my mind, the ambulance lights still turn the night red. It feels like ancient history and simultaneously, impossibly, like it just happened. I wonder how many of my memories are going to have that weird effect now.

"We were only thirteen," I say, as if that explains everything. "Afterward, I snuck into her hospital room and held her hand. She said she was sorry. She said she'd never leave me again. But…"

"But she did," Gen finishes.

For a few minutes, we walk without talking. Then she says, "Adam, are you doubting what you're doing here?"

"I don't know anymore. I don't even know up from down these days."

"I understand that feeling."

We reach the fence. As she always does, she kneels to take down the old flowers. But now, knowing what they mean, knowing *she* knows what they mean, changes everything.

There's so much I need to know. I blurt the words. "Are you sorry your dad brought you back?"

"Adam," she says, and I think it's a warning to back off. She takes the flowers to the cliff and throws them over. Then she looks at me. "But remember, I didn't kill myself."

The surrealness of this conversation makes me dizzy.

"But still?" I ask.

She sighs. "I'm glad I'm alive, if that's what you're asking. I don't want to be dead. But sometimes I hate what I am."

What, I think, *not* who.

"What are you?"

"A copy. A reprint. An echo." She shrugs, but the gesture doesn't seem as neutral as it does angry. "A girl left with the responsibility of trying to be somebody who's dead."

Tears shine in her eyes.

"I'm sorry," I say, but I'm not sure what for exactly. That she has to feel this way. That I asked. That her father ever dreamed up this craziness. Or maybe D: all of the above.

And even as I'm thinking all that, my stomach drops, because what does this mean for Marybeth?

A copy, I think. *A reprint. An echo.*

Gen clears her throat, breaking me out of my thoughts. "The worst is knowing that my father—that *her* father, the dead Genevieve's—he doesn't really love me. He loves *her*. And sometimes I don't think I'm her at all. Sometimes I don't want to be."

I don't know what to say. What it means for her kills me. What it might mean for me and for Marybeth kills me even more.

Finally, I say, "You're you, Gen. You're beautiful and wonderful and the best thing that's happened to me in a long damn time. If your dad doesn't love you for you, then that's his loss."

She looks down at the ground, and for a minute I think she's crying. I want to wrap my arms around her and comfort her the way she comforted me. But when she looks up, I see something hard in her eyes, something I recognize. It comes from having to look out for yourself for a long time.

"Yeah. *I'm me.*" She laughs. "But that's the thing, Adam. Maybe to me I am. But to everyone else, I'm her."

We stand here at the place where she died—or rather at the place where the first Genevieve died and the idea for this second Genevieve was born—and I hate that my selfish mind keeps going back to Marybeth.

"Gen? Do you think it's possible she was sorry about doing it? That at the very last second she changed her mind but it was just too late?"

She stares out over the water. "Sure. Yeah. It's possible. But even with bringing her back, that's something you're probably never going to know."

"No." I tip my head against Gen's. "I guess I won't."

She seems to think for a minute. Then she says, "Adam, there's somewhere I'd like to show you."

Chapter 59

We come to a wrought-iron archway so high it might have been made for giants to walk through. At the top, an arc of rusted letters form words in another language.

Gen pushes the gate, which creaks open halfway and then sticks. She angles sideways to get through, and I follow, metal pressing into my hips.

It isn't neat like the cemeteries back in the States, and it has the feel of someplace much older and somehow more—I don't know—intimate than the mapped-out, antiseptic ones like where LaLa and Jeddy are buried, like where Marybeth's birth mother lies six feet under. Like where Marybeth herself is.

Thoughts like that have no place here now, I warn myself.

But it's not like a switch in my brain that I can just flip off. It's more like a stain that I paint over, but it keeps showing through, no matter how many layers I cover it with.

Ahead of me, Gen walks the path. On either side, gravestones poke up from a sea of weeds, none of them at the same angle. I think of Jeddy's funeral, the way the white stones stood in perfect rows, as if death were something neat and ordered and controllable. As we move deeper into this true place of the dead, Gen veers off the path and wanders between the graves, her legs ending in a fringe of unmowed grass.

She stops by a grave with a small, graying stone, crumbling at the edges.

"Twelve," she says.

I come up beside her. "What?"

"This boy was only twelve when he died."

"Sad," I say. But it's just a word. I don't feel it. The bones beneath us are just things. I'm incapable of imagining them as more—a person, a child with cheeks brown from the island sun, a kid who laughed and played ball, who had a family who loved him, maybe a dog. No. They're just old bones.

Gen looks at me as if she knows what I'm thinking. But I can see from the turn of her lips, the flush on her cheeks that, to her, those bones mean something.

She moves on. I hesitate at the boy's grave, run my fingers over the etched words, so weathered I can't even make out his name.

"This woman was almost a hundred when she died," Gen says.

Her words speak of familiarity. She's looked at these stones before, I have no doubt.

I don't comment. Anything I'd say would feel false.

We walk deeper into the graveyard, Gen calling out ages, sometimes dates and names, from the stones we pass. There seems to be no rhyme or reason to the placement. Newer stones sit side by side with older ones. They don't form rows or circles. Here and there rotting fences mark family plots. We even pass a crypt, the front door sagging. Inside, a chair rests beside the stone vault for the dead, as if family might come to have lunch and a chat.

Finally, Gen stops at a tombstone that's shaped into a bench. She sits down on the edge, her butt barely touching the stone. Behind her, names and dates on the back tell me they were a husband and wife, who died the same day.

Gen swivels to look where I'm looking. "I've always wondered if they were in some kind of accident, or if one died and then the other followed, of a broken heart. Do you think that's possible?"

I look down. I want to tell her, *Yes, absolutely.* That sometimes you just can't go on without someone. But the words ball up in my throat and I can't, so I just shrug.

She pats the bench beside her, but I can't sit there, so I wander a little ways away and pretend to look at an overgrown bush with bright orange flowers that are just starting to close up for the night.

Gen gets up and joins me.

"I'm sorry," she says. "That was insensitive of me."

I smile at her. "It's okay. Really."

"It's just…" This time she looks away. "I get obsessed with this place. Who died at what age, how. I wonder about their lives, their deaths, the people who loved them."

She links her arm with mine, as if we, the warm and breathing, are united here among the dead. We walk some more. I glance back at the entrance gates. They're so far away now they look like miniatures, like we'd never fit back through them. The sun is setting behind a line of trees and starbursts of light shatter between the branches. It's beautiful, but it makes me hurt in some weird way. Or maybe it isn't the light that makes me hurt.

"I guess I wonder why I get to be here and they don't," she says, and then clarifies, "Living, I mean. Getting a second chance."

"You could go crazy asking that," I tell her.

She nods. "Like the questions you're asking yourself, right?"

She waits a minute, but I don't have an answer to that.

Then she says, "But still. Did I deserve it more than that boy? He was only twelve. And up there…" She points to a low hill. "There's a stone that's a tiny lamb, and a baby is buried there, Adam. Two weeks old. She never even had a *first* chance."

"Gen," I say.

She unlinks her arm from mine.

"Really though, when you think about it, I'm here and they're not, just because my dad has more money than God. Well, enough money to buy me back from death anyway. Money and maybe…" She hesitates as if she can't find the right words, and her cheeks puff up from the effort. "Maybe the biggest balls ever to think he can."

I almost want to laugh at such a crude thing coming out of Gen's mouth, but her face is so serious, and so is the thought behind it.

"And Sunshine," she says. I notice that she pointedly doesn't say "Marybeth" this time. "Did the world just love her enough to will her back from death, while that poor boy…and that poor baby and all these other people, all these other *dead* people…they'll stay there under the dirt forever until everybody's forgotten them?"

Her cheeks are red and blotchy, and her eyes shine with something like indignation.

"Wow." I blow out a breath. "That's quite a question."

Gen looks at me with those bright eyes, waiting for me to say something.

You do deserve it, I want to tell her. And that maybe it's more than just her dad who needs her to be here.

But before I can speak, she says, "I'm sorry. I don't expect you to answer that. The world is just so random." She looks back toward the setting sun, but the brilliant starbursts of light have disappeared, and all that's left is a deep red smudge behind the ragged edges of the palm leaves. "We should get back."

We walk back across the field of the long dead, not touching. Her distress is like a living thing, a dragon maybe, circling us, nipping to keep us apart. And maybe love or money, Genevieve or Marybeth or the twelve-year-old boy whose name I don't know, maybe the why of it doesn't make a bit of difference.

Eventually the sun disappears below the horizon, and in the spreading shadows, fireflies turn on their lights, winking green at the tree line. *Maybe*, I think, *each one is the soul of someone who's died, and they're waiting here for a body to be returned to.* Though the air is warm, I shiver.

At the gate, I stop. I take Gen's hand and turn her to face me. "The you who died, is she buried here?"

She looks back across the sprawling cemetery. It's mostly dark now, the more distant graves hidden by night. Finally, she shakes her head. "Not here. I've checked them all."

I look back too. For the first time, I realize that most of the graves are untended, the stones mossy, bouquets rotting in their plastic covers, planted flowers grown wild across the stones. I think of the flowers that Gen's father places at the site of her death again and again, and I think about Gen's question. Maybe it wasn't her father's abundance of money that brought her back. Maybe it was his love. Maybe his love was deep enough to change not only his own life and his daughter's, but mine too. Maybe his love was deep enough to change the whole natural order. And I know I need to ask him a question.

Chapter 60

"I need to see Mr. Grayson," I tell the front-desk guy. "It's important."

He looks at me as if I've just asked to see the pope, but his hand hovers over his phone. I think my request has stumped him.

"I'll do it if you won't."

Before he can stop me, I grab the phone and stab the button labeled Overhead Announcement.

"Reggie Grayson to the front desk immediately. This is Adam, Mr. Grayson. I need to talk to you."

The guy at the desk gapes at me as my voice booms through the compound. "I can't believe you did that."

"Not the first time I've heard that," I assure him. "Probably won't be the last either."

I lean against the wall to wait.

Probably not even a minute and a half goes by before Mr. Grayson is walking toward me.

"You're definitely an unorthodox young man," he says, but he smiles as if to say, *It's all good.* "Come on back to my suite."

I follow him through a different doorway and into the living area, where not too long ago we talked about the fact that Gen is a clone.

Once he shuts the door, I blurt out my question. "Why Sunshine?"

He tilts his head, that odd smile still on his face. "What are you asking, Adam?"

"I understand what Dr. Elloran is saying, about her being the perfect candidate for proving you can do what you say you can. But you chose her, right, Mr. Grayson? So I'm asking why you chose to resurrect Sunshine when you could have chosen anybody. She wasn't the only person in the world hooked up to a MAP machine."

He gestures for me to sit and I drop down on the same couch I sat on before. This time there is no coffee, no hesitation. And instead of sitting in the chair, he sits on the couch beside me.

"We already had the technology. It might not be legal in the States, but there's nothing stopping us from using it here. Sunshine was my gift to the world."

"That's it?" I raise my eyebrows. "Your gift to the world? That's awfully charitable of you."

"You'd mock my generosity, even though it's probably a bigger gift to you than anyone else?"

Is it? I want to ask. I think about what he told me the last time we talked, about how there will still be a beautiful girl buried six feet under.

I tip my head back against the cushions. How do I phrase this? I try to call up the image of Genevieve moving from grave to grave as she wondered why something can happen to one person and not another.

Mr. Grayson watches me with interested eyes. Something tells me he's been waiting for me to ask this question.

"What I mean…" I take a deep breath. "Is that you could have chosen anyone to bring back. You could have brought back a brilliant scientist who was on the verge of a cure for cancer, or Martin Luther King Jr., even if you couldn't re-create his memories, or…oh I don't know. But you chose Sunshine. I need to know why."

He surprises me by smiling. "Let me tell you a story, Adam."

"Please," I say.

"I nearly lost myself when my daughter died, Adam." He clears his throat. "This was in the days right after, you understand, before cloning and memory implantation was even on my radar. When all I could do was stand by that godforsaken bend in the road and cry."

I look away, up at the photos on the wall of the happy family that they must once have been.

"I drank too," he says. "Plenty. We stayed here on the island because I couldn't bear to leave the place where I'd lost my daughter. I had this weird idea that her soul would stay here and that if I left, I was abandoning her completely. Crazy, right?"

I look at him again, and he smiles his sad smile at me, and I think, *He's me. Mr. Grayson is me.*

"Losing someone you love makes you a little crazy," I say.

"My poor wife couldn't take it anymore and she packed up and went home. Or she went somewhere that wasn't here, anyway. But I was so lost that I hardly noticed.

"And then one day, I went into the local bar and they had a television on, and on it was this lovely young woman with the most beautiful voice." His own voice sounds far away now, and I realize that at this moment he's in that bar and he's hearing Sunshine for the first time. "There was something about the way she held herself, the way she stood on that stage, as if she were all alone in the world. Adam, I can't explain it, but she touched me. I felt connected to her. Like she understood my grief, understood my loss, and she was turning it all into something beautiful."

He looks at me, waiting.

"She did that for people," I say.

He nods. "She did. And in her way, she saved me. Because in that moment, I wasn't alone in my pain. And then I found my way back to myself, back to Genevieve."

He pauses.

"Then Sunshine died," he says. "She died so tragically, Adam. I was heartbroken like the rest of the world. Except for me, it was different. I thought maybe I could save her too."

"Then save her for real." I hear the plea in my voice and I don't even care. "Don't bring her back just to be miserable again. Bring back LaLa and Jeddy too."

He sighs, and then he says, "Do you know how Project Orpheus got its name, Adam?"

I shake my head.

"In Greek mythology," he says, "Orpheus was a legendary musician who loved his wife, Eurydice, dearly. When she died—bitten by a viper on her wedding day—he grieved so hard, playing such sad songs, that everyone was touched by his grief. Even the gods. And they told him to go to the underworld to find her and bring her back.

"So he did," Grayson says. "With his beautiful music, he softened even cold-hearted Hades, who agreed that Eurydice could return with him to the world above. But there was a condition. Eurydice was to walk behind him, and Orpheus, well, he couldn't look back to make sure she was still there. And he didn't."

"Except...?" I prompt

"Except he did. At the very last minute, when he was only a few feet away from the exit, he lost his faith. Orpheus looked back. And Eurydice, she was pulled back among the dead, lost forever."

Mr. Grayson sighs. "Adam, bringing back your friends, that's a beautiful idea. But we don't have their memories. We don't have their DNA. We don't have anything, really."

His words are so close to Dr. E's that I know he must have been talking to her. But hearing them from him is different somehow, as if it makes it the truth.

"I, of all people, don't want her to come back to a life of misery. But we can help her through it, Adam. You and me." He leans forward on the chair and clasps his hands together. "We're steps from the exit, Adam. Don't look back now."

Chapter 61

At 3:00 a.m. the phone rings. Not like I was sleeping anyway. I hurry into the other room and grab the receiver. At this hour, I know who it has to be.

"Gen. What's wrong?"

"You're awake. Good. Get dressed. I'll be right there."

Three minutes later there's a soft tap-tap at the door. I open it.

"What's going on?" I slip out into the hallway.

"Come on." She starts down the hall.

After a few turns, I figure out where we're going. My heart does too, and it's beating so loud I think it's going to wake up the whole fucking place. But we make it to the room where Gen works without Dr. E or Mr. Grayson or Rita screaming after us.

Gen whispers, "Wait around the corner. Give me five minutes and then come back here."

I nod and do as she says.

A minute later I hear the door open again. Voices break the quiet—Gen's and another I don't recognize—and then it closes. I wait a few minutes and then hurry back.

The door hisses open and Gen pulls me inside. My ears fill with the sound of liquid bubbling and even more, the sound of Marybeth's heartbeat, magnified. Behind Gen, light reflects from a curve of glass.

She puts one hand on my chest, holding me in place. I wonder if she can feel my heart pounding.

"I thought about what you said the other day, about seeing her outside of the sim," she says, "and I know she can't answer the questions you have, but…"

She pulls her hand back and steps aside, as if revealing a gift—which I guess is exactly what this is—bowing her head to give me privacy to process what I'm seeing.

A tall, cylindrical tank occupies the center of the room. Inside, bubbles rise through pale green fluid.

Among the bubbles, Marybeth floats. She wears a yellow bodysuit, and wires trail from her temples, her closed eyelids, the base of her skull, running up and out of the tank and into a bank of machines.

I walk toward the tank and put my hand against the glass. Though I expect it to be cold, it isn't. It's the exact temperature of my own skin.

She looks young, physically not much older than when I first met her. It's hard to reconcile the Marybeth here with the one I've been seeing in the sim room.

Behind her closed lids, her eyes move rapidly as she dreams what's not really a dream but her life. Or the life of her predecessor, really.

She smiles.

Where is she now? I wonder. Is she rehearsing with the band? Is she at the Galleria shopping with LaLa? Or maybe we're in my apartment, lying in bed, our bodies tangled together, and she's saying, *It's okay, Adam. Let's keep going tonight.* Does she feel the press of me against her even now, somewhere in a world that only exists in our memories?

My breath fogs the glass, veiling her face, and I'm suddenly, unbearably, sad.

"Marybeth," I say. I half expect her eyes to open, but they stay closed, her long lashes fluttering with the memories.

But are they memories, or only stories from someone else's life? Things that belong not to her, but to a girl who died, a girl who shares her DNA, but a stranger nonetheless?

Without them, would she become someone other than Sunshine? Other than Marybeth even?

"Adam?" Genevieve rests her hand on my arm. I'd forgotten she was there.

"Sorry. I was just…"

"It's okay. It's a lot to take in, right?" There's something weird in Gen's voice too. "I think about it sometimes, you know? Me floating in there, having the real Genevieve's memories put into me. The good ones and the bad ones. And I wonder what it would have been like if someone had let her—let that Genevieve—rest in peace."

She looks at me as if she's studying me for a test. "Whatever's inside of me—*me*, not her—that makes me alive and who I am, my soul maybe—I don't know—I wonder if it would have gone into another baby, if maybe I could have been anybody."

Anybody. I press my forehead against the glass of Marybeth's tank.

Gen squeezes my arm. "I'm going to take a walk for a minute, Adam. Would you keep an eye on her while I'm gone?"

And though my heart beats like a million moths trying to escape from inside me, I nod.

Chapter 62

The door opens and closes, and then I'm alone with Marybeth in this horrible monster movie room. For the first time, nobody's watching us, looking for cracks in me, waiting for me to screw up.

"I don't know what I'm doing, Marybeth," I tell her.

I kneel down and put both hands on the glass. I wish I could touch her. I wish I could hold her.

In the tank, she smiles, her cheeks rounding into apples, the lines of her face softening. She looks like an angel, her long dark hair flying up around her like strands of silk.

An image pops into my mind:

Marybeth in her coffin, her eyes closed, her hair spread out on a sky-blue satin pillow, so perfect that she can't possibly be dead, except that she's cold and hard and…

And then another:

The coffin being lowered into a dark hole, me at the edge, dropping in the first yellow rose, and it's falling, falling…

Jesus, I think. *Stop.*

The bubbles continue to rise around her, oxygen pouring into the tank to give her life. They surround her, and it's as if I'm seeing her through a veil.

"I followed you onto that stage, Marybeth. I followed you into that ridiculous fame we had. I would have followed you to the ends of the earth. And still it wasn't enough.

"Poor me. Right, MB? You had a hard life. Well you weren't the only one. You weren't the only one who lost your family, who lost LaLa and Jeddy. You weren't the only one who got stuck in shitty foster homes. You weren't the only one who had scars. You weren't the only one who'd ever thought about…

"But you quit, Marybeth. You quit us. You quit life. And you left me to live without you. You left me when you knew it was going to hurt me the most. When it would look like it was my fault and not yours."

She dreams on, oblivious to my words, oblivious to my pain.

"And I am so mad at you, Marybeth. I am so mad at you for leaving me here all alone, just like everyone else did."

My head throbs so hard that the world goes dark around the edges. I close my eyes and try to breathe.

"I need to know what you want," I finally say.

I wish I could ask not this Marybeth but the first one, the real…

I pull back from the glass.

Did I really just think that?

For a minute, I'm back in Mr. Grayson's suite and he's saying to me, "There will still be a beautiful young girl in the ground, and nothing will ever change that."

Is my mind going to replay that particular record for the rest of my life? Even after I have Marybeth back?

"Damn it!"

I pound my fist against the thick glass, just once, but the whole tank shudders. The clone doesn't so much as blink.

The clone, I think. *Not Marybeth. The clone.*

Stop it. Stop it, stop it, stop it.

I stare at the wires feeding her memories and experiences and thoughts. Who would she be without those? Would she still be the Marybeth I knew and loved…just unscarred? Or would new experiences make her someone I would never recognize?

My eyes sting.

Would she be happy without me, or would she still find her way back to loving me?

If she did, could I live up to it this time? And if she didn't, could I let her go?

A little voice in my head says, *You did once, didn't you?*

"It was a mistake," I tell the girl in the tank. "It was the biggest mistake I ever made."

Or is *this* the biggest mistake I've ever made?

The girl in the tank—whether it's really Marybeth, her soul returning as her body has returned, or only a photocopy—continues to dream, her lips curled up in the smallest of smiles. And I have no more answers than before.

Chapter 63

In the simulation, we walk toward the bus station. It's spring. The trees all have buds. Here and there tulips bloom red and yellow and white.

Marybeth wears a short denim skirt and a black T-shirt, but when I look at her, I keep seeing the girl in the tank, a curtain of bubbles across her face.

And this, I know, is it. The edge of the waterfall is right in front of us, and rather than a barrel, we're walking toward it, hand in hand.

In fact, the worst has already happened. The bus LaLa and Jeddy are on—the one MB and I couldn't take because we're not eighteen yet and had to wait for the final permission for our trip to the city to come from the Bureau of Unparented Minors, the good old useless BUM as Marybeth says, except this time maybe not so useless for us—is probably already at the center of the five-car pileup on the expressway. We just haven't gotten the call yet.

My grief threatens to bubble up. I know that the LaLa and Jeddy I've rehearsed with, hung out with, laughed with over the last few weeks have been only simulations. But the thought of hearing the news again, Marybeth's reaction, the funerals, everything I'm going to have to relive again…I don't just worry about Marybeth. I worry about myself too, if I'm strong enough to go through all that again.

In my mind, I hear Dr. E's mantra: *Stay with the memory.* I grit my teeth. You stay with the fucking memory, Dr. E.

In the simulation, Marybeth stands beside me, our fingers tangled. And my mind tells me, *This is Marybeth. Not a clone. This is really her.*

Maybe when you want something bad enough, you just will it to be true.

"It feels weird," she says.

"What's that?" I ask, reciting my line.

"This." She lets go of my hand and spins. And even though I know better, I think she knows. She knows what's happening to her, to us, to them. But even as I think it, I realize that the conversation matches the memory in my head. "Being happy," she says.

In less than an hour, my cell phone is going to ring, and it's going to be Jeddy's brother and he's going to tell us there was an accident and...

My heart squeezes and tears burn in my eyes. I duck my head to hide them as the words play over and over in my head. *Stay with the memory. Stay with the memory.*

"Adam?" She dips her own head to look at me. "What's wrong? Aren't you happy too?"

"Stay with the memory," Dr. E warns in my earpiece. "Don't deviate or you could short-circuit the whole memory process."

I swipe at my eyes. But Marybeth stops walking. Her eyes jitter, just the tiniest bit.

"Adam," Dr. E warns.

"Adam," Marybeth says.

I could change it all here. I could stop this. She never has to know about LaLa and Jeddy. I could let her have what Genevieve never did—a chance to be someone new, without the weight of the memories of the original Marybeth.

I could do it.

Right now, I could do it. And maybe she'd still find her way back to being mine somehow.

I hesitate.

Do it, a small voice in my head says, even as the push of the memory directs me to park my ass on the nearby bench, to tell her we're early, that we can wait here…or better yet, why don't we get food.

Do it, I think.

I wet my lips.

"Adam, unless you want to be on the next plane home, stay with the memory," Dr. E says.

I look at Marybeth. She's watching me, her eyebrows wrinkled up. Her eyes jitter again.

Do it.

"I…" I sink down into the bench. "Let's stop here for a minute. We're early."

I'm a coward. I can't do it.

"Better yet…" I swallow hard. "Why don't we get some food?"

The jittering in her eyes stops. She smiles. No, she grins. It's wide and it threatens to swallow me completely.

I love this girl.

She puts one hand on my chest. "Wait here."

I'm glad because the memory only tells me to nod. There's no way I can form words.

She turns, and I watch until she disappears into a deli down the road.

As soon as she does, Dr. E says in my ear, "End sim."

I stay sitting on the bench even as it becomes a blue cube, even as the tulips and the deli and the sidewalk disappear.

I don't need the sim for this. I don't need the wires and the electric poke.

This day is flash-burned into my memory.

A technician comes in to unwire me. But all I can think about is what happens next.

I close my eyes and remember.

* * *

When Marybeth returns she's carrying two bags. One is a brown paper deli sack. The other says Dollar Daze.

"I thought we could have a picnic," she says.

I raise my eyebrows. "Umm...where?"

She takes my hand, pulling me to my feet. We walk to the bus terminal, an old building with high, arched ceilings where everything echoes. Inside, we find a quiet corner, and she opens the Dollar Daze bag.

Marybeth tears open a package that holds a vinyl tablecloth that reeks like, well, vinyl, and spreads it on the floor. It's lumpy with permanent rectangle-shaped creases.

I laugh.

"Sit," she says.

So I sit, anchoring one edge of the stinky tablecloth with my ass.

She sets out two wrapped sandwiches. I smell peanut butter and jelly before I even open one.

Then she pulls out another package from the dollar-store bag.

"Plastic ants? For real?"

This time she laughs as she places them in a line that snakes toward the sandwiches. "It's a picnic, Adam. Go with it."

Out of the corner of my eye, I see an older couple sitting on one of the high-backed benches watching us, smiling. For some reason, it makes my stomach feel warm.

"And..." She wags another small plastic bag at me. "Dessert."

"Dessert too?"

"Yup." She struggles to tear into it, and it rips apart completely, candies spilling out. They're the kind with the wrappers painted to look like watermelons.

She sits across from me, on the other side of our makeshift picnic, and I think: *I love this girl, and she makes everything okay. All the foster families, all the failures, all the shit life has handed me. The fact that it brought me to her makes everything worthwhile.*

I can't help myself. I get to my knees and start to knee-walk across the tablecloth toward her.

"You're killing the ants," she says and presses her lips together like she's trying not to laugh.

I launch myself at her. With a little squeal she falls backward, beneath me, and I kiss her there, on the slippery vinyl, with the legs of plastic ants digging into my skin.

And then my cell phone rings.

* * *

"Adam?"

I open my eyes. There's no picnic, no Marybeth—she's probably been whisked back to her tank—no cell phone ringing. Just the blue sim room.

"Let's talk in my office," Dr. E says.

I follow her out and down the hall.

"You can't do that," she says when we're both sitting.

I know she means splitting away from the memory.

"You could ruin everything we've worked for," she says. "Why do we need to keep having this conversation?"

"I'm sorry."

"Are you?" she asks.

I stare at her and don't say anything, because the downturn of her lips tells me she already knows I'm not.

As if to complete the thought, she says, "I understand the temptation to want to change things. It gets hard from here. We all acknowledge that. What we're asking you to reenact isn't easy."

She purses her lips. I wait for her to continue.

"The easy thing would be to stop your part here, to let her continue on with the direct-feed memories, no sim room, no reenactment."

I think she's chosen her words carefully to elicit a reaction. I feel my blood pressure going up. "So she'd have to go through it alone, without me there."

"No, of course not. You wouldn't be there physically beside her. But they're memories, Adam, so you'd be there as part of the feed." There's something funny in her voice. "We'd rather have you in the sim with her, to cement those memories."

Because it's how Marybeth became Sunshine, and they want to make sure that that happens as it's supposed to.

I take a deep breath. "So what's the punch line?"

She smiles. "I'm willing to make a deal with you, Adam."

Why do I think this could be a deal with the devil?

"And that would be what?"

"We want to take her memories all the way to the time of her death. It will make it easier to account for, to the world…and to her…that there was an accident, that maybe she had some lost time, a coma and all that, you understand. And that when she woke up, she realized it was the perfect opportunity to leave fame behind, to fake her death and disappear."

"And the deal?"

"There's something that happened before she died, isn't there? Something that may have, let's say, *contributed* to her death."

All my vital organs turn to lead and fall down into my toes.

Because suddenly I understand.

"If you agree to get back into the sim and let things play out the way they're supposed to—the way they did—then we're willing to erase her memories of the day that you left her, Adam."

We stare at each other for a minute, and then she says, "But if you don't cooperate, we can always tell the world that her beloved Adam was ultimately the one responsible for her death."

And there it is, my biggest regret of all, flopping on the desk between us.

Dr. E stares at me, letting it sink in. And then she says, "And we can write you right out of her life in the process."

Chapter 64

The memory doesn't want to come. I've held it down for so long now. I look around Memory Room B, the place where so many of my memories have been harvested over the last few months. The couch is the same, the blue armchairs, the table covered with magazines, the photos on the wall. But somehow, I'm different. Older, I think, though I haven't spent a birthday here. And when I look at the pictures of Sunshine, the hurt isn't so flash-bright. Maybe it's because we're at the end—our new beginning—or maybe it's just because that's what happens with time.

I want to tell Dr. E to just take the damn memory that I know she's planning to hold hostage until I play my role like a good boy all the way to the end. Do what she wants, and Marybeth never has to relive this. Screw it up, and I lose Marybeth forever, but in a different way.

I don't want to remember. But I think I need to own this. Because it is mine. And because in remembering, it is my shame and my punishment, and it is my penance, but it is, maybe, my redemption too.

I close my eyes and lean back in the chair, and I force myself to remember.

* * *

Marybeth sits in the window seat of the tour bus's bedroom, her legs tucked beneath her. Shadows of raindrops run down her face like tears, but she isn't crying. She never cries, not even as she watches me jam clothes into a duffle bag.

"I can't do it anymore, Marybeth," I say.

I want her to beg me not to go. I want her to tell me that she'll stop being Sunshine and be Marybeth again, that we can run away somewhere and hide from the world and just heal together, start our lives for real instead of living this sham that they've become. But she only nods, still staring out the window, watching the rain or the groupies gathered over by the fence, as if she doesn't even have words for me in this moment.

I sling my duffle bag over one shoulder and I open the door of the bus. For a minute, I don't think my legs are going to cooperate, but then I'm walking down the stairs and the door is closing behind me.

And it's done.

I keep my eyes closed while Dr. E unhooks me from the wires. She says nothing, and I keep my eyes closed as I hear the door open and shut. I keep my eyes closed for a long time after that.

* * *

When evening comes, I lie in bed on top of the covers, ignoring the ringing of the phone, and then later, ignoring the knock on my door. The thought of seeing Gen makes my cheeks burn. If she doesn't already know, it will be spelled out in blotches on my face.

I left Marybeth when she needed me the most.

Chapter 65

In the sim, we hold hands. Tightly. As if we're all each other has left after the bus crash stole our surrogate musical family forever. We're at the first of the funerals, this one for LaLa.

It's an overcast day, the clouds so low we could probably pull them apart if we stretched. Everyone clusters beneath the canopy, their heads bowed. A lot of people. LaLa had been loved.

Beside me, Marybeth wears the yellow dress, even though I begged her not to, that yellow dress that after today will never stop reminding me of funerals.

In my ear, Dr. E says, "Remember what we talked about, Adam. Stay with the memory." As if I could forget.

So I try, even if I might squeeze Marybeth's hand harder this time around.

Marybeth looks straight ahead. Sorrow is visible in her eyes and in the set of her mouth, but she doesn't cry. I remember wishing she would, because as long as she didn't, I couldn't either.

When the ceremony ends, the reverend nods to her, and Marybeth steps forward. I frown. At the time, I'd had no idea what was happening.

She takes her place beside him.

As much as I want to resist, the lure of the memory is strong, a riptide of a pull, and finally I let myself go with it.

"Marybeth Travers would like to leave us with a song," the reverend says.

I can't imagine how she'll be able to get out any notes, to sing on-key, to stand in front of all these people without falling apart. *She won't go through with it*, I think. *She's just going to turn and flee the gravesite.*

But there's something determined in her expression, and then she starts to sing. She starts off hesitantly, wobbling through the first few notes. But then she finds her stride and her voice is strong and so filled with grief and loss that it touches me right to my core until I want to drop to my knees.

It's a song I've never heard before, a folksy ballad about a girl who journeys to the moon and then falls back to earth so that all that remains of her is dust.

The song is strange and beautiful, and I'm captivated. And when I look around at the other mourners, I can see that they are too, standing there with tears in their eyes and on their cheeks. Only when the final notes fade away do people seem to breathe again.

Afterward, Marybeth silently walks past the mourners and onto the cemetery path. I follow quietly, waiting for her to fall apart, waiting to put my arms around her and comfort her, to comfort both of us. But she only walks, her yellow dress so out of place in the cemetery, and I follow.

* * *

"Great job, Adam," Dr. E says as she unhooks me.

"Yeah. Fantastic." I tear off the rest of the wires and walk out of the sim room.

But I've done as she's asked, and she can't complain.

* * *

In the sim, we repeat the routine at Jeddy's funeral the next day. This time she sings about a boy who grew sunflowers as tall as skyscrapers. And just like before, the crowd of mourners stands enchanted, lost in emotion.

It was as if grief had transformed her into something else, some beautiful light that everyone couldn't help but look at.

Chapter 66

I don't know how I got here, but I'm standing in the room where Marybeth 2.0 floats in her tank, eyes closed, lips pressed tightly together. Whatever she's reliving right now isn't pleasant.

"Probably that day Daddy Jacobsen made me clean the bathroom floor with my favorite dress because I got a C on my math quiz."

I jump at the voice. A second Marybeth stands beside the one in the tank. My chest squeezes seeing them next to each other.

I turn to leave. I can't do this right now. But when I open the door to the hallway, I hear bubbling, like Marybeth's tank, only a hundred times over. My feet drag like my shoes are anchors, but I force myself forward, into a room filled with rows of tanks. In each, a clone of Marybeth floats.

I approach the closest one. The Marybeth inside is identical to the Marybeth standing beside me. Her eyes are open, staring through the pale fluid as if she's actually seeing me, rather than whatever exists inside the memory that's currently being piped into her.

"Can she…?" I put my hands against the glass. But up close I see the faraway look in her eyes that I know so well, and my mind supplies an image of her sitting in the tour bus, her dress traded for jeans, her head tipped against the tinted windows, looking out at something only she can see.

In the next tank, the clone is younger, but only slightly, and in the next, younger still. I can pick out the ages of each by her hair length, the roundness of her cheeks, her height. The Marybeths get younger, until they're younger than the first time I met her. I see Marybeth at maybe the age of seven or eight, a hand-shaped bruise on her bare arm. I see Marybeth at around four or five, her hair short and choppy, as if she cut it herself. In some of the tanks, she's nothing more than a baby.

I walk to the next, and the next, and the next, studying the Marybeths in each one.

The Marybeths.

At what point would it make a difference to stop the memories? When we were with the band? Before I met them? The day I met her? Or before? Or was it something just inside her? A ticking time bomb that started the day a sperm met an egg, something in her genetic code that'll be there no matter what I do?

I bang my fist against the nearest tank. The Marybeth inside it opens her eyes.

"I wouldn't do that," she says. Her voice is Dr. E.'s. "Do you want to fuck this up too?"

Even as she speaks, a crack appears in the tank, spider-webbing out. I back away from the tank, only to bump into the one behind me. There's a sharp pop, and a crack opens in that one too.

And then it's a chain reaction. No matter which way I turn, the tanks are breaking. They're breaking, and it's my fault.

Chapter 67

"Are you avoiding me?" Gen calls through my apartment door. "I haven't seen you for days."

I look up from strumming random chords on my guitar.

When I don't answer, she says, "Are you going to make me start bringing you fancy milk shakes now, because I'm not really down with that."

Some days I feel like I'm caught in a tangle of memories and dreams and impossible science that's so deep I'm lost in it. But Gen's words cut through, and I can't help but laugh. I set my guitar aside and get up to open the door.

"Can I come in?" she asks.

I let her in and close the door behind her. She sits on the arm of the couch, but I stay standing, looking down at my feet.

"What's going on, Adam?"

I shrug. "Nothing."

"Seriously? You're going to tell me 'nothing'?"

"I just have a lot on my mind."

"A lot that you can't even tell Clone Girl Number One?"

I smile just a little. "Maybe tomorrow."

Genevieve sighs. Finally, she gets up and puts one hand on my cheek. Her skin feels cool against mine, as if I'm feverish. Maybe I am.

"It's almost over, Adam." She smiles and I get the feeling there's so much more she wants to say. "You know where to find me if you want to talk."

She heads for the door, opens it, and hovers there, as if she hates to leave.

"Gen?" I say.

She tips her head to one side.

"Am I taking away from who she was by doing this?"

"I don't know, Adam. I wish I did."

* * *

In the dream, I sit onstage beside Marybeth. No, Sunshine. Sorry, Sunshine. Because nobody cares about Marybeth, right?

The stage is small and round, an island in the dark sea of some random concert hall. Only the tiny, flickering holoflames—sold at the concessions before the show—light the darkness as they wave, held by unseen hands, as if to say, *We understand what it is to hurt, we understand what it is to lose.*

Sunshine stands in the spotlight and sings. Her eyes focus not on the audience but somewhere else. Maybe another lifetime.

I don't think she even knows I'm there.

And yet I don't want the concert to end, because even this isn't as bad as afterward, in the tour bus, where we've gone past grief, past sadness, into a place of grayness, nothingness, limbo. A place where we don't even have each other.

In the dream, as my fingers find the right chords on the guitar, my mind says: *It's time to leave, Adam; it's time to let her go.*

* * *

When I wake, I kick off the covers and get up. I know what I need from Gen.

A few minutes later, I'm knocking at the door of the room where she works, and this time I don't care who sees me.

From behind the door, footsteps approach, and then Gen opens it. She starts to push me back. "Adam, you can't be here."

"I need to know what she was thinking, Gen. I need to know what her last thoughts were. Do you know how to work the machines in there?"

"Adam, I..." she starts. "You can't..."

Then I realize why she was pushing me back. Because Rita is standing behind her, her face stern.

Oh shit.

I hold my breath for a second, and then I say, "I'm sorry. I just had a bad dream. I didn't mean to..."

I wait for Rita to grab my ear and drag me off to Dr. E's office so they can make the final decision to implant that hostage memory and put me on that plane home, writing me out of Marybeth's life forever.

But she only takes a single step out and looks both ways down the hall.

"Get in here," she says. "And be quick about it."

Chapter 68

"Why are you helping me?" I ask.

Rita continues to wire me up. "I'm not," she says and doesn't elaborate.

"What do you mean 'you're not'?" I'm fully awake now and wired in more ways than one. Gen stands to one side, silent, hands crossed over her stomach. She looks worried, and baffled.

"I'm not. Let's leave it at that."

But I can't. "So who are you helping?"

Even helping me—despite her claim otherwise—she isn't going to win any Kindness of the Year awards.

"You ask a lot of questions, kid," she says.

"And you weren't always like this," I say.

Rita stops what she's doing and stares at me.

"I saw your pictures. You used to smile. You have people who love you."

"Had," she says. "I *had* people who loved me. Life is cruel, Adam. You aren't the only one who's lived with loss."

I don't know what to say to that, so I don't.

"So you want to know what I think? I think what Sunshine did was selfish and stupid. You have a world of people who love you and you go and kill yourself. We get one life, Adam, and if you throw it away, that's on you. You don't get second chances."

"But what we're doing here—"

"We?" She shakes her head with a little tut-tut. "You, my friend, are a passenger in this car ride. And so am I."

"How are you a passenger?" I ask. "You work here. You're a part of this."

She nods. "I'm a part of it because once upon a time I believed in what we were doing. Because I thought if I brought my expertise I could maybe have my turn in line, bring back my loved one."

"The man in the picture," I say.

"If it's any of your business," she says, which is probably the closest she's going to come to a yes. "And who died of cancer, I might add."

She says the word "cancer" like it's a badge of honor.

"What we're doing here should be reserved for people who 'lost' their lives. Murder victims. People who died in car accidents, or of cancer. People who deserve a second chance. But now we're bringing back superstars. And look at how most of them died. Suicides. Drug overdoses. They didn't lose their lives. They threw them away. That's not what I signed on for."

I feel anger building inside me. I want to correct her, to tell her that Mr. Grayson has his reasons that are none of *her* business. But with Gen standing here, it's not something I want to get into.

"You don't know anything about Marybeth," I say, "about what her life was like."

"She was orphaned?" She jams a wire onto my temple and another, so hard I think she'll leave thumb-shaped bruises. "She had a miserable childhood? Lost her bandmates? Life gave her lemons and all that crap. It's tragic. I get it. But that's life. And at some point you have to decide whether you're going to be a victim or you're going to be a survivor."

"Decide? You make it sound so damn easy." The anger that's been burning low beneath my skin flares up. "Who are you to judge? You didn't live through what she lived through. You had one loss. One. Not a lifetime of them."

"And what about you, Adam Rhodes, orphan, lost your band-mates, lost the love of your life? You're still standing, aren't you? You chose to survive."

Gen looks from me to Rita and back again, hugging her arms around herself.

No, I want to say. *Maybe I'm still standing, but I'm so angry and scared and sad and guilty that most days I can't bear it.*

"I didn't choose anything," I say. "Maybe that's even worse."

Rita stares at me, hands on her hips. "Well then maybe it's time you did make a choice."

She jams two more wires onto my head and then turns to the computer and types something in.

"You should have all the available information before you make any decision. That's why I'm helping you, if that's what you choose to call it. Now if you want the memories, I need a locator, an index to match her memories to yours, time-wise."

"Meaning?" I ask.

"Meaning I first need you to remember, to pick a memory from close to the end, so I can show you her memories of it. Are you ready?"

Am I? It's a good question.

But I have to do this, so I grab the arms of the chair and lean back and force myself to breathe. And, once again, I remember leaving Marybeth.

"Okay," Rita says. "I've got it. Here we go."

I wait and breathe. Gen continues to stand back, as if she doesn't know her place here. I want to reassure her, but I can't even reassure myself.

I expect it to be like last time, that the memories won't come until later. But maybe because I've done it before and I'm primed for it, the memory starts immediately.

Again, there's that disorienting shift in perception that makes the tour bus look bigger, skewed. Emptier.

My stomach plummets. It's emptier because I'm gone, because she's alone.

Marybeth walks the length of the bus, one hand trailing the wall. She looks at the refrigerator, at the bed, at the mirror over the bathroom sink.

I see her face reflected back, and I am her, and for a minute I—me, Marybeth—linger there looking at someone who's become a stranger. I touch my face, try to feel something of the person I've become. But there's nothing but a hollow.

She—no, I—walk to the bedroom, where I lie on the bed and stare at the patterns the rain makes on the wall.

And there's something else there that I can't immediately identify.

And then I do.

It's relief.

Because she no longer has to keep going for me.

Marybeth closes her eyes and falls into a dreamless sleep.

There's a moment of nothingness, and I'm floating, or falling. I'm not sure which.

Rita's voice says, "Hang on a second, Adam."

The dark resolves into early morning. Outside the bus, the sky is peach and purple. For a minute, Marybeth lies in bed, listening to the stillness of the world.

There's a stillness inside her too.

She gets up and dresses in jeans and a sweatshirt, very

un-Sunshine-like clothes. She gathers her hair into a ponytail and puts on a baseball cap and big, dark sunglasses. In the bathroom, she finds the antidepressants in the medicine cabinet. She dissolves a handful in hot water and washes them down the drain so it will look like she's been taking them. Then she swallows three.

She checks to make sure nobody is up and about yet and then she slips out.

Disguised, she takes a cab to the beach, watching the scenery go by. Her thoughts are few. Memories mostly.

Me and her that day at the beach so long ago, the little red boat, our first kiss, the first time we made love.

The taxi driver leaves her off at the beach, where a sign reads: No Lifeguard on Duty. She tips him well, just the tiniest bit self-satisfied that he has no clue who she is.

Marybeth kicks off her shoes, which she drops along the board-walk that leads through the dunes. Already she feels the antidepressants moving through her system, slowing her down, making her fuzzy.

The beach is empty. Seagulls fly figure eights overhead, diving for oysters in the shallows and dropping them on the rocks to crack them open.

She knows this beach, knows where the currents run strong at high tide, and she walks there, letting the water run up over her ankles. The cold sting of the water makes her sigh.

She thinks about me, wonders where I am, what I'm doing. She worries about what this will do to me.

But she thinks I'll be okay. After all, I made the decision to leave.

"I'm sorry, Adam," she says, as if she's trying the words out loud. "I love you."

The part of me that's still me, not lost in Marybeth's memory, wants to shout at her that this is dumb, that it doesn't solve anything, that I won't be okay.

But I'm caught in the memory, and the water washes around her, pulling at her feet and legs.

If I do it this way, it's the ocean's decision, she thinks. *I'm not giving myself to the ocean. It's taking me.*

Her arms pinwheel as the tide comes in, the sand being sucked away beneath her toes and heels. She walks out. The ground drops out from under her. And then she's falling.

Do you regret it, Marybeth? I listen closely to her thoughts. This is what I need to know. *At that very last minute, did you regret it?*

The current pulls her out and her waterlogged jeans weigh her down. The water is icy. It numbs her hands, her legs, her face. Her stomach cramps with the cold. She coughs out water.

And then she's under the surface, and still the current is pulling, pulling. In the now, I feel myself choking, gagging. I hear Gen's voice crying out, Rita's voice, still calm, saying, "Adam, do you want me to pull you out of it?"

I shake my head. I need to know. *What are you thinking, Marybeth?*

But I can't breathe because she can't breathe. And I can't hear her thoughts for my own panic because I'm drowning. I'm drowning.

Chapter 69

In the sim, Marybeth takes the phone from my hand and hangs it up. "I want to go onstage," she says. "I want to perform."

Trying not to think about everything that happened last night, I go with the memory.

"Marybeth," I say as gently as I can, "Constellation is gone."

I think she's in shock, worn out from the funerals, on the edge of collapse. I sit beside her on the bed and brush her hair back from her face. "The band is gone."

"You and me." She looks right at me, and her eyes are clear. She's retreated into this weird shell of calmness. "I want us to perform, Adam. I'll sing and you'll play guitar. As a tribute to LaLa and Jeddy. As a tribute to our band."

I look at Marybeth.

No, I remind myself, *not Marybeth*. The clone of Marybeth. A copy burdened with the heartaches that belonged to Marybeth and Marybeth alone.

"We have to, Adam," she says.

But they're the original Marybeth's words, not her own. Not really. And we don't have to. Not this time.

I think about Genevieve, who wishes more than anything that she could be someone new and not have the burden of her original's memories and experiences, the burden of expectation.

"We don't have to, MB. We could run away. We could start fresh. Just you and me." The words come out in a rush.

I realize I've totally jarred us both from the simulation. In my mind, the memory continues playing. In the memory, I'm agreeing with her, going along because I will do anything for her. But in reality, everything has suddenly changed.

And this, I understand, is doing anything for her.

This is giving her up.

"Adam, don't you dare do this now," Dr. E warns in my earpiece. "We have a deal. You are going to ruin everything."

Yes, Dr. E. I certainly hope so.

Marybeth frowns as if she's suddenly confused. "Did something happen?"

Please let her memories be coming undone. Please let them unravel until she's nothing but a blank.

But there's something else there too, that weird jitter in her eyes. Stronger now. Like a seizure but...

I want to laugh, but I'm afraid I'll start to cry if I do. *Did something happen? Two years have happened, MB. Deaths and grief and fame and suicide and...well, everything.*

The memory tells me to nod, to tell her that of course I'll go onstage, whatever she wants, whatever will make this easier for her.

I know how this spins out. I've replayed these moments hundreds of times. Tonight I take her hand and go onstage and she sings, not the songs we always played with the band but the ones she sang at the funerals, and more, songs I never knew existed. And I play along on the guitar as best I can, missing notes here and there, pretending to know what I'm doing. And it didn't matter, not one bit, because the audience had been hypnotized. They fell in love with her instantly, Marybeth wearing her yellow dress and her grief, her words and music touching people as only music can.

I think about the man in the audience who called Marybeth

Sunshine for the first time, the talent scout who took her by the hand and told her he would make her a star when all she could think about was honoring our friends, and the day we met Jack, who would become our manager and, in some way, our friend.

I've always wondered if this was the moment that changed everything, if she never would have become Sunshine if I hadn't agreed to this.

In the sim, Marybeth is watching me with that mixture of grief and hope that I know so well.

"Adam, you will be on a plane tomorrow," Dr. E yells in my ear. "And you will be written out of her life forever. Stay with the goddamn memory!"

Instead, I grab Marybeth's hand and hold as still as I possibly can and let the memory spin away and away and away.

"You might not understand this now, but you are not Marybeth. You are whoever you want to be, and this is my gift to you, because I love you. And I hope if you remember one thing, it's that I love you."

"Adam," Dr. E says, "*Don't you dare do this!*"

But I am. I am doing this.

Marybeth looks confused. Then there's that jitter in her eyes again, worse this time. Back and forth. Back and forth.

Abruptly, the memory is gone.

Marybeth and I are left standing in the blue room.

She looks around, taking it in. Her mouth hangs open. Her eyes jitter.

Then she collapses.

A door opens and Dr. E rushes in. Someone yanks me away from Marybeth.

Dr. E leans over MB, checking her pulse, listening to her heart.

"Is she alive?" I ask. "Please, Dr. E. Is she alive?"

She only says, "Get him out of here."

Someone pushes me out of the blue room and closes the door.

With my heart pounding, I run.

Chapter 70

I pound at Genevieve's door. Christ but I'm always pounding on somebody's door. She opens it after a minute, looking a little wild-eyed. Probably expecting another drunk attack.

"Adam, what is it?"

"Can you get me to a phone? One that'll dial back to the States."

"I…" She frowns. "Yeah. I guess. Why?"

"Please, Gen. I promise I'll tell you later, but we need to do it quick."

"All right." She comes out into the hall. "Come on."

I follow her, waiting for someone to yell, *Stop!*

When I realize she's led me to her father's suite, my heart pounds even harder. Is she going to turn me in?

Then she says, "My key card may not get me everywhere, but it does get me into Daddy's apartment."

"Won't he be there?"

"Nah. He's probably in his office planning who to resurrect next. I'm thinking David Bowie."

I know she's wrong. I remember the kindness in his voice and I want to tell her she's wrong about her father.

Or that she doesn't know him as well as she thinks.

Or maybe it's just that I understand Mr. Grayson, with his good intentions and his grief. I might just as well be Mr. Grayson.

I bounce on my heels, anxious, as Gen slides her key card through the slot by the door. The door opens. She holds a finger to her lips.

"Daddy!" She calls in. "Dad! Can I use your shower? I'm not getting any hot water again."

When there's no answer, she says, "Yeah. Not here," and we step inside.

"The phone's in his sitting room," she says. "Dial nine first. Adam, who are you calling?"

I squeeze her hand. "I need to do this first."

"Or what's going to happen?"

"Gen, please."

She nods.

I find the phone, take a deep breath, and punch in the number I forced myself to memorize before I came here, in case of emergency. Then I hold my breath until he answers.

"This better be good," my manager's voice says.

The familiarity of it washes over me.

"Jack," I say. "It's Adam."

"Jesus H., Adam. Where are you?"

"I'll tell you everything," I say, realizing they're the same words I just spoke to Gen. "But right now I need you to work your magic for me."

There's no answer for a minute and I think, *He's done with me; like everyone else, he's written me off.*

Please, Jack, I know I've been a shit, but not you too.

Then he says, "I have been worried sick about you, kiddo. You tell Jack what you need and I will make it happen. Tell me where you are, Adam, and I will come get you myself."

It's exactly what I wanted to hear. I let out a breath and think about the threat I made a long time ago to Dr. Elloran.

In my memory, she says to me, *And you're going to tell them to go where, Adam?*

To the island, I think. *To the island where a billionaire's daughter died in a car accident six years ago. The name is Grayson. Reggie. And Genevieve.*

I close my eyes and I think about landmarks. The landing strip. The old marina.

"Adam?" Jack prompts.

I blow out a breath. "Do you have a piece of paper?"

Chapter 71

"You're leaving?" Gen says.

We're still in her dad's apartment, and I keep looking over my shoulder to check the front door.

"Yes." Now that it's set in motion, I feel this weird mix of fear and relief and regret. Looking at her, I also feel a deep, deep sadness. "Tonight."

"In the middle of the night?" She crosses her arms over her chest. Pink splotches bloom on her cheeks. "And some guy is sending a boat?"

"Jack," I say. "Our manager."

Mine and Sunshine's.

"So does Jack know why you're asking him to do this?"

"No. And he knows better than to ask. Well, sometimes, anyway."

"Great. Got it." Anger radiates from her with each word.

"Gen, listen to me." I put one hand on each of her arms and lean down so we're eye to eye. "I blew the simulation today. I deviated from the memory. Completely."

Her eyes get wide. "Marybeth?"

I shake my head. "I don't know. She collapsed. But she was alive when they threw me out."

"I'll find out."

I hug her. I can't help myself.

"What are they going to do to you, Adam?" she asks.

"Put me on a plane in the morning," I say. "Write me out of her life forever."

"So why the boat?" Almost as soon as she asks, her lips make an O. "You're going to take Marybeth."

Chapter 72

I sit on the beach, looking out over the water and watching the sun burn a path across the sky, waiting for some Project Orpheus SWAT team to fan out from the tree line and gun me down. Or maybe Dr. E herself, Uzi in hand, screaming, "You didn't stay with the memory!"

But nobody comes. Not even Gen. In the pit of my stomach, a combination of thoughts and memories and worries churns and grumbles.

I want a drink, but I breathe through it and watch the waves roll in and out, and the urge passes. It's a beautiful beach, white sand, seashells the size of my fist, the surf strong. Marybeth would have loved this.

I think about how it would feel to let the water take me, wading in until my clothes would get soaked and my arms and legs would become stone, until finally I'd go under and wouldn't come up.

But I don't think I could. I don't think that possibility exists inside of me, no matter what.

I remember that day, waking up in a hotel room alone. Alone. Because I'd left her.

And here I'd finally had this thing that I wanted. Escape from the never-ending grief and the nothingness that we'd become. And suddenly all I'd wanted was Marybeth.

I'd repacked my duffle, and I'd come back, only to find the bus empty. Then my cell phone had rung, not Marybeth's voice on the other end but a stranger, saying, "I'm so sorry to have to tell you this."

Our driver had rushed me to the hospital. I don't think I breathed the entire ride. She was in a coma by the time I reached her, hooked up to the damn MAP machine.

But at least I'd held her hand when she took her final breath.

I hope she isn't dying now without me.

* * *

I don't know how many hours pass, but finally the sun falls toward the horizon, turning the water to gold.

Behind me, someone clears her throat. I turn, sure it's Dr. E— Uzi or not—to tell me that Marybeth is dead, that I've killed her, but it's Gen.

She sits beside me. "I can't stay long or they'll come looking for me. They think you're in town, drinking." She gives me half a smile. "I can't imagine where they could get such a crazy idea."

"Marybeth…Is she…"

"She's alive. You didn't kill her, just…short-circuited her I guess."

I sigh out a breath. "Thank you."

"And her memories are intact. You didn't ruin everything."

My heart sinks. I didn't undo anything.

"Just don't go back to your room. Dr. Elloran is on a rampage."

They'll be watching for me, I think. Of course they will. How did I think I could get Marybeth out of there? Just walk hand in hand with her out the front door? And now, even if I do, what is this going to do to her?

Genevieve shifts until she's kneeling in front of me. She rocks back onto her heels and lowers her eyes. "I wish I'd met you under different circumstances, Adam. I'm going to miss you."

"I'm going to miss you too," I say.

She nods. Then she takes something from the pocket of her blouse and presses it into my hand.

Her smile is sad. "I'm sure yours was deactivated. This will get you in."

I look at the name on it: Reggie Grayson.

"Daddy's spare," she says. "You're not the only one who can steal key cards."

"But I can't set foot in that building, Gen. They'll never let me near her."

"I know," she says. "But *Daddy's* key card will get you in *Daddy's* entrance. Do you know where that is?"

I nod.

She takes off her watch and straps it to my wrist. "There's a second door to the nursery just inside that entrance. Only my father's key card opens it. Meet me there at two a.m. Hopefully by then they'll figure you're sleeping it off or you did something even more stupid."

I look at her, this amazing girl who's become my friend and who, under other circumstances, could have been so much more, and I know there is no way I'll ever be able to tell her how grateful I am for this. For everything.

"Thank you." I squeeze her hand.

She dips her head and smiles. Then she gets up to go.

On impulse, I jump to my feet and catch her by the arm. "Come with us, Gen."

She sighs. "I can't, Adam. This is for you and Marybeth." Tears brighten her eyes. "Besides, my dad would probably just clone another me, and the world isn't ready for two Genevieve Graysons." She tries to laugh and can't quite manage it.

"Your father loves you." I touch her cheek and my hand lingers there. "You should be honest with him."

Then I lean in and kiss her one last time. For a second, she doesn't respond, except for a soft gasp, and then she does.

It's a soft kiss, quick and light. I cup my hand at the back of her head, where the edge of the dragonfly barrette digs into my thumb. Then for a minute more we tip our foreheads against each other and just breathe together.

I love Marybeth. With my whole heart and soul, I love Marybeth.

But in another lifetime, I could have loved this girl too.

My heart breaks when she pulls away.

Chapter 73

Before I head back, I visit the place where the first Genevieve died. The wind blows in hard off the water, a little cool and smelling of salt.

In my mind, I replay Gen's words. *Her memories are intact.*

Nothing's changed. We've only come full circle, Marybeth and I, back to the edge of that cliff. And whether it's tonight when I plunge her, unprepared, into a world that she abandoned a long time ago, or whether it's tomorrow and she walks into the sim without the real me, to step on the stage and transform into Sunshine, it's going to happen.

I scream as loud as I can, but the wind swallows it.

I can go tonight. I can get on the boat that Jack sends and I can let him set me up in a new life. With the money from Sunshine's estate, I can go anywhere, be anyone.

But it won't change anything for Marybeth. No matter what anyone says, I know that.

I think about what Gen said that day, the day I almost found the strength to let Marybeth go.

Whatever's inside of me, she'd said, *that makes me alive and me, my soul maybe—I don't know—I wonder if it would have gone into another baby somewhere, if maybe I could have been anybody.*

Anybody. Maybe somebody who could be happy.

I shake the words away. My watch says it's 1:45. I need to get going.

I find Gen's journal back in its hiding spot and tear out a single page. With the pen that's tucked in beside it, I write: I'M SORRY.

Then I fold it up and tie it to the fence where there are, even now, fresh flowers to mark the tragedy that happened here.

* * *

I approach the compound like I'm walking through a field of land mines. One wrong step and the whole world will blow up around me.

But it doesn't, and Mr. Grayson's key card grants me access to the building.

Inside, like Gen said, is the door to Marybeth's nursery. I hold my breath when I access the room, sure that Dr. E or Mr. Grayson will be waiting for me. But when the door opens, it's Gen who pulls me inside.

My teeth chatter. I'm so scared.

The room looks the same. I don't know why I expected it wouldn't. That's the way it is sometimes when terrible things happen. You expect the whole world to have changed, when really the only thing that's changed is you.

Marybeth floats in the tank amid her veil of bubbles. Alive. Her memories intact.

"I've been here before for the transition," Gen says. "To get her out of the tank. I think I know how to do it safely. Are you ready?"

I move toward the tank. Even though Marybeth's eyes are closed, I see her sadness. It's in her face, the slope of her shoulders.

She's just one more lost girl, one more kid the world failed and forgot.

Looking at her, so close to me and yet separated by a huge gulf, I feel helpless.

"Adam," Gen says from behind me, her voice tight. "We need to hurry."

I turn to look at her. Suddenly there are three Gens, four, a whole prism of Gens through the tears in my eyes.

"What's wrong?" she asks.

"I can't do this, Gen. I can't do this to her."

"What?" She frowns. "You can't take her with you?"

"I can't take her, Gen. But I can't leave her either."

From the O of Gen's mouth, I know she understands what I'm saying.

"Do you know what you're saying? Are you sure?"

How could I ever be sure? But it's never really been my choice, has it? It's Marybeth's. And though I might hate it with everything inside of me, she made that choice a long time ago.

If I could have been there, at the beach in that moment, if I could have saved her then, I would have. I would have grabbed her and pulled her back kicking and screaming. I would have held on to her forever to save her, or I would have gone under with her, trying.

But I wasn't there. And it's over. It's been over for a long time. I just couldn't accept it.

Gen steps toward me, but I hold up a hand to stop her. I need to be strong, and if she hugs me, comforts me, I won't be able to do this.

All around the room, the machines continue their steady parade of lights and soft beeps. In the tank, Marybeth dreams her dream that isn't a dream. Or maybe for her it really is. Maybe it's nothing more than the dream of another girl who has long since left this world.

If you're really in there somewhere, Marybeth, I think, *the original Marybeth, my Marybeth—I love you and I am so mad at you for leaving me and I'm trying so hard to forgive you. I think, one day, maybe I will.*

Maybe in time I'll forgive myself too. For everything.

I lick my lips and taste the salt of my tears. My throat aches.

I move around the tank to where the hoses connect. My hand hovers, not knowing. Gen comes closer. She hesitates and then guides my hand to the thickest of the tubes.

"Will it be painful?" I ask.

She sighs. "I don't know. I hope not."

I take the tube securely in my hand. Behind me, Gen's breath is as ragged as mine.

With my other hand I place a kiss on my fingers. Then I press my fingers to the tank. To the glass that separates me from this girl who I love with my whole heart, this girl so long in the ground.

"I would have done anything for you." The words choke me. "But I needed you too, you know? I needed you too."

My hands shake. My whole body shakes. My throat is too closed to let me breathe.

I twist the hose. It uncouples from the tank and drops to the floor with a hiss. In the place where it was, the small opening seals shut, only a few tablespoons of the fluid leaking out.

Instantly, the room fills with shrieking of alarms. In my shock over what I've done, I stand there dumbfounded.

Gen's hand flies up to her mouth. Her eyes meet mine.

From the hallway, I hear a commotion. Then the door opens and Dr. E and Rita pour in. A second later, the other door bangs open and Mr. Grayson rushes in.

Seeing her father, Genevieve takes a step backward, one hand over her heart.

But right now, all eyes are on me.

Chapter 74

The whole world exists as noise. The ear-splitting shriek of the alarm, the hiss of the escaping air, which I couldn't possibly hear over everything else, and yet I do.

And I think time has stopped completely, except for the hose on the floor, which twists and flips like something alive.

Then Rita pushes past Genevieve to the bank of computers, and with a few keystrokes the alarm cuts off. The abrupt silence is thick and somehow even louder than the alarm. My ears feel stuffed with cotton.

Still, I think I can hear the heartbeats of everyone in the room. Even Marybeth's as it slows down.

I killed her, I think.

Mr. Grayson stands in the doorway, unmoving, except for his head, which swivels to look at me, and then at Marybeth, and then at his daughter. I mean the clone of his daughter.

It's Dr. E who moves toward me, her eyes focused past me at the fallen hose.

"Step aside, Adam," she commands. "You don't know what you're doing."

I square my shoulders. "I do know what I'm doing, and I can't let you change it."

"This is really what you want to do?" Dr. E takes another step toward me. I see her weighing her options. But I'm bigger than her and determined, and I think she knows it.

"Adam," she says, "Think about this. If not for yourself, if not for Marybeth, then for all the other people who lost someone who this technology will be able to bring back. The children of soldiers killed in wars who will be given the chance to have a daddy."

I open my mouth to call bullshit, because I don't think Dr. E gives a damn about those children or anyone else other than herself and her own path to fame and fortune. But it's Rita who speaks first, and I was so intently focused on Dr. Elloran that I jump at her voice.

"Sure, Trixie," she says. "If those families have the money to pay for this. Soldiers aren't getting the same salary as rock stars these days, in case you hadn't noticed."

Dr. E seems as surprised as anyone at Rita's words, and she stands there open-mouthed staring at Rita.

So do I.

"You'd throw away all our work for this juvenile delinquent?" Dr. E asks.

"I would throw away all our work to do the right thing," Rita fires back.

"The right thing for whom?" Dr. E says.

My hands clench into fists. Beside me, Marybeth is dying for the second time, and I can't even say a real good-bye to her.

I look from Rita to Dr. E and back again, and words bubble up inside of me. "Not everything is right or wrong. Sometimes we make our own choices and we have to live with them. Or die with them. Marybeth made hers a long time ago. Don't you get that?"

I wait. For what, I'm not sure. And it isn't until I see Dr. E's gaze flick to a point behind me that I realize that in the distraction, Mr. Grayson has come around and reconnected the hose.

"That's enough," he says, in the voice of a man used to being in charge.

Everything inside me crumbles. One more time I failed to stop something from happening. One ultimate fuckup.

"No," a girl says, her voice so hard-edged that for a minute I think it's Marybeth 2.0 speaking up for herself. "That is not enough."

But it isn't. Of course it isn't. It's Genevieve.

All eyes turn to her as she steps forward. I think she's coming to comfort me, but instead her eyes are focused on her father.

"You shouldn't be involved in this." Though he speaks to her, he shoots me a look, as if I'm to blame for everything. "This has nothing to do with you, Genevieve."

She stands firm. I see the set of her shoulders. "But it does," she says.

She comes to stand beside me and squeezes my hand. With each second that passes, the hose breathes life-giving air into the tank, bringing the Marybeth clone one step closer to the world that her predecessor gave up.

I'm sorry, MB.

Gen lets go of my hand and faces her father.

"It has everything to do with me, Daddy," she says. "Because I know what I am. And I know I'm not her."

Mr. Grayson's face changes. I think he ages twenty years in a matter of seconds, and he goes from looking like the man in charge, to a man out of control and terrified.

He looks at Rita, at Dr. E. "Go," he says. "This doesn't concern you anymore."

"But we need to make sure there's no permanent damage to the clone," Dr. E protests.

"Go," he says again, his tone like steel.

This time Dr. E doesn't argue. And Rita…I'm not sure I'll ever understand her completely.

"Am I the same girl, Dad? Am I the Genevieve who sat on your knee when I was little? Or am I someone else? I've been trying to figure it out."

"Gen." He reaches out to her, but she shakes her head.

"Forgive me, Daddy, because I want to be someone else. I want to be someone whose life is a blank slate, someone who isn't expected to be this one specific person just because of her DNA and some artificial memories."

"I'm so sorry, baby." He breathes the words. "I am so very, very sorry. I was only trying to do what was best. For you. For us."

She nods. Her face is all sadness. "Then don't do this to Marybeth. She was never meant to be Sunshine, Daddy. Don't write her life the same way again."

I look between them, father and daughter. Or father and clone of daughter. Both broken, maybe beyond repair. But they are still family.

I look at Marybeth, floating in her tank. She still looks so young, practically a little girl, her body not yet aged to the time when her two lives will converge.

All Mr. Grayson wanted was to give Genevieve a second chance. All I wanted was to give Marybeth the same.

Were we so wrong to try?

In my head, I hear what Mr. Grayson said in our last conversation. *I thought maybe I could save her too.* In my head, I hear Genevieve say, *Don't write her life the same way again.*

Something in my mind clicks.

"Mr. Grayson?"

He looks at me with tears in his eyes. "Pull the plug if that's what you think is best for her."

Is this a man I can trust? I think it is. And sometimes, I'm beginning to realize, you have to take a chance.

I meet his eyes, and there are tears in mine too. "Mr. Grayson, what if there were something else we could do?"

Chapter 75

They let me carry Marybeth into the simulation room. Her head rests against my shoulder. Her breath is on my neck. She's so light in my arms, her body still boyish with childhood.

She isn't awake, but she isn't dreaming either. This moment is probably the only true moment I will ever have with this new Marybeth, a moment without the weight of memories, a moment when it is just me and her in the here and now.

I try to memorize it. To memorize her. To make this a memory not of pain, but of love.

Mr. Grayson opens the door for us. He bows his head, as if showing respect for the sacrifice I'm about to make. *He's a good man,* I think, *even if—as Gen says—he doesn't always use the best judgment. Who does, really?*

We step inside the sim room. Mr. Grayson. Genevieve. Rita. Me, carrying Marybeth.

I don't know where Dr. E is and, honestly, I don't care.

Inside the room, impossibly, is the ocean. It's not the pale, tropical sea that I've come to know here on the island. Rather, it's the dark, white-capped waters of the Mid-Atlantic coast. It stretches forever.

I turn in a circle. I can see the boardwalk where they sell ice-cream bars and prepackaged Italian ices with wooden spoons taped to the top. I can see the underpass that leads from the parking lot. And I think, far out on the water, I even see a small red-and-yellow boat.

My throat closes.

Thank you for this, Rita. I hope I think it loud enough for her to hear.

"I wish Marybeth could see this one more time," I say. Because soon, like so many things, it will be gone from her memory forever.

Mr. Grayson claps me on my free shoulder, a gesture that makes me think of fathers and sons. "I'll take her here one day, Adam," he promises. "I can give her that."

I nod my thanks.

"You can set her down," Rita says.

I turn to her. "I'd like to hold her, if it's okay."

She smiles. "No harm in that." Even Rita's hard edges seem to be wearing down.

I kneel and then work my way into a sitting position, still holding Marybeth against me, wanting to hold on to her as long as I can.

Rita kneels beside us and begins wiring Marybeth. Despite the judgment she was quick to pass on her earlier, Rita is gentle with her, carefully brushing hair away from her forehead before she sticks the receivers in place.

When she's done, she stands, brushing sand off her legs, as if it's not all just an illusion, and steps back. "You're certain about this?"

No, I want to tell her. *I'm not certain at all. Who am I to make this decision for Marybeth? Who am I to make any decision at all? It's her life.*

And me…I'm not even the master of my own life most days.

But I also think I'm at least partially responsible for her life now. Because I made the most selfish decision of all, to bring her back from the dead.

But maybe also because I'm the one who loves her the most.

"I'm sure," I say.

Rita nods. "Then let's start."

Mr. Grayson puts an arm around Genevieve, "I think this is just for Adam and Marybeth, sweetheart," he says.

I like the way he calls her Marybeth for the first time.

Gen leans into him, and my heart squeezes. They will be a family.

But she stops before they leave, to bend down and kiss the top of my head. "We'll be in the waiting room. You're not alone."

They leave. Mr. Grayson. Genevieve. Rita. And it's just me and Marybeth.

The sand is soft and warm beneath us, the sky cloudless, the sun strong. I close my eyes and feel it on my eyelids. I hear the white noise of the waves and the cry of seagulls. The salt from the breeze stiffens the skin of my cheeks.

I open my eyes and breathe deeply and wait for our lives to be undone for the final time.

"Beginning memory reversal," Rita's voice says through the overhead. There's no need for an earpiece today, because Marybeth will sleep through the process, mercifully oblivious.

"I love you," I tell Marybeth. "If there were one thing you could remember, I wish it could be that."

In my arms, she flinches. It's just a small flinch, and maybe I've only imagined it. Or maybe it's me who's flinching.

But I know a memory is gone. Maybe a hundred memories. Or a thousand.

I can't possibly know which memories are disappearing as they go, because there are years' worth, a lifetime. Not Marybeth's lifetime and not my lifetime, but the lifetime of *us*. And yet I imagine I do.

At first it's easy. With each flinch, I imagine memories of endless concert halls disappearing, memories of crowds and memories of paparazzi and memories of pain.

I imagine her unbecoming Sunshine, her memories leaving until she is once again only Marybeth, LaLa's and Jeddy's funerals, their deaths, her grief erased.

And me, I think. *And me.*

Sharing the hole-in-the-wall apartment post–foster care.

Winter afternoons at Java Bean and summer nights at Smitty's Point.

The first time I told her I loved her.

Our first kiss.

The day we met.

I bow my head over her and listen to her heart beating against mine, her body strong, even as the Marybeth I know, the Marybeth I hoped to have again, dies.

But I think I see her face smooth out as the weight of her memories—as the weight of her predecessor's memories—are lifted from her. And I hope it's not only my imagination.

Finally, Rita's voice comes over the speaker, seeming to come right out of the sky like the voice of God. "It's done."

How quickly everything can change.

If Marybeth woke up now and saw me, I would be a stranger to her.

I sit there and rock her, and the simulated ocean continues to roll in and out, and then the room is just a room again, nothing but walls and lumps, everything a shade of blue that makes my eyes burn.

The door opens and footsteps approach. Mr. Grayson puts one hand on my shoulder and asks, "May I take her now?"

Chapter 76

Gen comes to sit beside me. She doesn't say anything, doesn't even touch me. She just sits there in the shadow of my silence.

Marybeth will never know me, I think.

She will never love me.

There will never be a little red boat that says ADAM ♥ MARYBETH.

We will never have a happily ever after.

Someday there will be new memories to take the place of these. Another first kiss. Another boy to hold her hand. Things I can't, in this moment, even begin to imagine for her.

A new hollow opens up inside me. There are so many of them now.

"Did it work?" I finally ask.

"Rita says her memories up to age eleven are intact, but beyond that she seems to be a blank slate." Gen shrugs. "She's in another section of the simulator with my father now."

I nod, imagining a memory that never really existed rolling forward, Mr. Grayson in the simulator with her instead of me. Creating the beginning of a new future for an eleven-year-old Marybeth with her new, adoptive father.

I wish I could give her to him as a baby, before the world started to wear her down. But physically, that isn't possible. Physically, she's already been aged too far. She'll even be a little bit tall for an eleven-year-old, an early bloomer. They can't reverse the aging process, of course.

She'll be a challenge, I want to tell him. *At eleven, she has more than her fair share of scars. She might wear too much yellow and you might find her keeping pet spiders in her room. And she'll test you at every turn. But she's worth it. And her edges will soften once she lets you in.*

I think he's up for the task. I've seen his capacity to love. I think with Mr. Grayson, she'll have a fighting chance.

And I trust him.

Because, as I'd come to realize, in some way, he could be me.

Tomorrow she will wake up in a bungalow on the other side of the island in a room that overlooks the ocean, on the first day of their celebratory adoption vacation. Maybe she'll spend the day collecting shells. Maybe they'll go home, far away from this place of ghosts, and he'll get her a kitten. And she'll have the best big sister ever.

In Marybeth's new world, I do not exist. In her new world, I will never exist, except for a face that maybe she'll see one day in an old video clip, after everyone tells her about the amazing singer she so closely resembles.

"Your boat will be waiting," Gen says finally, pulling me from my thoughts.

"I guess so," I say.

She squeezes my hand. "I don't want you to leave."

I look around me at the blue simulation room where I've relived so much. "I have to. There's no place for me here now."

Genevieve nods. "I know."

She stands and helps me to my feet. I think we both know I have to do this before neither of us have the strength.

"I'll walk you to the door," she says.

* * *

The compound is silent. Everyone else—except Dr. E, of course—is seeing Marybeth into her new life.

We reach the back door.

I don't bother with my bag, or with the guitar. I'd rather go forward with nothing. Except…

"Come with me, Gen," I say.

The words come from nowhere but also from someplace deep inside me.

I hold out my hand. "Please. If you come with me, you can be anyone you want to be."

In the silence, I swear I hear both our hearts beating.

Genevieve takes my hand. And I know she's going to say yes.

She smiles but then she says, "I'm sorry, Adam. I can't."

* * *

I'm alone.

The moon is full and tints everything blue. I walk through the woods, onto the airstrip and then past it to another path.

It's hard to believe it's still night, that a month of nights haven't passed since I pulled the hose out of Marybeth's clone's tank.

I think a lifetime has passed since Dr. Elloran showed up at my doorstep with the offer of a lifetime.

And now, again, I'm alone.

Finally, the path opens up, and I step out onto the sagging wood of the old dock. A red boat shines in the moonlight, waiting to take me…somewhere.

On deck, a man motions for me to board. I take a deep breath and climb onto the boat.

Suddenly, there's a flurry of motion in the woods behind the dock. I turn to look just as a dark shape bursts out from the tree line.

"Wait!"

Genevieve.

Something inside of me shifts. My knees wobble.

She stands on the dock, facing me, her breath ragged.

"Tell me again," she says.

I swallow hard. "You can be anyone you want to be. Please, Gen. I want you to come."

Meeting my eyes, she unclips the dragonfly barrette from her hair and throws it, as far out as she can, into the water.

"Yes," she says.

Chapter 77

Out on the open water, the night is cool and the wind off the ocean strong. We sit on the deck and Genevieve watches the island disappear behind us.

"Are you cold?" I ask her.

"A little," she says.

I get up and find a blanket and wrap it around her shoulders. She leans against me.

"I'm sorry things didn't turn out the way you'd hoped, Adam," she says, "with Marybeth."

I nod, my throat too closed to speak. This is what grief feels like without the chemical comfort from a bottle. It's heavy and raw and swells inside me, until I think I might break in half to get it out of me. But I let myself feel it.

The truth is that I lost Marybeth a long time ago. What I lost now was just a false dream, a hope that I was never really meant to have.

I'm sorry for Mr. Grayson, that he'll have to lose Genevieve again just like I had to lose Marybeth twice. But it took me that to understand that you can't go back. You can only go forward the best way you can, even when it seems impossible.

And he'll have Marybeth to look after now, a girl who genuinely needs him.

When I look at Gen tonight, I don't see a dead girl. Instead, I see a lightness about her, a bright, vibrant young woman who's ready to enjoy all the happiness—all the possibilities—the world has to offer her. This is a gift that Marybeth—through Sunshine's estate—can give her. I think Marybeth would have liked that.

And I think Mr. Grayson will understand.

The day I met Marybeth, I'd been planning to run away. The night before, my foster mother had told me I was rotten to the core, that nobody would ever care about me. Then I'd met Marybeth, and everything changed.

She was wrong, my foster mother. Two of the most amazing girls in the world have loved me. When I look at Genevieve, I see it in her eyes, in her smile, in how she looks at me.

I look back one last time at the island. It's no more than a speck now, dark land against dark water. Then I turn away. I won't look back again.

Gen squeezes my hand.

I almost open my mouth to tell her I love her too. Because I think I do. But it isn't quite right. Not just yet, anyway.

And though I know I'll still have this sadness inside of me for a very long time, when I look at the seat across from us, by the light of the full moon, the Hope-Ghost shimmers back into life. It smiles at me, waves as if we're old friends, and then walks toward me. Finally, I hold out my arms and let it become a part of me.

Acknowledgments

Once upon a time I took to calling *Resurrecting Sunshine* "the book that would not die" (though not entirely without affection). Now here it is making its way out into the world, and I have so many people to thank.

To my amazing agent, Brianne Johnson of Writers House, who is as kind as she is fierce, thank you. Under her editorial guidance I wrote some of my favorite scenes in the book. Bri, you are the best! Thank you also to my film agent, Dana Spector of Paradigm.

To Erika David and Lee Kelly—CPs, accountabilibuddies, friends—you are the best! Erika, without you, this book, quite simply, would not exist. Thank you for believing in *Sunshine* even when I didn't, and thank you for your endless enthusiasm no matter how many drafts I threw at you. And to Holly Hughes, thank you not only for beta reading, but for being a great friend and the best cheerleader ever.

To all the talented writers from *Neverwhere* and its many in-carnations (Kori, Jeff, Wendy, Ken, Dawn, Julie, Jim, Gyppy), thank you! Yours are the voices I hear when I strive to be better. Thank you especially to Jeff Lindsey and Wendy Ribelin, who gave me feedback on early chapters. And a special thank you to Kori Henning, trusted critique partner and friend. It's you I go to when I want the unvarnished truth, and that is priceless.

And how do I even begin to thank my beloved Herded Kittens? Not only are you the best writing group ever, but people I'm proud to call friends: Michelle Mead, Linda Hanlon, Ian Wickstead, Richard Mirabella, Mark Irish, Irene Kipp, Shiloh Delawder, Heather Versace, Lobsang Camacho, Patrick McGriff, Marita Casey-Russo, and honorary member Claire Mead. I'm grateful for every one of you.

Thank you to Kim Sabatini and all the Hudson Valley Shop Talkers. You are all so inspirational. And a special thank-you to Jalissa Corrie, my friend and beta reader extraordinaire. You rock!

Thank you to Kendra Levin for the best-ever introduction to writing YA fiction, and to all my amazing writing teachers, especially Doris Brennan and R. B. Weber. Thank you to the Sweet Sixteens, to my wonderful ABNA friends (who are the true prize in that contest), to the awesome short story editors I've had the opportunity to work with, and to everyone at NaNoWriMo. Without NaNoWriMo, I may never even have written a book! Thank you, also, to Mónica Bustamante Wagner and Stacey Lee for picking me for your team in the Writer's Voice and enabling me connect with my dream agent.

Love and thank you to my family for teaching me to embrace the chaos! To my parents, Beryl and Ernie Sorensen, to my brothers, Ryan and Erik, and to my sister-in-law, Missy, who is the sister I always wanted, I love you all! Thank you, too, to my in-laws, Donald and Irene Koosis, for always supporting me.

And to Aron Koosis, the love of my life…throughout everything, your belief in me has never wavered. Thank you for keeping me steady and for cheering me on and for sharing this journey with me always. There's nobody I'd rather walk it with.

Thank you to my editor, Wendy McClure, for her wisdom and insight, and for taking a chance on *Sunshine*. And thank you to the unstoppable team at Albert Whitman & Company:

Kristin Zelazko, Annette Hobbs-Magier, Tracie Schneider, Laurel Symonds, Jordan Kost, and everyone else who has worked so hard to make my book a reality.

I feel like I could write forever and still not have enough time and space to thank everyone who has shared this journey with me. But you know who you are, so THANK YOU!

In addition to always loving books, **Lisa A. Koosis** is a confirmed science geek, a hopeless beachcomber, and an animal lover. Her prize-winning short stories have appeared in numerous journals, podcasts, and anthologies. Although a Long Islander at heart, these days she lives in New York's Hudson Valley with her family (both two- and four-legged). *Resurrecting Sunshine* is her first novel.